Turpentown

Randy Harris

Thanks Claire

CHAPTER ONE

"Received from Henry Clayton, the sum of ninety-six dollars to pay the commissary debts including Ten Dollars per head for five Negro bucks and one Negress, wife of Willy Forrester. All Negroes are in good health and free from malaria, typhoid or any sickness keeping them from steady work.
Signed, Carl Latham,
Pine Ridge Turpentine Camp"

"You got to rewrite this," Henry said.

"What the hell for?" Carl asked.

"Because it reads like a bill of sale," Henry replied. "That'd get me fined down in Florida."

"But I've writ nine lots just like that. Ain't no one got pissy about it, til you."

Henry frowned down at the parcel and then asked, "You send any to Florida, yet?"

"No. Yer the first…mostly Georgia."

Henry kept staring down his counterpart from a different state until he saw he was beginning to understand and then smiled.

"You take out the part where you said 'including Ten Dollars per head' and just write, 'Received from Henry Clayton the sum of ninety-six dollars to pay the commissary debt for 5 Negro bucks and one Negress, wife of Willy Forrester. All Negroes are in good health and free from malaria, typhoid or any sickness keeping them from steady work.' If this reads anything like a bill of sale, I get fined and probably could spend some time in the pokey."

"Okay, I'll rewrite it," Carl said.

"Seems like a lot of money," Henry said.

"It *is* a lot of money, Henry. But it's money well spent. You got five healthy bucks. Three are good chippers, two are pullers and all five are good dippers. Those are five of the best niggers I have."

"What about the negress," Henry asked. "Will she whore out?"

"I don't think so. Have you seen Willy? He's a big 'ol boy...and they're in love," Carl explained.

"I need another whore. What can she do?"

Carl pulled a pack of Lucky Strike cigarettes out of his pocket and pulled one out. He offered Henry one before he stuck it in his mouth and struck a match across the top of his desk. From the small scorched marks there, it was a practice he had repeated many times over several years. Henry smoked his pipe on occasions, but only smoked cigarettes on rare occasions.

"She can dip cups, skin rabbits and cook like no other woman," Carl said. "Muffins, pork steaks, hoecakes, taters, greens and peach pie. Them two is just good all round...get ya another whore."

Henry scratched his stubble of a beard, pondering then smiled over at Carl.

"You sumbitch. You had to bring food in it, didn't ya?"

"Did it work?"

"Rewrite the damn paper, so's I can start heading back," Henry grinned.

Carl smiled, as he took the paper back from Henry. He retrieved another piece of parchment from his rickety, old desk then peered closely at the words and copied it down without the "including ten Dollars per head" clause. He was a smart man, but couldn't read all that well. He copied down most everything he needed to write in life. His love letters never won him much favor with the ladies, though.

"What are you gonna do with yourself after turpentinin all these years?" Henry asked.

"Well, you know there just ain't much gum left in these trees around here. I have one last crop of about seven-thousand trees on the southwest plat. Other'n that, it's all old-growth, longleaf pine. I got two mills set up to plank them all and that will keep me going for say, another six to eight months. I should make enough money after the last tree is planked to settle down

6

and drink m'self to death. It's a shame the lumbering part don't last as long as the sap does in them trees."

After finishing the parchment, he handed it and the individual debt sheets to Henry and then asked, "Are you ready to go meet the brood?"

"I reckon I am," Henry said as he inspected the documents. "Where will they be?"

"Well, being as today is Sunday, they should just about be getting outta church," Carl said.

"Ya'll have a church?"

"No, but they hold services in the jook. One of the bucks got his certificate for preachin," Carl replied.

The two men picked up their belongings and headed out the back door of the foreman's house. Outside, Henry saw the woodsrider's shack and barn far to the left. He figured it to be about 8 a.m. The air was crisp and felt good. The woodsrider was standing on his porch, stretching in the rising, morning sun. Henry guessed he had just finished breakfast as the smell of bacon and hoe cakes still filled the air.

"Josh," Carl yelled over. "Run get me Willy, Stella, Curtis, Louis, Charles and Wilson."

"Big Curtis or Little Curtis," Josh yelled back.

"Little."

"Little?" Henry asked.

"Don't worry," Carl replied. "Have I ever let you down?"

"You never sold me bucks before."

"That's true," he grinned. "Meet us in the barn, Josh!"

"Yessir!"

When the group gathered in the woodsrider's barn, Henry saw what was so funny about "Little" Curtis. He was as big as a mountain! Once there, the pack gathered around as Carl waited for them to settle down.

Everyone knew the pine sap was about gone. Soon the longleaf pines would be harvested for their lumber until the stumpers could come in to dig up the last of the tree stumps. Every precious drop of resin left would be boiled out. The first and the last of the pine sap were considered the most potent.

Turpentine distilled from stumps was used almost exclusively for medicinal purposes, thus the most expensive. It also meant the life of the crop had passed and the lumbering phase required far less workers than the *turpentinin* phase, which was the sap extraction. The country was in the midst of what was being referred to as the "Great Depression" and most people were just happy to have enough to eat. Fortunately for some, the turpentine industry was not nearly as affected by the bad times as most other industries. The turpentine industry was already "bad times."

"People, this here is your new foreman," Carl began. The crowd immediately straightened up and paid attention. Some grinned slightly, while bystanders, not called to this meeting, lit cigarettes and listened quietly. "His name is Mr. Henry, but you can call him 'Bosm,' just like you do me. He has paid your commissary debts and you're now indebted to him. As ya'll know, I can't keep as many niggers here, cuz the tree gum has nearly run out and we don't need so many souls to do the lumbering. He will be taking ya'll to Florida to his turpentine camp, where ya'll will do the same fine work for him as you've done for me these many years."

"Florida?" some thought aloud "How far away is that? Will we like it? Will there be enough work?" So many questions, but such a relief to know they will still have work!

"Bossm," Little Curtis asked, "will we git time to say goodbye to everyone? We sho enuff appreciate the chance to keep workin', but we's been here fo so long, so very long...gonna miss some of the folks."

"We've been through some hard times together," Carl said, "but we made it...when many, many others did not. I know ya'll will do well down in Florida. Ya'll have ONE HOUR to gather your possessions and say goodbye."

The group scrambled to get out the door. Carl was a little saddened at the lack of ceremony their departure had embraced, but understood the desperation of their response. He turned towards Henry.

"That'll be ninety-six dollars, my friend."

"Will you take scrip?" Henry asked.

Immediately, Carl's smile faded, but realized Henry was joking. "Scrip" was company coins or printed company currency, which were virtually worthless unless used in the company store of the camp issuing them. Workers were paid with scrip to keep them dependent entirely on the company for the necessities of life. Turpentine Camps, along with other industries of the time, would also pay a worker less than it took for them to survive, but offered credit. Once a worker owed the company store, it was virtually impossible to leave, as state laws did not allow a worker to leave a company where they were indebted. It was modern day slavery of the times.

"What sort of scrip you using down at West Tocoi?" he asked.

"Five and ten-cent stamped coin," Henry said as he counted out and handed Carl ninety-six dollars in folded, U.S. currency. "It's cheaper than the printed stuff and harder to lose. We had a feller press a bunch of slugs for us a year-or-so ago, so until we need more than eighty six workers, we have enough to cycle round. The hard part is finding the workers."

"How much housing ya got?" Carl asked.

"We have my house, which is a two bedroom with a brick chimney, the woodsrider's house, a cinder block worker's quarters we built last year because of a surplus of block, and about ten shanties."

"Where'd ya get the cinder block?"

"A ship busted up during a storm and pretty much ran aground down by the West Tocoi docks. I got a good price on a shitload of them. Actually, I didn't pay a dime," Henry said smiling. "The trick was getting them back to the camp. That took a while. We used crushed cinders for the mortar. My woodsrider knew concrete work, so we got us a seven-unit workers quarters and commissary for about nothing."

"I could use one of those around here," Carl said.

"Next time we have a ship run aground, filled with cinder block, I'll grab ya some."

9

They both had a good laugh at the thought of this. Most camps had either stationary, wooden shanties or "skids," which were small shacks built on skids and dragged from one crop to another. At West Tocoi, they used wooden shanties, which were two rooms, a small brick fireplace, kitchen and a wooden toilet enclosure in the corner of one room. Workers were used to the odors and used newspaper to cover cracks in the walls. Rats were commonplace in most shanties.

It usually took about a year or so to totally work a crop of ten-thousand trees. Each crop would last about six seasons. Workers were assigned groups, who spent most of their time walking from tree to tree, either chipping, hacking, scraping or dipping. Hackers chiseled the bark from the tree, exposing the bare pine wood beneath. A chipper would chip angled grooves called "streaks" into the bare wood, where the pine sap or *resin* would seep out. Flat, tin "gutters" directed the oozing sap down to the collection pot below.

During the cooler months, the sap would thicken. A scraper would scrape the gum or hardened resin down the flat "catface" of a tree, into a box or Herty cup. Scrapers also did the *pulling*, using long-handled hacks to reach up high, to both chip and pull resin from the catface. "Chip boards" were used to cover the Herty cup and prevent bark and wood chips from mixing with the sap. Dippers gathered the collected resin from the collection pots on the trees about every eight days.

Outside Carl and Henry heard the gathering of the new workers for the West Tocoi Turpentine Camp. As they stepped outside Carl remarked on Henry's truck, a 1931 Chevrolet flatbed with side rails.

"How'd you manage to get such a fine looking truck?"

"Hell, that ain't my truck. We only have wagons back at West Tocoi. The truck belongs to Larry Larson, the National Holdings Company Manager. He oversees eight camps, so moves around a lot. Occasionally, when he's needing' a day or two off to rest, he'll let me drive the truck. He insisted I bring the truck up here to fetch these niggers and get them back to camp the quicker the better. He also wanted me to pick up some

10

seawater on the way back."

Once the crew was loaded up, Carl and Henry bid each other farewell. Henry got into the driver's seat and had Little Curtis ride shotgun. Henry and his truck bed of workers were almost a mile down the trail when Carl scooped himself some grounds to brew a pot of coffee. With his back to the door, an unexpected visitor slips up behind him and holds a knife next to his neck.

"I'm expectin' you got yo self some cash for them niggers that just rode away," the visitor asked in a heavy voice. Carl recognized him right away as one of the trouble-makers of the camp. "I suspect I'll let you give that to me so's I don't cut ya."

Carl flung the coffee pot over his shoulder, hitting the would-be thief in the face, but as he staggered back, sliced the side of Carl's neck, causing blood to gush forth. Carl turned, stepped forward and wrapped one massive hand around his attacker's throat, pinning him against the wall. Try as he might, the attacker could not break his grip.

Turpentine camp foremen were known throughout the industry for their toughness. They had to be the toughest of them all. Turpentine workers knew the foreman as "The Man" because of his ability to put any man down who started trouble. The workers both feared and respected him. There was only so much a man could do, however, when trouble snuck up from behind.

As Carl bled to death, he slowly slid to the floor. His attacker finally freed himself and ran away, after taking the money pouch from the desk drawer. Two days later he was arrested while seeking medical attention for a crushed larynx and was hung after a short hearing, in front of the Wilford County Courthouse two weeks later. The Rockwell Holding Company, out of New York, would miss one of its most valued turpentine foremen.

It was no secret that turpentine camps were some of the most violent workplaces that ever existed in civilized America. The work was hard and although the peonage system of employment was outlawed by congress in 1867, its basic

11

applications were still employed by turpentine camps throughout the south. The workers were basically indentured servants. Nobody really cared what went on twenty miles out in the deep forest, especially if it involved Negroes, and only then if it involved murder.

Henry looked back at his workers as they drove on slowly in complete silence for two hours. They were already indebted to the West Tocoi Turpentine Company and he needed to size them up and start planning on where they would stay, what their assignment would be, and which ones he could count on. Little Curtis sat next to him. He noticed earlier that he had calluses between his middle fingers, indicating he had driven a wagon for many years. He turned slightly to face his crew through the back window of the truck.

"Listen up, everyone," he shouted. "I need to get some basic information from ya'll and lay down the law."

Most everyone turned towards him, except for Little Curtis sitting next to him. He stared straight ahead, down the road.

"I am Mr. Henry or Bossm, whichever you prefer. If you do your job and what yer told, we get along just fine. But if you get lazy or fuck with me in any way, I will beat the livin' shit outta you. Ya'll got that?"

A few shook their heads in agreement and mumbled yessah.

"What, goddammit?!" he screamed.

"Yessah, Mr. Henry!" they shouted, almost in unison.

"That's better," Henry said. "Now, who here are my chippers?"

The crew looked at each other and most of them raised their hand.

"Hackers?" Henry asked.

Again, most of the crew looked at each other then raised their hands.

"You mean *all* of you are chippers and hackers? You're all scrapers and dippers too, I suppose?"

"Yessah," Willy offered quietly.

12

"What?"

"I mean, yessah, Bossm," he stammered, a little louder. "Me and the rest here pert near know how to do all of dat, sir."

Henry smiled at this latest revelation. He had known some talented niggers before, but if this entire lot knew chipping, scraping, hacking *and* dipping, he had made a good business deal!

"Okay," he said. "We'll see how ya'll do when we get to the camp. Did everyone git fed this morn'?"

After a slight hesitation, Stella bravely raised her hand.

"What is it...*Sheila*, is it?" Henry wasn't much used to a Negress speaking up.

"Yessah, Mr. Henry...my name is Stella. I cooked brefest for most everone here dis mawnin. I also packed two bags wit vittles fer the ride. We didn't knows win we gonna gits to eat again. I brung some cornbreh, hoe cakes, sweet taters and three jars of pot lickers from the greens las' night."

A cook, thought Henry! This day was getting better by the mile. The cook they had at West Tocoi in the blockhouse was a lazy bitch and he's had to slap her for being sassy on more than one occasion. Guess she won't be so high-n-mighty now...

"We'll eat after we git to the beach in a couple hours. We'll be just above Charleston," he said. The look on Louis' face told Henry he was confused. "What's the matter, Louis?"

"Oh, nuttin, Bossm. I jest never bin to a beach befo." Henry looked at Louis in disbelief.

"You ain't never been to the beach or seen the ocean?"

"No sah," he admitted quietly.

"Me either, sah," another admitted.

"What?" Henry said. "Okay, who all ain't been to the ocean?"

Of the six, only Wilson had ever been to the beach. He was once sent to work a steamer transporting Naval Pitch down to Florida when it was still a popular commodity and there were far less mills down south. Once the sap started running out in the Carolinas, more and more camps started popping up in South Georgia and Florida. Turpentinin a crop of pine trees was, in

13

essence, a death sentence for that area of forest. It wasn't economically feasible to plant new growth trees, so more longleaf pine crops were streaked in other camps to the south.

"Well, my niggers, ya'll are in for a treat!" Henry smiled. It was the first time they had seen him smile...and it scared them a little.

"We'll get to the beach a little above Charleston," he continued. "I need to fetch a half-keg of sea water for our woodsrider back at the camp. We'll stay there long enough for ya'll to take a piss in the ocean then we'll head down south, gas up the truck and catch a steamer out of Charleston down to Jacksonville. From there we board a flat car down to West Tocoi, which is where the camp is. Any questions?"

Everyone looked at each other with a rather surprised look, not expecting solicitation of their questions. Henry noticed that immediately and took it as a sign of leniency. He regained his composure with a follow up.

"And anyone getting back to the truck late will git a couple loose teeth for it, including you, Missy," he barked.

Willy did not like anyone speaking to his wife in this manner, but held his words as he had learned to do for many years. They were both in their early thirties and had been married ten years.

"Don't worry, Mr. Henry," Stella said. "I ain't never late for hardly anything."

Henry mumbled his acknowledgement and the group continued their southeast trek to North Charleston. He reminded himself not to be too neighborly with his workers and never show affection. He had a position in life, which required a foreman's image to be maintained and personal feelings ignored.

True to his word they arrived at the beach in a little under two agonizing hours. Henry pulled the truck up behind some small sand dunes, which was as far as they were going to get to the beach in this area. Again, Henry turned to his crew.

"Now before ya'll go running over there, let's git a couple things straight. First, if you don't know how to swim, don't go far out in the water. That water has currents in it, which is to say it can drag your ass out and you could drown. You are not allowed to drown until you pay off your debt to me and The West Tocoi Turpentine Company. Everybody understand that?"

"Yessah, Mr. Henry."

"Second…we'll will be leaving here in about one hour, so don't go off too far where's ya can't hear me. Third…if'n you see any white folks, don't say nothing. Don't look at em and don't speak. I don't know how folks are up around here."

"Yessah, Mr. Henry."

"Okay," he said, looking around. "Let's go see the ocean."

They crawled out of the truck and walked slowly across the small mound of sand dunes. At the top, at least three of the workers let out an audible gasp. Louis raised his arms straight in there air and yelled out, as he ran towards the water, followed by Wilson and Charles. Willy and Stella just stood there, hugging each other as they scanned the beach looking first to the north then to the south. Little Curtis, held back as the others moved forward at different paces. Henry turned around and peered at him with idle curiosity.

"Little Curtis…you comin?" he asked.

"Mr. Henry?" he asked. Henry noticed there were actually tears in his eyes. "Kin I stay here. Is that okay?"

"Why do you want to hold back?" Henry asked. He was becoming a little suspicious.

"It's too big, Bossm…too big. It scares me."

Henry thought about it for a while, and then thought he understood. These niggers have never been to something that was too big to behold in just one look. The ocean was huge, and he could almost feel the panic Little Curtis was feeling, as he had felt the same panic as a child.

"You stay here and watch the truck," he said. It was one of the first times in a long time, that he could remember coming close to trusting a black man. Turning, he headed for the water as Little Curtis sat down on the dune to watch the others.

15

Louis was still screaming, with his arms raised as he ran in large loops from the water's edge to the dunes. It was pure exhilaration, a feeling that most people of color had never experienced before in their lives.

Henry enjoyed the cool ocean air for a time and then just watched the crew take it all in. Willy and Stella held each other tight as they tip-toed through the water and occasionally looked up to admire the vastness of God's creation. Charles and Wilson were walking knee-deep out in the waves as Louis settled down and began to head back towards the dunes where they had accessed the beach.

Pulling out his pocket watch, Henry glanced down then call back to Little Curtis, "Hey, go fetch that half-keg in the wagon!"

"Yessah," Little Curtis yelled back. "Right away, Mister Henry!"

Little Curtis retrieved the keg and brought it back to Henry then stood there staring down.

"Something on your mind?" Henry asked.

"Mr. Henry?" he asked.

"Yes, what is it?"

"Since I is the only Curtis here wif us…could I be called jes' Curtis?" he asked.

Henry looked over at his troubled crew member then asked, "Little…um, Curtis, I didn't know that it bothered you."

"I knowed we needed to keep us straight and dat's alright, but if'n there's jes me, I'd be proud to jes to be "Curtis" again. Besides," he added, "I have always been bigger than Curtis."

Henry smiled then said, "Curtis" it is! Now take that keg down to the water and git me some sea water. Ms. Delores wants some back at the mill for different things. Get one of the boys if'n needed."

"Yessah!" Curtis smiled, as he stood tall. "Right away, Mr. Henry!"

Curtis headed off in the direction of the ocean at a healthy pace. Henry figured he wouldn't need any help with it either. He smiled then looked after the others. Shading his eyes from the sun, he peered down the beach and saw a group of people spreading blankets several hundred yards away. They appeared to be staring back in their direction. One from the group appeared to be walking towards them.

Curtis had filled the keg and was heading back to the dunes. He didn't want to spend any more time near the water than he had to. The stranger caught up with Curtis and grabbed his shirt sleeve.

"Boy? What are you doing here?" he demanded. "Where you going with that?"

"Sah," Curtis stammered. "I was tol' to fetch this."

"Who told you that, nigger?"

"I told him to do that," Henry said as he, in turn, grabbed the stranger's arm. "And if you don't turn him loose, so we can hit the road, I'm going to have him stuff *you* in that barrel."

The stranger turned to look at Henry and saw the terrible fire in his eyes. He turned Curtis loose immediately and tried to pull away from Henry.

"Sorry," he said as he struggled to free himself. "I just wanted to know what was going on."

"What is going on," said Henry through clenched teeth. "Is none of your fucking business. Now get your ass back down the beach to your faggot friends and we'll be on our way."

"No need to get all huffy, Mister," the stranger said, as he hurried away. He feared for his safety and was happy to back down from this one.

Henry motioned for the rest to head back to the truck as he and Curtis did the same.

"Thank you, Mr. Henry. I's sorry that had to happen," he said.

"Curtis, you ain't done nothing wrong. That man was just a nosey little bitch, trying to be a big shot."

"Yessah," Curtis smiled. He never heard a white man referred to another white man as "bitch" before. He found it amusing.

Back at the truck, Henry informed the others that Little

Curtis would now be known as just plain "Curtis." He then hurried everyone into the truck and they were on their way once more. When Curtis looked back to the bed of the truck, anyone looking in his direction would lend him their smile of approval. Curtis felt blessed and thankful that he had summoned the courage to mention it to the camp foreman.

Within forty-five minutes after continuing their journey, Henry and Curtis gazed out upon the first signs of Charleston. At the northern mouth of the bay, Henry made his way to one of the many ship moors, seeking a particular cargo vessel, which could accommodate the loading of their truck for transport down to Jacksonville, Florida. They already had a term contract with the Magnolia Marine Company, so the trip would be without any up-front costs. In Jacksonville, they would switch to a train for the remainder of their journey to West Tocoi. The train station was several miles south of the turpentine camp.

Once loaded aboard a freighter, along with four other trucks and crews heading south, they were soon steaming for Jacksonville. Two of the other trucks were also carrying negroes south to work in the turpentine camps. Most of them gathered along the railing as they watched the sea swirl by, and chattered about their good fortune of having work after their previous camps had dried out. Henry watched them closely as a sheep herder would, tending his flock. He could really use a nap right now, so instructed Curtis to wake him when they approached the port. He leaned back against the seat, pulled his straw hat down and fell asleep. He dreamed...

"Boy, can't you git nuthin' straight?" an old man screamed as he grabbed the young boy's arm. Henry felt a familiar pain shoot down his arm. The old man then slammed the two inch branch of a tree limb into the side of his leg, rising ancient pains there as well. Henry twitched as his dream relived memories of his youth. His father often used limbs of trees as disciplinary tools on his two children. "I told you youngins to git them weeds pulled in the garden!"

18

"But daddy, we were just getting a drink of water," Henry's older sister replied. To his horror, he watched his father grab his sister roughly up by the arm, bending it back in an unnatural way, causing her to cry out in pain.

"No...stop it! Stop it, Pa!" Henry begged. Unknowingly, he stepped backward in fear, as if to avoid the scene. He tripped over a cinder block barrier and fell backwards into a deep trash pit as his arms flailed in empty space. "Papa!"

"Mr. Henry? We're here!" came a voice from above. "Mr. Henry?"

Henry bolted upright, still sitting in the seat of the flatbed truck. Looking over, he saw Curtis at his side, shaking his arm.

"The cap'n says we're coming up on Jacksonville," he said. "You can sees the train up a ways, close to the loading docks."

Henry shook the cobwebs out of his head and looked around. Most of the negroes were still over by the boat's railing, looking out ahead. He looked back at Curtis and asked, "Was I talking in my sleep?"

"No sah," Curtis lied. "Not that I heared."

He felt he should just keep quiet about Mr. Henry calling out to his papa. There were too many other things to think about right then.

"Tell the others to come here," Henry said.

"Yessah."

Curtis went to fetch the others as Henry composed himself and thought of what he would say to the workers. As they gathered around, Henry waiting for them to quiet down then held up his hand.

"When we pull into dock," he began. "ya'll will have to wait by the side as the truck is hoisted off this boat and placed on a flatcar with the train. Since there are no passenger cars with this train, we will load onto the flatcar and ride with the truck down to West Tocoi. After the truck is taken off there, we all load up and drive the rest of the way north to the camp. Any questions?"

19

"No sah," they replied in unison.

"Good," Henry said. "Stella, now would be a good time to hand out some of the vittles you brought along."

"Yessah, Mr. Henry." Stella said. She didn't mention she had already handed out a good portion to the crew. "Did you want sumthin' Mr. Henry?"

"No, I'll get some tack at the office on the docks. I had a big breakfast this morning," he lied.

"Okay, Mr. Henry."

Two hours later, they were unloading the truck from the flatcar of the St. Johns Railroad. Once unloaded, Henry had the crew climb up unto the flatbed of the truck once more then told Curtis to drive. He wanted to see how well he could handle the truck because he may need an additional driver sometime in the future. Soon they began the final, seven-mile leg of their journey back north to the West Tocoi Turpentine Corporation. Curtis was as good a driver as any other he knew.

CHAPTER TWO

Little Thomas Wright looked down and picked at the tiny thorns which stuck in his body in different areas. His stubby, little fingers weren't the best for getting the smaller ones out, but he did the best he could and they didn't bother him anymore. He's been getting stickers and thorns in his skin for as long as he could remember. On his arm he saw another tick. He thumped it and it tried to crawl away, so plucked it off and crushed it on a small rock. If it had not moved, he knew it was burrowed in. Momma would then have to remove it with a drop of turpentine as she stretched the skin, until it let loose and could be plucked.

Standing up, he turned to head back to the shanty. He knew when it got dark, momma would want him home. He heard something in the distant and turned his head to get a better listen. It was the truck engine! Mr. Henry was back! Soon, more workers would be here and moving into the camp! He hoped there would be more children with them. There were only fourteen here now and the older ones hardly ever played with kids his age. He was five years old and most of the rest were ten or older. He was the only one not yet working either as a fetcher, tallyman or raker, besides the babies. He was hoping this year they would let him start raking. The trees needed the fallen pine needles raked back from the base of the tree in case of fire, which was a common occurrence in southern forests.

As the truck drove near, Thomas saw one worker in the front cab, with five more riding in the flatbed. He didn't see any new children. He ran towards the workers quarters to tell the others.

Looking at his pocket watch, Henry saw that it was now 6:45pm. He knew that nobody had worked today and that most everyone ate at 7:00pm or thereabouts. He left word that morning he would be bringing six niggers back from North Carolina and that they would probably be hungry, so make sure enough is cooked to feed them.

21

The worker's quarters currently consisted of ten shanties, which were small huts. They could hold four to six workers and each had a small, brick fireplace for warmth. The road adjacent and bisecting the crop of ten-thousand trees was referred to as skid row. This was because in many camps, shanties were built on skids and pulled along this trail to be near the work. At West Tocoi, they had stationary shanties close to the main road.

Additionally, there was the cinder block worker's quarters adjacent to the main road. It was seven units with the commissary on the end. He had Curtis pull up in front of the these quarters.

"Okay, everybody out," Henry commanded.

They all shuffled out, groaning a bit as muscles stretched out. They peered over at the cinder block structure then looked back at Henry.

"This is the West Tocoi Turpentine Camp. We've been working this area for going on four seasons now and still on our first set of crops. We have the usual ten-thousand trees per crop and we're currently working two crops." he said. "We have two sets of worker's quarters. The block house right in front of you has seven apartments, with three rooms in each apartment and the commissary. Willy, you, Stella, Curtis, Louis and Charles will be in the one apartment, next to the commissary, and Wilson will be moving to a shanty in the back."

Henry looked over his shoulder and noticed a small crowd gathering to greet the newcomers, including Ben Carter, his woodsrider.

"Stella, you'll be cooking in your kitchen for the cinder block building crews and helping Mrs. Carter stock the commissary," Henry continued. He heard a small, insignificant gasp behind him and figured it to be Kendra, the current cook for the cinder block quarters. He was tired of her attitude and constant complaining. She would either go to whoring out or out to dipping if she wanted to stay here.

"The rest of you," he continued, "will rotate to different crews, depending on where we need you and where I say your skills are. We work cant to cant like ya'll did up north."

22

"Cant-to-cant" was turpentine camp terminology for *can't* see in the morning until you *can't* see at night. It meant sunrise to sunset.

"Your woodsrider here is Ben Carter and you best do as he says! Times are changing in this industry and camp workers don't get whipped nearly as much as they did five or ten years ago, but that don't mean you won't feel a cane across your back if need be, you got it?"

"Yessah, Mr. Henry," everyone replied.

"Now I don't know everything about turpentinin' up north, but down here you don't get locked in your quarters at night and you won't be working with no state prisoners. We're in our fourth season of first crop drifts and have another three-hundred-thousand acres or four-hundred-thousand trees left to work. You will NOT leave this property as long as you are indebted to the commissary. It is not only against the law, but some years back a County Sheriff was killed by a young buck from a turpentine camp up the road. The locals 'round here don't take kindly to niggers, especially ones that work in turpentine camps. If they catch you off the property, they will most likely lynch you. Do ya'll understand that?"

Henry let that set in for a moment. He wanted his workers to know of the violent history of the industry, but they would be safe and would have plenty of work for many years to come.

"Also," he continued, "if you want shoes, you can buy them through the commissary for what we pay for them. We don't make no money off shoes."

Most of the new crew had shoes, although they were worn out and tattered. The prospect of a new pair of shoes made many of them smile.

"Kendra, after you show Miss Stella around, you'll be moving over to the jook house and starting now, you will receive your pay in the form of cross-time slips," Henry continued. The jook house was where the workers gathered to sing, drink, gamble and even have sex in the back room with one of the designated *whores*. A *cross-time* slip was given to the Negro

23

bucks for the whore to record her time spent with him. "Misty, you make room for her."

"Yessah, Mr. Henry," Misty replied.

"Mr. Henry!" Kendra shrieked from behind him. "I's ain't no whore!"

"Kendra," Henry replied in a cold, fearsome voice. "You'll do as you're told. If you expect to get credit for your food and stay here, you WILL do as you're told."

He turned around and looked her square in the eyes.

"We both know you've done been sleeping with at least four other nigger bucks that I know about, you bitch," he said. "Now you'll be earning your keep or I'll be calling the law who will be damned pissed about having to come clear down here to carry your ungrateful, no-job ass back to the county jail. Five, ten years ago, you would have received fifty lashes just for running your mouth!"

Kendra, along with everyone else who had heard the exchange knew Henry meant every word of what he said. Kendra stepped back and stared down at the ground. She knew she had little choice, but to comply. She also knew that he was right about the four bucks, but didn't know which of the seven she was sleeping with, he was referring to.

"Yessah," she half whispered.

Misty and the other whore, Taylor glared at Kendra for *giving it out*. Their survival depended on them laying with the bucks of the camp and recording their encounters on the cross-time slips.

Henry turned back to the crowd. He wanted to finish up his talk and get over to his house. He stomach was growling loudly and he was in need of some home cooking.

"One other thing I wanted to tell ya'll. We don't have hardly any trouble in this camp and by God, we're not going to start. There are no guns allowed in camp, cept for me and the woodsrider. You can gamble and you can get liquored up on Saturday nights and off season, but don't start no shit or you could face the smiling end of Miss Browning here," he said as he patted his shotgun. "We have whores here for the bucks, so you

24

best not be taking what you don't have permission to tap. The sun is going down, so all you new workers will need to get settled in. Everyone go about your duties tomorrow and I'll meet with the new workers during the morning *cant* to assign their duties. We'll meet behind the block house there.

Any questions?"

Curtis raised his hand reluctantly.

"Curtis, yeah?"

"Bossm, I don't sees any still around. Where's she at?"

"Good eyes, Curtis," Henry replied. "I was wondering if anyone would notice. Up until early last year we had two backwoods fire stills. Then, a large distillery opened up in Jacksonville and somebody with more brains than me, figured we'd make more money of we just barreled up the raw resin and shipped it north. They can distill it up there a whole lot quicker and we can work through a whole lot more trees. Keep in mind that this is only our fourth season open. We still use one of the fire still tubs to clean the Herty cups."

Henry looked around and waited for any responses.

Finally, after a short time, he asked, "Any more questions? No? Okay, ya'll go eat, now! I'm hungry too!"

"Ben," he added. "You want to make sure everyone knows where to go? I gotta get something to eat before I fall out."

"You got it, Henry," Ben said.

The foreman's house was about an eighth of a mile up the road. Henry walked the short distance then slipped in the back door. He walked through the small, enclosed porch and saw his wife, Delores, standing in the kitchen, basting a small roast in the oven. The woodsrider's house and his were the only two in the camp with electricity. Power poles were run down to West Tocoi train station and steamboat port three years ago. Both families knew how fortunate they were to have an electric fan.

Still, the fans basically moved hot air around, until the cool air of the evening rolled in. Henry could see the sweat pouring off his wife as she kept dinner warm for her husband until he got home.

"That for me?" he asked, startling her.

"Oh, good grief, Henry," she scolded. "You scared the crap out of me!"

"I expected my dinner to be on the table," he joked. "I may have to whup you after dinner."

"Henry Clayton, you know you better beat me to death if you ever decide to whip me," she said. "Otherwise, you know you gotta sleep sometime." She smiled affectionately at her husband and stepped over for a kiss and loving embrace.

"How did it go today? Get your new workers?" she asked, looking up into his tired eyes.

"Yeah, it went fairly well." he replied then added, "You know…we stopped by the ocean, north of Charleston this morning. Most of them never seen it before. It was quite a sight to see them people so excited about a bunch of water."

"Well, I was the same way when I first saw the ocean," she admitted as she pulled the roast out of the oven and set it on the table. "And I'd be willing to bet you thought it was quite a sight yourself."

"Yeah, I reckon so," Henry said. "Damn woman! Them taters sure look good!"

"I hope so!" she said. "The boy from Gustafson's Dairy stopped by on his way to Tocoi, this morning. I bought some butter and you some fresh buttermilk. I would have got some cheese, but didn't want to spend too much grocery money."

"Buttermilk!" Henry exclaimed. "Ain't had that in a while."

"I know!"

They both enjoyed a hearty meal of roast beef, mashed potatoes, gravy, biscuits, fresh buttermilk and snap beans from the garden. After dinner, Henry pushed himself back away from the table and rubbed his belly.

"Damn, that was good." he smiled. "You wanna listen to some radio before bed? I could see if we could pick up that Jacksonville station again. Who was that guy, "Bob Hope?"

"You sure you ain't too tired?"

26

"Naah, I'm okay!"

"Well then, sure! Let me clean up the kitchen a bit and you can go warm up the RCA."

"Sounds like a plan." he said. In the distance he could hear a fiddle playing, back at the jook. Camden was the camp's fiddle player. Once he had rosined up his bow, it wasn't long until toes were tapping and bodies were swaying. Henry figured his new niggers were now a part of the crew and were getting to know each other. He just hoped he didn't have any trouble makers in the brood.

At the jook, some were dancing, while others were smoking cigarettes, and drinking tea or coffee. Many sat at tables, having just finished dinner. Some workers played cards, while others enjoyed a game of dominoes. A young buck named *Memphis* sat in the corner next to the fiddler and strummed a rhythm on his old, beat-up guitar. It only had four strings left, but Memphis still made it sound sweet. Many of the workers danced to the harmony the two instruments produced.

Willy and Stella sat with Curtis, Wilson and Misty, but none of them stayed too long. Tomorrow would be the start of a new week and new duties for the ones just arriving. They all felt at ease with each other and spoke openly about the assigned duties, Florida weather and working conditions. The newcomers felt nothing would change much, except for the weather. They were still undecided about Mr. Henry, but felt he was playing his role and understood his commitment. They, like most of the others, were grateful to have a place to sleep and food to eat. Life would carry on.

Daniel, a short, cocky buck smiled over at Kendra, who recognized the look immediately.

"What say you and me go to the back room for a spell?" he asked.

"You got a cross-time slip?" she asked. "You know I is a camp whore now. You was there today."

"You gonna charge me?" he asked. "I thought you liked being with me."

"Times have changed," she replied. "You got to pay fer it now, like any other buck. How else am I gonna eat?"

"Shiiit," he said, shaking his head. "If'n I gots to pay for it, I'll git me some from Misty or Taylor. They gots the goods on yo ass."

Kendra's hand was resting on the table close to a steak knife. Her hand began sliding ever so slowly over towards the knife, a movement which had not gone unnoticed by Daniel.

"Ya know," he said. "I think I'll jes' go see what the folks outside are doing. It's getting a might stuffy in here."

"That's prolly the best idea you had all day, you dumbass nigger."

Daniel rose and headed out the door, where he saw a group standing over by a small fire. The fire was lit not so much for warmth, but more for the repelling effects it had on mosquitoes, so he headed over to join them.

As he was walking out, Ben Carter was walking in. He looked around the room and just stood there. The room grew silent. The woodsrider of a turpentine camp was always a white man, and made sure everyone kept working during the day. He carried a Henry rifle on horseback and was not afraid to smack a worker on the back with a five foot length of bamboo he carried around with him.

"I don't know about ya'll," he said. "But today has been a long day for me, so I'm probably hitting the rack here shortly. I hope everyone has gotten to meet the new workers we got today. You new niggers will meet me behind the cinder blocks. Stella, Kendra will be showing you around the kitchen and commissary tomorrow. The rest of you will be getting your assignments in the morning."

Ben looked around to make sure everyone understood then said, "Okay, let's get some rest."

Slowly, everyone filed out and headed for their quarters assignment. The jook was the second shanty in the first row, so it was only a short walk back to the cinder block building. Willy, Stella, Curtis, Louis and Charles would be sharing the three room unit next to the commissary. So it was only a short walk back for them. Willy and Stella had dropped their two canvas sack of clothes in the middle room where they'd be sleeping. Curtis, Louis and Charles would be in the front room. When they entered the back door, they noticed Kendra exiting the middle room and heading towards the front door.

"Everyone check your stuff," Louis said as he rushed to block Kendra's exit.

"I didn't take any of your shit," she said as she turned to face Louis.

"What are you doing in here?" Stella asked. She noticed her bag was open.

"This used to be my room," she said. "Until you got here."

"Is all of your stuff out now?" Stella asked.

"Yes," she said.

"Good," Willy said." Now get your ass out of our rooms and don't get caught in here again. We treat all workers as best we can, but if you ever get caught stealing from your neighbor, it won't be a good scene, so let's not go that road."

"Don't worry, my big buck…you won't see me near here again. I'm now back in the shanties."

"Then, goodbye," Wilson said. He didn't trust her either.

After Kendra was gone they looked at each other and promised to watch each other's stuff. Stella would be here most of the day cooking meals for the cinder block tenants and possibly watching the commissary. She'd heard Mr. Henry talk about that yesterday, but wasn't sure what that would mean. All but two of the cinder block apartments were now occupied.

Back at the foreman's house, Henry went in and turned on the radio. It usually took a few minutes for the vacuum tubes to warm up, so figured he had time to go take a leak. Later, as he and Delores listened to Bob Hope on the airways, they smiled at his audio routine. He wasn't often you could find an opportunity to smile, so they enjoyed the evening and went to bed at eight o'clock. Morning cant came awful early sometimes. Henry usually got up at five a.m. on weekdays.

As he drift off to sleep…he dreamt. He dreamt of his last encounter with his dad. He had just hit Henry in the jaw with his favorite thick branch, splitting it open. He then threw the branch at Henry, but missed.

"Where's your sister at," his dad asked in a drunken slur. He turned to go look for her, when Henry picked up the branch and ran after his father.

"No Pa, you leave her alone!" he screamed as he slammed the branch against the side of his father's head. His dad staggered to one side then fell on the ground. The branch had fractured his father's skull and he would never be the same after that. From that day forward, he could no longer speak and was confined to a wheel chair.

Considering the beatings the siblings received, the law did not charge Henry with anything, as they knew the history of violence they endured. Within days they were sent to live with his aunt. She was kind and took care of Henry and his sister until they were both able to move away on their own. Last he heard, his sister lived somewhere up in Georgia. Occasionally, he'd get a letter from her. Still, he had the nightmares and headaches. Henry was whispering to his pa to leave them alone when his wife woke him up.

"Henry, wake up." She whispered. "you're having another bad dream."

Henry woke up and got out of bed then poured himself a drink of buttermilk. He went back and sat on the couch and fell back to sleep. Delores let him sleep there. She knew it meant a sore back in the morning, but for some reason, he didn't have the dreams there.

Morning came and Henry was shaving as Delores cooked hoe cakes, grits, white bacon and coffee. As they ate they could hear the woodsrider rousting the workers with the morning cant bell. Workers would soon start to travel out towards the drifts, which were about three, haphazard rows of trees they were assigned. Each worker turpentined around five-hundred trees at one time, depending on their skill. This kept them constantly

30

moving slowly forward with either chipping, hacking, dipping or scraping.

Workers may have wives and children who usually cooked or tended gardens that each one was allowed to grow as long as it wasn't bigger than the area of the shanty. Wives could occasionally dip turpentine cups and their younger children could run water to the workers. The older children could serve as tallymen or were assigned to rake around the trees, keeping pine needles away from the base. Fires were common in the longleaf pine forests, but did little damage if the property was maintained properly.

Pigs were raised on the far end of the property, to the side of the block house. Food was provided pro-bono, except for vegetables. Each worker had a monthly allotment of food, which was recorded by Claire, the woodsrider's wife, who worked in the commissary. The commissary also sold toiletries, candy, tobacco, dry goods and even furniture if ordered through the massive catalogue. All purchases were either by scrip or added to a workers debt. Items considered a "luxury" were not allowed to be debited and those with too much debt were limited to scrip-only purchases.

Claire kept her pit bull Pete, with her at all times. He had been a birthday present from Ben a couple years ago. She felt safer in the camp during times she was alone, when Pete was with her. Their other pit bull was named Bonnie, who followed Ben around as he rode his horse. Both dogs were fiercely loyal and would rip a man's leg to shreds in defense of their masters.

The camp had two horses and twelve mules. One horse was for the woodsrider and his daily ride-arounds and the second horse and mules were for pulling wagons full of barrels. The wagon horse was generally used for the supply wagon as it was faster than the mules and less stubborn. Wagons ran back and forth to both active crops of ten thousand trees, covering about fifty to sixty acres each. The woodsrider covered all hundred-plus acres being worked at any given time.

31

CHAPTER THREE

"Okay, I'm heading out," Henry yelled as he grabbed his grub sack. He never knew how far out he'd be until he read the tallyman's report after the woodsrider had checked it for accuracy, so he carried a burlap sack of vittles.

Behind the cinder block building Henry met with the new workers. They had full bellies and seemed anxious to get going, which Henry viewed as a positive sign. From the window he could see Stella smiling over at her man, who in turn, smiled back. She was cleaning up the cooking area, which Henry reckoned, hadn't been done in a while.

"Willy, you gonna be able to concentrate on your work?" he asked.

"Yessah," Willy smiled as he turned towards Henry. "You just give me tree and task and I'll show you what I can do. I gots my tools and I'm ready to go."

"You already checked out your tools?" Henry asked. "Who showed you how to do that? You need to take directions from either the woodsrider or me, from now on."

Willy, realizing the confusion, was quick to explain, "Oh nah, Mr. Henry. I gots my own tools. I bought them two or three years ago. Can't rightly remember. Had to save me up some scrip to do it, but I gots em."

"You bought your own tools?" Henry asked incredulously.

"Yessah," he replied. Henry noticed the others were nodding their heads in agreement as if to validate Willy's claim. He gained a newfound respect for this man. If he was that motivated about turpentinin, he should be a fairly skilled worker and Henry was now anxious to see how well he would do.

"Okay…we'll see how good you are with them tools."

Henry noticed Willy did have some high quality tools with worn, but sturdy handles and sharp looking edges.

"Does anyone else have their own tools?"

32

"Nossah," came the general response.

"Then the rest of you can check your tools out at the far end of the cinder block house. Eric is down there waiting on ya'll now."

They all turned to see Eric smiling back at them. When not checking out tools, Eric tended the livestock and kept the stable clean. He was also the blacksmith for the camp. In a turpentine camp, the more skills you possessed, the more valuable you were to the company. During good times, this usually meant you also got more pay, but during the depression, it simply meant you got the job over someone with lesser qualifications.

"Okay," Henry continued. "Charles, I need you dippin' today. We have six drifts still needing dipping. Everyone, remember to holler out your name, so's the tallyman can mark your name. She already has everyone's name on her list. Louis and Wilson, you two will be hacking bark today."

Henry looked over at Willy and said, "And Willy, you and Curtis will be chippin' today, so show me what ya got. The woodsrider will be back directly to show you where your drifts will be today. Mostly, your drifts will be three trees wide here at West Tocoi. That may be less if we're close to the edge of the crop, but you'll still get the same amount of trees."

"Yessah," every nodded, acknowledging they understood.

"Did everyone bring vittles for the field?" Henry asked.

Everyone, but Wilson nodded their head yes. Henry looked at Wilson. "You didn't bring a vittle sack for the field?"

"I forgot about that," Wilson replied.

"He can have half of mine," Willy offered. Henry was really beginning to like this nigger.

"Hell no, Willy," Henry said. "Hell, the kitchen is just right there. Hey Stella!!"

Stella's head poked out the window, "Yes, Mr. Henry?"

"You got any left-over vittles for Wilson, here? He forgot to pick any up."

"Yes, Mr. Henry! I got's his sack right here! I was

33

wonderin' if'n he was gonna pick it up or not."

Henry looked back at Wilson, who grinned his embarrassment.

"Go git yer sack," he said.

Wilson ran and fetched his vittle sack, and then returned just as the woodsrider was getting back to take the other workers to their drifts. He was followed by the wagon used to carry workers back and forth to the crops furthest out. Others would walk to their nearby assignments.

"Load em up, boys," Ben said. "The rest of the camp is already at work."

Henry went over and spoke with Ben, to let him know what assignments he had given out. He told Ben about Willy having his own tools.

"No shit?" Ben asked. He had never seen a nigger with his own tools either. He peered over at Willy who had already loaded up into the wagon. "Well, maybe that's a good sign. We could use some smooth sailing."

"Amen to that," Henry agreed. "Amen to that."

After the crew had checked out their tools from Eric, the wagon was loaded. Ben told the driver to head for the new hack drifts. This is where the bark was being stripped off the trees to give workers access to the virgin wood beneath. Once the bark was stripped, creating a *streak*, the chippers would follow behind to start gouging the v-shaped notches in the tree, where the sap would seep out then ooze down the notch across the tin "gutter," directing the resin into the Herty cup.

Slashes in a tree showed the boundaries for every worker's drift, which was his area of assignment.

Wilson and Louis were the first two to be dropped off. As they grabbed their tools and exited the wagon, Ben looked down from his horse and said, "Louis, your drift is the first three rows, beginning with the first slash. Wilson, you have the next three rows over. Remember, more hacking, less yacking. Holler out your name after each tree is streaked so the tallyman can mark it."

"Yessah," they smiled. They were anxious to get to work and see if these trees were any different that the longleaf pine trees up in North Carolina.

The wagon and woodsrider on horseback moved on. They rode between the rows and up. Willy and Curtis would start chipping in trees that were already streaked and ready for slanted groves to be cut to direct the flow of sap into the cups. All the trees worked at West Tocoi were in the fourth year of bleeding and still had another two to three years left. The catface was about eye level at this time, with next year probably requiring pull-hacking, which meant the use of a longer pull-blade on the end of an extended handle or pole.

Behind them, they heard an occasional shout-out as Louis and Wilson shouted out their name to be tallied, and the return shout of the tallyman acknowledging their declaration. The tallyman placed a dot by each name as they were shouted to keep track of each worker's progress. After each tree was hacked clean of its bark in the catfaced area, the process was repeated. There were three tallymen, all between the ages of fourteen and sixteen, two of which were females.

"Louis!" a voice shouted.

"Louis!" came the reply.

"Mathew!" came a fainter shout, further down.

"Mathew!" came the reply.

"Wilson!" another voice shouted.

"Wilson!" came the reply.

This process continued until the wagon was out of hearing range. The tallyman was usually positioned midway between streak groups, in order to hear from as many shout outs as possible.

Soon, the wagon carrying the remaining workers came to the end of the worked trees, so they cut over to the previous day's work, which was void of bark in the catfaced area. Again, the woodsrider looked back at the wagon.

"Curtis, Willy…you're up."

Willy and Curtis grabbed their tools and stood at the

35

beginning of their assigned drifts as they watched the wagon pull away with Charles. The rows went on as far as they could see. Curtis looked over at his rows then smiled at Willy.

"May the best man win," he said as he hurried to the first streak in his drift.

"Wait!" Willy complained. "I didn't know we was racing!"

"Then you better hurry, my bitch!" Curtis laughed.

Together, they attacked their drifts with equal determination, easily slicing through virgin wood of a freshly hacked catface. The gutters and Herty cups had already been moved up by the hacking crew, which was not a requirement of them, but more of a sign of respect and comradery amongst camp workers. Hackers knew moving the cups would make the chippers work go faster and didn't slow them down all that much.

Their assigned tallyman, a fourteen year old girl recorded their progress.

"Willy!" he shouted, calling out his own name.

"Willy!" came the reply.

"Curtis!"

"Curtis!" came the reply.

It didn't take long for both men to be soaked in sweat as their coveralls, hardened by years of dripping resin, stuck to their skin. They focused solely on making double rows of even, slanted lines at proper the depth. They worked like men possessed, but after one hour Willy started pulling ahead. This encouraged Curtis to chip even faster, which in turn, sped Willy up. They smiled the whole time they worked and enjoyed the friendly competition.

Around eleven o'clock, Curtis asked Willy, "My bitch, are you gonna slow down long enough to grub?"

"Ain't time to grub," Willy chuckled. "Grubbin' fer sissies…who's the bitch now?"

So, that's the way it's gonna be, thought Curtis. Fine then!

They worked on at a blistering pace. Finally, Willy

36

frowned and slowed to a stop. Curtis, thankful for a change in pace, slowed down as well.

"Ya know," Willy called back over his shoulder. "I don't mind bustin' my ass and leaving you in the dust, but if'n we keep dis pace up, we'll need to work like dis ever day."

This stopped Curtis in his tracks. He looked serious then finally smiled and reached down into his bag. He grabbed a cold hoe cake out of his sack.

"Ya know, you got that right," he admitted. "Shit, too late now. Look!"

Willy looked back behind them and saw what Curtis was concerned about. The woodsrider had ridden up behind them and was studying the trees they had chipped. He slowly made his way up their drifts until he was next to them.

"Dayum, son!" Ben said. The pit bull, Bonnie was trotting alongside of him. "I was expectin' to see you two back yonder and I git here to find you way the fuck up here! I thought the tally sheets was wrong! I ain't never seen two niggers chip this fast. You boys sure you ain't got any help out here?"

"Nossah," Willy said, as he munched on some fried, white corn bread. "We was jes taking a little breather and grabbin' a bite. We thought maybe we should ease back a might, so's not to get burnt out."

"Makes no nevermind to me," Ben said. "You *will* burn yerself out if you push too hard. I seen it before. Keep in mind, though, that you get paid by what the tally sheets say…and I check those like a hawk."

"Yes, Mr. Ben," Willy said. Curtis shook his head in agreement. "We'll give you our best and do whatever we can for the company."

"I like that," Ben said. He had been around long enough and worked other camps, so wasn't a stranger to some of the horror stories that had gone on in the past. He has witnessed the turpentine industry coming out of a dark era and he welcomed it. Last year, he proved to the company which owned West Tocoi, that beatings and degradation did not motivate workers to work harder or faster. He proved that by comparing tally sheets, increased production was promoted and sustained by positive motivation.

"Welp, boys," he continued. "I'll have to go check on the others. Keep up that pace! It's almost two…you only got another four hours or so."

"Yessah, Mr. Ben," Willy smiled.

Charles was assigned dipping in another part of the same crop of trees. That meant he would be collecting sap by scraping and emptying Herty Cups. A wagon had placed empty 40 gallon barrels about every twenty-five yards in those areas being dipped. Charles worked two drifts of six rows of trees, carrying a five gallon wooden pail with him. He would scrape the catface of any sap still oozing, downward into the cup then empty the cup into his pail. At every tree he completed, he would shout-out to the tallyman, who placed a dot by his name. Once his pail was nearly full, he would walk to the nearest barrel and empty the contents. Once the barrel was full, he would shout-out "barrel" and a wagon, pulled by four stout mules would eventually arrive, pulling two poles. The poles were used to roll the heavy barrels up into the wagon for transport.

The wagon would carry the barrels to the West Tocoi loading dock and stored in a designated spot. It made no sense to unload the barrels at the camp, only to reload them for transport to the steamship loading docks. Two wagons drawn by four mules made a constant loop from the crops being worked to the docks and the barrels were stored there until the steamship pulled in to pick up cargo. The wagon driver would have the dock master sign the inventory and then head back for another load.

Ben turned and was riding away as the water wagon pulled up behind him. This was the first Willy and Curtis had seen it today, so rushed over to get a drink. They both grabbed a ladle hanging on the side of the bucket and drank. Marcus, the boy driving the wagon was only fifteen, but had already proven his skills with a horse-drawn wagon or team of mules. He turned towards Willy as he drank.

"Mr. Willy?" he asked.

"Yeah, boy?"

"Margaret's in trouble," the boy stammered.

"Why you say that, boy?" Willy asked.

Both men stared at Chris. He was usually quiet and hardly ever said a word.

"Mr. Willy, she's my girlfrin', and that buck, Daniel, is trying to have his way with her."

Margaret was the fourteen-year-old girl serving as their tallyman this day. She was young, pretty and innocent. They had only seen her briefly the day before, as she stood with the other youth of the camp.

"What?" Curtis asked. He didn't like this buck Daniel, even though he had only met him yesterday. "Where they at?"

"Curtis," Willy said. "I'm a few trees ahead of you. I'll go see 'bout this."

Curtis was furious and wanted to handle this himself, but heard wisdom in Willy's words. Willy placed his hand on his forearm, as if to calm him. Willy, saw the rage in his eyes.

"Okay, go!" Curtis said.

Willy turned towards Marcus and asked, "Where."

"Midway back," Curtis said. "At the edge of this crop…she's taking tally."

Will sprinted off as Curtis and Marcus looked at each other. Marcus saw the rage as well.

"Thank you, Mr. Curtis…for caring like dat."

"Willy will take care of it," Curtis replied. Of that he was sure.

Willy could hear the interaction way before he could see it. Margaret was crying and pleading with her aggressor to leave her alone.

"Mr. Daniel," she begged. "My tally…I'm getting b'hind."

Rounding the last row and behind a tree, Willy saw Daniel had pinned the youngster to a tree and was forcing his hand down the front of her shirt. She struggled to free herself, but he was much stronger than she was. Willy walked up behind

Daniel, grabbed him by the collar of his shirt, and slung him back through the next row of trees, eight feet away.

"Back, your ass off, buck!" Daniel hissed and he lunged at Willy. Willy leveled the hot headed attacker with one massive right hook to the jaw, knocking him flat. Willy turned to Margaret.

"Girl, go over two or three rows and catch up your tally. Can you remember the calls?" he asked.

"Yessah," she cried. "I gots them in m' head, I jes' could'n write them down. He hit Marcus!"

"Marcus is alright. Move down the line and get your tally writ. Me and junior here will have a talk."

Margaret moved away as Daniel started to moan. She picked up her tally pad and marked the call-outs she still had in her mind as she walked away. Daniel instinctively, bolted upright when his head had cleared. He tried to sit up, but Willy pushed him back and kept him pinned with his knee on his chest.

"Now look here, nigger," Willy said as he leaned down to within inches of his face. "You ever touch that child again and I'll put you in the ground, boy! Don't make no nevermind to me. I've been to the house before and I'll damn sure go back if it means wiping some shit like you off the land."

"I hear ya! Now git off my chest!" Daniel said. He had considered saying something smart about Willy's wife, but decided he would just keep his mouth shut for now. He tried pushing Willy off, but was pinned down. Willy harbored years of frustration at having to deal with stupid jackasses like this, who felt it was their God-given right to push people around and take what they wanted.

"Do we unnerstand each other?" Willy asked.

"Yeah, yeah," Daniel quipped.

Willy slapped Daniel with a thunderous blow, causing a small trickle of blood to ooze from his nose.

"I don't think you do unnerstand, buck!"

"Okay! Okay!" Daniel pleaded. "I'll behave. I won't touch that girl again. Let me up!"

Willy, helped him up, which surprised Daniel, then

pushed him along.

"Now git back to your drift," Willy said. "Don't ever make that mistake again. She's only a child."

Daniel hurried away, holding the side of his face. Willy doubted he had learned anything and fully expected he would be dealing with him again.

The day dragged on slowly and, in spite of the interruption, Willy and Curtis still had the most call-outs. As they walked back to meet the wagon, they peered inside the cups beneath their scrapes and saw the gum already collecting there. It would take about three days for them to become full enough to dip. During the cooler months, it could take four, maybe five. In mid-November or early December, they would quit for the winter until March. During the winter months, they would still receive daily rations of food, but no payment for work, unless they worked through the winter, scraping the hardened resin. Workers usually stockpiled such luxuries as coffee, toilet paper and soap to last them through the winter.

That evening after dinner, Henry worked the books, tallied the sheets and recorded commissary transactions to be balanced with payouts on the last Saturday of the month. He wished like hell they could afford a book keeper. Peering through cracked reading glasses, he whistled quietly as he noticed the numbers on the tally sheets. He picked up the sheets, and then grabbed his hat.

"Delores, I'm headed over to Ben's for a spell."

"Okay," she replied, as she washed dishes. "Take a lantern and watch out for snakes. If you ain't done so yet, you may want a dab of turpentine oil...the skeeters are bad."

"I'm good," Henry said. "Be back in a few."

Delores knew that a "few" probably meant an hour or so.

"I may go to bed early tonight. A bit tired from unloading stock at the commissary today."

"Didn't Eric help you?" he asked.

"Yes, but we got some canned goods today. Also got more canned hot peppers!"

41

"Okay, seeyas in a while."

Henry walked across the road to the woodsrider's quarters. Both pit bulls initially barked at him then came up with wagging tails after seeing who it was. He saw light in the stable, so went straight there. Ben was working on his saddle, tightening down new straps on the rigging dees. Ben was always proud of his mount and gear, so kept them in the best shape possible.

"Looks good," Henry said from the gate.

"A man ain't deservin' of respect if he can't keep his rig lookin' respectful." Ben said without looking up. Henry was impressed that his sudden appearance in the doorway hadn't startled him.

"Sounds like words of wisdom," Henry admitted. He never thought about it like that, but considered the logic of the statement. "Did you have a good supper?"

"Mighty fine," Ben replied. "Claire fixed me up a mess of beans n' corncakes. She's got some apple pie left in there if yer hungry."

"Damn, that sounds good," Henry admitted. "But Delores about busted my gut with tonight's supper."

"Aiighttt." Ben said, as he looked down at the documents in Henry's hand. "Is there a problem?

"I was looking at the tally sheets today," Henry said. "Are these numbers right? Eight niggers today at over ninety trees, with Willy and Curtis chipping over one hundred and twenty? Is this right?"

"Yup," Ben replied. "I check them myself, three times. I couldn't believe it either, but them boys were on fire today."

"Did they skip any streaks? Were they cutting shallow?"

"Henry, I rode the drifts all day. After seeing how fast they were going, I looked hard for cheats, but they chipped good," Ben said. "And the hackers were stripping bark faster than I've ever seen."

"Well, I'm glad to hear it," Henry said. "This industry sure is changing. It's gotten a whole lot more civilized than it was, even five years ago! When was the last time you had to beat any nigger?"

"Not since last year," Ben replied. "Hell, maybe two. Don't get me wrong, I'll beat the shit out of anyone starts trouble or doesn't do their job. I just haven't had any *reason* to in a while."

"That's what I'm saying. I don't know if people are changing or we are changing, but production is up. We have fewer workers and streak more trees than we did at the last mill."

"Hell, this is 1935!" Ben said. "Who knows what the next five-ten years will bring…"

"Are we getting soft?" Henry asked.

"No, boss, I just think the world is moving along."

"Them new workers have sure been through some shit, though," Henry said quietly. "Have you seen the scars on Wilson's back? That boy has been beaten pretty bad."

"Yeah, I saw that," Ben said. "He seems to be no worse for the wear."

"I'll bet he's got plenty of left-over, pissed-off in him." Henry said. "We best just keep an eye on him for a spell."

"Will do. He hacked good today, but I *will* watch him."

"Good enough," Henry said as he rose. "Now I got to git back and git some rest. I'll see you in the morning."

"Good night, Henry," Ben said. He placed his saddle back on the rack then started brushing down School Duster, the camp's thoroughbred Appaloosa. He loved this horse and took good care of her.

Willy was sitting on the bench in front of the cinder block house, when he spotted Henry walking back across the road to his house. He was going to speak with him in the morning, but felt now was as good a time as any, so got up and walked up to him.

"Evening, Mr. Henry."

"Good evening, Willy." Henry said.

"Can I speak to ya?"

"Sure thing," said Henry. "What's on your mind."

"Can we talk jes between us, sir?" Willy asked.

"If we need to talk confidential, come with me over to

43

my front porch. Voices carry in Florida dark."

When they reached his porch, Henry sat in one of the lawn chairs and invited Willy to do the same.

"Now how can I help you, Willy?"

"Sir, it's about a young buck, Daniel." Willy said. "I had to punch him down a little today. He was trying to force himself on one of the girls taking tally today. Margaret is her name."

"The Margaret who is 14 years old?"

"Yessah, that's the one."

Henry felt angry and was quick to react. "Let me get my gun and we'll go pay him a visit," Henry said. He started to rise, but Willy asked him to hear what he had to say.

"Mr. Henry, yer the Man and I respect you for dat," he said. "But if'n we can, could you let *us* handle this? Us black folks can deal with this buck and keep it over there. They would respect you for dat."

He motioned towards the quarters and Henry understood what he was asking. He also understood that Willy was paying him the respect of keeping him aware of the situation. Henry sat back in his chair.

"Willy, I understand, he said. "Do what you got to do. If it gets more serious, come and get me and we'll see where we need to take this thing."

Willy smiled and stood. "Thank you Bossm. Thank you for listening. I wanted you to know."

"No," Henry said as he stood up. "Thank *you* for keeping me in on this and I'll let you and your people handle it, unless you tell me different."

Willy held out his hand, and Henry firmly shook it.

The two parted better men. Unknowingly, they had risen above pettiness and a social hierarchy enough to handle a situation without considering differences. Neither of them understood it, but both embraced it in exactly the same way. They were proud.

Henry slept well that night. Willy, drenched in sweat, spent most of the night fanning mosquitos off of his wife.

44

CHAPTER FOUR

An early morning mist hugged the damp ground as Stella squinting in the first glimmer of light and made her way to the shallow water well behind the cinder block building. The air was cool, there were no mosquitoes and the only sound breaking the serenity of the morning was the bellow of an occasional bullfrog calling out for a mate. On a morning like this, there was no suffering and no injustice. There was only a pleasant solitude embracing the camp and the people living there. She dipped her wooden pail and filled it halfway.

She loved this time of the morning and hummed quietly as she walked back. It was the most peaceful time of the day to her. Soon she would present her husband and the rest of the cinder block building dwellers a country breakfast of fried eggs, grits and fresh biscuits. Her unit was the same as the other six, three-room dwellings in the cinder block building. The only difference was, in theirs, the room in the back served as the kitchen where breakfast was cooked for all the cinder block building dwellers.

Later, after the woodsrider rang the morning wake-up, the remaining women of the camp, living in the wooden shanties were the first to rise. They started their morning ritual of cooking breakfast as the men and children began crawling out of their bunks or off the floor mats they used for beds. The air began to fill with the smell of fried breakfast foods and the sounds of idle chatter throughout the camp. Some women had to rouse those too stubborn to pull themselves away from the relative comfort of the beds. The routine was exactly the same, Monday through Saturday beginning in early March and lasting until mid-November. During the cold winter months, only scraping was productive. The pine sap hardly flowed and many workers rested or made do with other activities.

After breakfast, and just as the first rays of sun began to

peek through the tall, majestic longleaf pines, men began walking towards their drifts as others hopped in wagons taking them to areas farther out. Dippers were dropped off at drifts ready to have their sap collected, chippers were dropped off at trees hacked bare to start gouging, and the hackers approached virgin pines to scrape the bark down to the bare wood. The younger workers began filling up their water kegs and the coopers returned to the previous day's efforts of building the barrels. Eric had already handed out the worker's tools and was now cleaning out the stable, slopping the pigs engaged in other daily routines.

Ben made his rounds with Bonnie, his pit bull. He checked tallies, quality of work and made sure everyone was where they were supposed to be. Each worker knew their job and each knew the laws of the camp. You did not slow down at any time except to get a drink or urinate. You could only urinate in the field. The other, you had to wait until evening cant and waited in line if you wanted the privacy of an outhouse. If you smoked cigarettes, you smoked as you worked and kept your smokes in your feed sack to keep them dry. Otherwise, they would be soaked as your body drenched your clothes with sweat.

By nine o'clock, considerable work had already taken place. It was Saturday, so everyone would be off at noon. The three tallymen were kept busy with call-outs. Back at the commissary, Henry was checking the current inventory and ordering supplies, as Delores and Claire checked in the mail-ordered supplies they had received the evening before. In the distance he heard the familiar hum of the National Holdings Company's truck. He listened intently for a time, and then stepped outside to greet the Company Manager. The company office was in Jacksonville to the north and Larry was just down week before last, so Henry wondered what brought him down so soon.

"Top of the morning to ya," Henry smiled.

"And to you, as well," Larry replied. "Got something in the back for you..."

Henry met Larry at the back of the truck, where something was covered up with a canvas. Larry threw back the canvas, exposing two large blocks of ice.

"Oh my gosh!" Henry said then called inside. "Delores! Larry brought us some ice!"

"Wonderful!" Delores said. "Bring it on in, I'll have the ice bin open and ready for you!"

Henry and Larry teamed up with the two sets of ice prongs Larry had brought then carried the heavy blocks into the building, one-at-a-time. Delores and Claire pulled the heavy lid off the double-insulated wooden bin. As the men placed the blocks into the bin, Delores covered them with sea water before the cover was put back on.

"Thank you, ladies," Larry said, as the two men walked back outside. "You got a good woman, there."

"Don't I know it," Henry said. "How's everything going?"

Henry was more than a little curious at what had brung Larry clear down here. Surely, not just to deliver a couple blocks of ice.

"Everything is going well," Larry said. "Production is up at all the camps due to the heat. The sap is flowing well."

"Yeah," Henry replied. "We hack a virgin tree today and the sap about leaps out at you."

"I wish it was *that* good," Larry smiled. "Still…can't complain."

Henry hated it when Larry played coy. He knew something was up and was anxious to find out what. He continued to smile at Larry as he enjoyed tormenting his highest producing camp foreman. Then Larry's smile turned into a slight frown as he looked down at the ground. Here it comes, Henry thought.

"Henry, I *do* have one problem," he finally admitted. God, how he was enjoying this!

"What's that?" Henry practically begged.

"I need a ride back to Green Cove Springs," he said solemnly.

47

"What?" Henry asked. He wasn't getting it. "What's wrong with the truck?"

Henry started looking over the truck as Larry grabbed his arm.

"Because, this ain't *my* truck anymore," Larry smiled. "This truck now belongs to the West Tocoi Turpentine Corporation."

Henry looked at Larry incredulously. He finally got it.

"You're kidding?" he asked.

"Nope," Larry smiled. "We figured it was about time West Tocoi had their own truck. Your numbers are the best of all eight camps and we've had the least problems with your site. In fact, if it weren't for the funds being transferred from the clerk at the West Tocoi Harbor, we wouldn't even know ya'll were still down here."

"Why, thank you!" Henry said, grinning. His mind was already racing forward with everything they would be able to do with this new asset. He reached over and shook Larry's hand. "Thank you!"

"You deserve it," Larry said. "Now, if you don't mind, I really *do* need to get back to Green Cove Springs. By the way, there are four, five gallon cans of gas in the bed, and a half barrel of spring water."

"Thanks, Larry," Henry said.

The two men then unloaded the gas and water. The water was considerably heavier because it held thirty gallons. They toted it over to the side of the commissary. Fresh spring water in this area was quite a treat. All they had to drink was from the shallow water well and it was a bit rank, at times. Delores, Claire and a few of the Negroes boiled theirs before drinking, but most did not.

As Henry drove Larry back to Green Coves Springs, Delores and Claire finished up Henry's inventory and placed the mail orders on shelves. It was mostly clothes, which some of the workers had ordered. There were a couple shirts, but mostly children's clothes. Of the eighty-six Negro workers living at the

48

camp, fourteen of them were children. Some of their mothers were dippers, which was the least physical of the turpentine camp assignments, while others simply watched the children, did household chores or worked in the gardens.

That afternoon, one of the young mothers noticed that a few of the children had not been as active as they usually were, even in the summer heat nearing one hundred degrees. She approached Thomas, the five-year old, and felt his forehead; he was burning up.

"Thomas, do you feel alright?" she asked.

"Naah," he said. "I feels sick."

"Well come over here and drink some water," she replied then turned to the other children. "Everybody go sit under the shady tree."

She picked up Thomas and carried him over to the back entrance to the commissary. Claire was sweeping and Delores was just leaving.

"Miss Claire?" the young mother asked.

"Yes, Kathy, is it?"

"My name is Karen, Miss Claire. I think this baby is sick. Can you check his tempture?" she pleaded.

Claire looked at Thomas, who looked a little pale, even for a black child. Delores decided to stay and see about the boy.

"Yes!" she said. "Lay him over here on this blanket!"

Before Karen could lay the child down, he was vomiting in her arms and onto the ground. Karen waited until she thought he was through then laid him down and wiped off his mouth with a rag that Delores had soaked in water for her.

"Thank you, ma'am." Karen said gratefully.

Claire had gotten the make-shift doctors bag they kept under the counter and rummaged through it. She found the thermometer and the small jar of Vaseline.

"Here's a thermometer," Claire said. "All we have is rectal."

"Thank you ma'am," Karen said, as she took the thermometer. She dipped it into the jar Delores had opened then inserted it into the boy. Karen watch the magnified side of the thermometer as it rose quickly. She looked up at Claire; her face a mask of concern.

""What's it at?" Claire asked.

"It ain't stopped, yet…but it's at 103 now!" Karen said. After another minute, Karen pulled out the thermometer.

"Miss Claire, my eyes ain't so clear," she said. " but it looks like 104 to me. Could you double check it for me?"

Claire took the thermometer and verified the temperature at 104.6 degrees. The three women look at each other. Delores dipped a large ladle into the water the water bin. She covered the boy in a small blanket then poured the cool water over him.

"Someone's going to have to go after a doctor!" Delores said.

Claire bolted for the side door and said, "I'll ring the come-quick bell. That'll bring Ben."

"Good idea," Delores said. Just as she said that, two more children stood at the back door looking for Karen. They looked sick as well. Delores looked up at Karen.

"Karen, take that pad and four more blankets two apartments down, where no one is sleeping yet," she said. "Make a bed for these children then get a fresh pail from under the shelf and fill it with fresh water from the well…" and then stopped herself.

"Better still," she continued. "Fetch us a half pail of the spring water on the side. Let's get these babies t' bed!"

"Yes ma'am!" Karen said and hurried over to grab a pail. By that time, Stella had returned from their apartment next to the commissary.

"Anything I can do to help?" she asked after seeing what was going on.

"Yes! Stella! Can you carry young Thomas here to the apartment on the other side of ya'll, and get them a bed set up. We got three very sick kids here, and I fear there will be more."

"Right away!" Stella said as she bolted into action.

Across the road Karen heard the come-quick bell being

rung as she ran to fill the pail with some spring water from the spring water barrel that Larry brought with him from Green Cove Springs. Claire rang the bell three, followed by two rings, which told Ben to come quick! In the distance she heard Ben riding up the side path and a very healthy pace. As he neared the side of the cinder block building, he saw Claire waving him over to the commissary end. He got there just as Karen was returning with the water.

"Mr. Ben, can you to run git the Doctor?" Karen said. "These kids are real sick. They got 104 degree temperature and vomiting."

"Are you sure it's not the flu?" he asked.

"Not with 104 degree fever and vomiting," Claire said as she came up from behind him. Ben very rarely saw his wife this worried. "It's serious."

"Okay!" he said. "Where's Henry?"

"He went to Green Cove Springs with Larry Larson in his truck." Claire said.

"Okay, maybe I'll see him there. I'll be back in a bit."

"We got some sick children," Karen said as she ran down to where they were bedding the children down. She placed the pail on the floor next to the wall and looked over at Delores.

"All three's about the same," Delores said. "Karen honey, go check out back where the children play and see if we have any more sick kids."

"Yes ma'am," Karen replied. She ran out back and headed for where the children usually play. They seemed okay, so she headed for her own shanty where the ten month old was sleeping. She saw two more mothers out back of the shanties and yelled for them to check all children for fever. As she entered her shanty, she rushed to her baby's crib and scooped her baby up.

"Thank you, Jesus," she whimpered. "Thank you, Jesus!"

Her baby felt normal, so she gently lay him back down in his makeshift crib. She then turned and went back outside. There were now three mothers gathered there, with one of them holding Beth, her four year old. Her face looked worried and that

51

was all Karen needed to know.

"Fran? Yo baby have the fever?" She asked.

Fran shook her head "yes."

"Okay," Karen said. "Take her over to the cinder block house, three apartments down, next to Stella's." Fran turned and ran.

Karen looked over to her neighbor and asked the young girl standing there if she would watch her baby and come get her if she felt hot. She said that she would, so she headed back to the commissary as well.

Six miles up the road, towards Green Cove Springs, Ben was just meeting up with Henry who was returning back, after dropping off Larry. Henry stopped the truck as Ben came galloping up.

"What the hell has gotten you all fired up?" he asked. "You'll need to walk the horse a bit to cool him down."

"Henry, there's several children sick, back at the camp! 104 degree fever and throwing up."

"Well, shit!" Henry said. "Ben you git back to the camp and I'll go fetch Doc Bradley. I just seen him headed to the drugstore for lunch."

"Okay," Ben said as he turned the horse around. "I'll meet you back at the camp."

Ben turned around and headed back to the camp.

Back in Green Cove Springs, Henry found Doc Bradley walking up the steps to his office. He turned around and smiled.

"Showing off the new truck?" he asked.

"Doc," Henry shouted. "We got problems back at the camp. High-fevers and vomiting...at least five kids."

"How high?"

"104 degrees and over."

"Be right there," Doc exclaimed. He rushed inside his office and grabbed his bag. He started to head out the door, then thought about something, headed back in and grabbed a few boxes from his medicine closet and another carrying bag from under the shelves. Soon, he and Henry were headed back to the camp.

"Was there any chills, sweats or diarrhea?" the Doctor asked.

"Doc, I don't know," Henry replied. "Ben caught me on the way back and said a lot of kids were sick, with fever and vomiting."

"Okay. Sounds like food poisoning, but we'll see."

The truck moved along at a healthy pace. It was a nice day, but neither man noticed the weather. They each had their concerns of how the next few days could play out.

Delores was standing out in front of the cinder block building as she waited for the truck. She heard it coming for several hundred yards before it actually arrived. The worried look on her face told Henry something was really wrong.

"How bad is it," Henry asked.

"Five children are sick and two adults." she said.

"Two adults?" Doc Bradley asked?

"Yessir," Delores replied.

"Shit," the doctor mumbled. That meant there was less of a chance that it was a childhood illness and something more serious.

The doctor was led to the room where the children were bedded down. He could hear someone out back, throwing up. He went over to Thomas and felt his chest, looked into his eyes and probed around his abdomen. Thomas' mother looked on intently.

"Who is this boy's mother?" he asked.

"I am," she replied.

"What has he eaten since last night's supper?"

"He wasn't hungry last night, Doctor. He said his tummy hurt." the worried mother said.

"And is any of the sick adults available?"

Delores said, "There's one out back. I'll get him to the window."

A middle-aged man appeared in the back window, looking sickly. The doctor rose and went over to the window.

"When did you start feeling bad?" he asked the man.

"Yesserday morn," the man said, then hurried away from the window to vomit next to a tree. As the doctor looked over by the man, he noticed a circular shaped hole, with a small stone border around it. He turned to face Delores.

"Where do these people get their drinking water?" he asked, almost dreading the answer.

"From the well out back," Delores replied as two of the ladies nodded their heads in agreement.

"I'll be right back," the doctor said.

He went out back and peered into the shallow water well. He shook his head and came back into the building. He placed one of his carry bags on the table, opened it and pulled out a microscope. He placed it on the table by the window. He went over to the sick man, lifted up his hand and pricked one of his fingers. After smearing a slide with a little of his blood, he went back inside, over to the microscope and inserted the slide. He then adjusted the reflective mirror on the bottom and peered into the eyepiece.

After a short period, Doctor Bradley stepped back then looked over at Henry. He motioned for him to step outside and lead him away from earshot of the others.

"God dammit, Henry," he said. "Didn't the health department come out here and inspect this site before you moved any people into these structures?"

"No," Henry said. "Were they suppose to? What the hell is the problem?"

"Malaria," the doctor said. "Malaria is spread through mosquito bites and shallow water wells, which breed mosquito larvae, like the ones you currently have in your well. That's the main reason why that type of well has been illegal since the mid-twenties, which was the last time we had a malaria outbreak in this area."

"Malaria? I didn't know, Doc," Henry said. "I got all the permits for the building and occupancy."

"I'm sure you did," he replied. "I'll be speaking with them tomorrow. Some asshole didn't do their job because they were too lazy to drive clear down here to check this place out. The forms they use are too vague. Under "water source", you probably wrote "well" and they just assumed you *drilled* a well."

"So what do we do about it?" Henry asked.

"Someone needs to run me back to my office to pick up some quinine medication for those who are already showing symptoms and we need to run to Jacksonville for a preventative version of the same drug," he replied. "Additionally, you need to dump a gallon of turpentine in that well, right now. You will need to have that filled and you will need to drill a well for your water needs. And for the love of God, Henry, when are you going to get a phone line down here?"

"They're running lines next week," Henry replied. "I already have orders for three phones. I'll have one of the workers dump some turp in and tell everyone to use the water out of the springs water barrel."

"Good, now let's get back and get that medication, so I can get it in these folks as soon as possible. The sooner we get these people on meds, the better!"

Henry left orders with Ben about the water and updated Claire and Delores about what was going on. Doc Bradley said malaria wasn't contagious, but they could still have a few that would get sick if they were in the "incubation" period. Henry and the doctor headed back to Green Cove Springs to pick up the medication. Doctor Bradley felt guilty that he had not noticed the shallow water well before, even though he had been there three times to deliver babies.

Later that evening, after everyone had taken their pill or received a shot, Margaret sat on Henry and Delores's back porch. Wednesdays were the nights Delores would teach some schooling to those with the desire to learn. Delores had already taught her basic math, which was why she was the best tallyman they had. Now, she was into her second year of English and reading. Delores was amazed at how well she learned basic schooling, but Henry thought it was a waste of time. Still, he felt it best to allow Delores her pet projects. She was a teacher when he first met her and sometimes felt a little guilty taking her away from something she loved so dearly. Delores secretly felt the Negro was every bit as intelligent as the white man, and even more so in many cases.

Margaret lived with her mother, three brothers and her brother's friend Marcus, whose parents had died in a fire when he was five. Margaret and Marcus were friends, but Marcus liked to call her his "girlfriend." Margaret didn't quite see it that way, but allowed Marcus to play the part. Her mom had threatened Marcus with a painful death if he ever tried to promote their relationship to a more physical level.

Margaret's daddy had died when she was eight years old. They were clearing a dead tree that had been struck by lightning. Two mules were hooked up to it to pull it over, but it twisted when it broke and fell a little to the side, on top of Margaret's father. He lived a little while after he had been crushed, but mostly to let his children and wife know he was carrying their love with him to be with Jesus. His absence made life harder, but the two oldest sons were already turpentinin, and the younger brother was hauling water for the camp. As a family, they did what they had to do to survive.

Margaret slept with her mom in the back room of a cinder block apartment near the end. Her brothers and Marcus slept in the middle room and a married couple with two children in the front. At thirteen, Margaret could already cook as well and any of the adults by the time she was twelve, could read better than most adults. Even though Delores would home-school any of the children who wanted to learn, Margaret was usually the only one to show up. Delores was amazed at how fast she learned and truly believed that she was very close to knowing as much as herself in just about every subject.

"Miss Delores?" Margaret asked. "Do you think God knows when we're sick down here?"

"God knows everything," Delores replied.

"Do you think he makes Negroes suffer more than white people?"

"Why no, Margaret. I don't think any such thing."

"Then why wasn't any white people taken sick?" she asked.

"Margaret, does your mother boil your water before your family drinks it?"

"Yes ma'am."

"Well, the water had bad things in it that made people sick. When we boiled our water, it killed the bad things and didn't hurt us." Delores said. "Margaret, a very long time ago, there was a terrible disease called the "the plague." It killed over 25 million people of all color and races. Sometimes there's reasons for things to happen the way they do, that we don't know about. We just need to put our faith in God and do the best we can on this Earth."

"Yes ma'am," Margaret said as she looked down at her book. Miss Delores was having her read "Abraham Lincoln, The Prairie Years and The War Years, by Carl Sandburg." She began reading quietly.

"Miss Delores?" she asked.

"Yes, Margaret?"

"Thank you for being so kind to me."

Delores had not expected the gesture and looked over at her student.

"Margaret, can I ask a favor from you?"

Margaret looked up, surprised. "Why yes, Miss Delores."

"Would you give me a hug?"

"Why yes, Miss Delores!"

Margaret set the book down and went over next to Delores. She wrapped her arms around her and hugged her like there were absolutely no differences in the world between the two. A single tear rolled down Delores's cheek. If she and Henry had been able to have children, she thought, she would have wanted her child to have a soul like Margaret's.

The next ten days were touch and go for two of the children, including Thomas. Their fevers would spike, then drop to almost normal, then spike again. The Negroes in the camp prayed in their make-shift church on Sunday mornings in the jook joint. They prayed for the health of all who gathered there in his name. They prayed for smooth-flowing pine sap and a bountiful harvest to provide them with higher tallies and more credit. Most of all, they prayed for their souls and acceptance into heaven to be with Jesus Christ, after they had departed this Earth and all the suffering here. In church, Margaret prayed for a place in heaven for Miss Delores as well.

Fortunately, after three weeks' time, everyone seemed much better and in relatively good health. The well had been filled and a deep-water well would be drilled the following month. Until then, they would drink the fresh spring water from Green Cove Springs. Henry was glad he had gotten a company truck, as he was putting it through its paces.

The phone lines had been run, connecting Green Cove Springs with the West Tocoi steamer dock. The Turpentine Camp received its three lines, with one phone in the Foreman's house, one in the woodsrider house and one in the commissary. The county even placed a street light right next to the cinder block house, giving the workers living there a way to see without the use of kerosene lanterns. The workers sleeping in the front of the building complained it was too much light and made feed sack curtains to cover their windows. It was still too hot to shut the wooden shutters. Henry had the cooper build some benches for the front of the building so workers could sit out there at night, instead of in the back, where it was still dark and the mosquitos were worse. Nearly everyone had shoes now, and it seemed like every month a new gadget would show up in the mail-order catalog in the commissary.

It seemed you could get just about everything in cans nowadays. The commissary currently stocked the usual variety of canned goods from vegetables and fruits, to canned meats and even canned milk. It maintained well-stocked shelves with just about anything. Most canned goods sold at seven cents a can for vegetables and nine cents a can for meats. For those who couldn't afford the luxury of a can opener, the commissary would even open the can for a penny each.

CHAPTER FIVE

Ben finished his breakfast then pushed himself back from the table and looked at his watch. He had another twelve minutes before he sounded the morning cant. Claire was busy clearing away the dishes and stacking them by the sink.

Ben had been working in the turpentine industry ever since he was seventeen and a woodsrider since he was twenty. He had shied away from working in his father's hardware store and preferred work outdoors, especially if it involved riding a horse. He had seen the beatings and had used the bamboo cane to encourage work and discourage laziness. It was part of the job and the sad reality of life in a turpentine camp. He had witnessed fist had, the darks days of the industry and slow decline of turpentine pitch since the evolution of the steel ships. He had seen it all.

At 5:10am he rang the morning wake up; one ring, followed by two rings. Around the camp, faint sounds of movement filtered through the darkness, mostly wives getting up to start breakfast for their husbands. Ben stood on his front porch and smoked a couple cigarettes as he watched oil lamps begin to flicker in windows across the camp. He snuffed out his cigarette then headed over to the stable to ready his horse for today's activities.

He met with the workers behind their quarters. After making sure everyone knew their assignments and were on their way, he waited for Henry to walk over from his place. They were going to discuss the placement of the water well being drilled that day. Ben had a book, which recommended pipe diameters, depth and placement specs. He wanted to have a well drilled over three years ago, when the shallow water well had been dug manually, but there was a three month back log. The manually dig was supposed to have been temporary, until a crew could come out, but for some reason it never happened.

Henry arrived, so they discussed and decided on a location, depth and diameter before the drilling crew arrived an hour later. Ben felt Henry had all that he needed from him, so headed out to the crops to oversee the workers. Henry spoke with the drilling crew for a short time after they arrived, then stepped back and allowed them room to do their work. A few of the camp children gathered nearby, but stayed well out of the way. The well drilling diesel was loud and exciting!

The well would be drilled in a location which would provide deep water delivery to both the foreman's quarters and the cinder block house. This would remove the threat of bacteria and mosquito contamination, and provide clean drinking water.

Ben arrived out at crop two, nearly a half mile away from the main camp. He first checked the tally sheets of the nearby tallyman then rode along a couple drifts to check the streaks for proper depth and angle.

"Streaks looking good, Curtis." he said, as he passed. He could depend on Curtis for good work. They had several good workers with them now, and Curtis was still one of the best.

"Preciate it Bossm," Curtis replied.

At the end of that drift, he saw a hawk perched on a low branch. He was surprised to see a hawk this close to workers. Curtis was only about twenty yards back. Hawks were usually a bit more skittish with people around.

Ben stopped his horse and went to dismount to take a leak. Just as his foot hit the ground, he heard the unmistakable chattering of a rattlesnake and, at the same time, a piercing jab in the calf of his leg causing him to jump. The horse was startled and bolted, with his foot still in the left-side stirrup. This twisted him around forward and threw him to the ground. The snake turned loose of his leg and wound up coiled and hissing very close to Ben's face. Initially, Ben had yelled out in pain, but now kept as still as death as he stared directly at the snake a mere foot from his face.

Just as he thought the snake would surely strike again, a hacker's blade stabbed down, pinning the snake's head to the ground. Just as fast, an arm reached down, grabbed the body and pulling it back, tore it away from the snakes head. Curtis threw the body several feet away then stomped on the snake's head, ensuring its death. He then leaned down next to Ben.

"Did it get ya?" he asked.

"Fraid so," Ben said. "Back of my right leg about halfway up."

Curtis stood up.

"Tally! Snake! Snake! Snake! Curtis!" he yelled as loud as he could. The nearest tallyman was Margaret. She knew immediately what *that* yell meant.

"Snake, snake, snake....Curtis!" she yelled back.

Curtis pulled his pocket knife out and started cutting up the back of Ben's pant leg. Sure enough, two small trickles of blood streamed down the back of Ben's leg, verifying twin piercings deep enough to inject venom into Ben's blood stream.

"I'm gonna have to cut you, Ben. It's gonna hurt, but be as still as you kin."

Ben looked around at Curtis and smiled. "Do whatever you got to do,' he grimaced.

Curtis cut an "x" with just the pointed tip of his knife into both of the fang punctures on Ben's leg. He knew not to slash the wound as that would make suction less effective. Curtis then lean forward and placed his mouth carefully on one wound, then the other, sucking as hard as he possibly could. Ben yelled out slightly.

Margaret had run twenty yards over to where Marcus was hauling water up her row.

"Snakebite! One drift over....straight ahead...Curtis!! GO!" she ordered.

As Marcus slapped the mule into a faster gate, Margaret, pulled the water barrel off the wagon as it moved forward. The water wagons weren't very big and they would need all the room possible to carry a man back to the quarters.

Once, the wagon was gone, Margaret took off running back to the cinder block house, where she knew Mr. Henry

61

would be with the drilling rig. Within minutes she could see him up ahead and screamed, "Snakebite!"

Henry barely heard her shrill, but calm voice above the diesel, and saw the urgency on her face. He went over and hit the kill switch.

"Hey, you son-of-a-bitch!" the operator yelled. *Nobody* touched *his* equipment but him!

Henry cupped his ear so Margaret would understand he had not heard her.

"Snakebite!" she screamed again.

Henry bolted for the truck behind him, started it up, then popped the clutch and sped forward. Instead of climbing in, Margaret jump up on the doorstep of the truck as it rolled by, and held onto the rearview mirror frame. Henry had not seen the rider-less horse of Ben's as it passed on the other side of the cinder block house.

"Who got bit?" Henry asked.

"Curtis, Mr. Henry." She had no way of knowing Curtis had yelled his name so that help would come to *his* area. If he had yelled Ben's name, they wouldn't have any idea where he might be. Ben's job kept him roaming the entire day.

"Shhhit!" Henry said.

"He'll be straight ahead and over one row, I think."

The next cutover, Henry moved to the next row and sped up. Up ahead he could see Curtis, waving his arms. Why the fuck is he moving around like that, Henry wondered. When they got closer, he saw.

"It's Mr. Ben," Margaret said.

"Yes, I see that!"

Henry made a big loop around the men huddled by the tree and stopped right next to them, with the truck pointed back towards the camp.

"Where's he bit?" he asked, knowing it was probably the leg.

"On the leg," Curtis said. "I done cut him and sucked as best I could." Ben was looking a little pale.

"Sorry, Henry…didn't see the damn thing," he said.

"Shuddup, Ben. It's very important for you to relax right now. Try not to move any muscles. Everybody just be calm," Henry said. He wanted Ben's heart rate to remain as close to normal as possible. He learned years ago, that once snake bit, the faster a heart beats, the faster it pumps poison throughout your body.

"Okay, Curtis, you know what we're going to do. We're going lift him up and keep his head above his legs. Margaret, get up there and wad that tarp in a pile so's we can put Ben's head on it."

"Yessah," Margaret said as she climbed up into the truck. Two other workers had gotten there and together, they lifted Ben and placed him face-down on the wooden bed of the truck, keeping his head elevated on the tarp.

Once he was there, Henry said, "Curtis, you jump up there with him and keep him still as we head for Green Cove."

"Yessah," Curtis said as he jumped up into the bed. Henry fired up the truck and headed down the row of trees as fast as he could safely go. As they approached the cinder block house, he saw his wife standing there and yelled at her as he drove by, "Call Doc Bradley! Tell him rattlesnake bite and we're headed his way!"

Delores shook her head that she understood then ran towards their house as they passed.

During the heavy bumps the truck endured, Curtis placed his arms around Ben, grabbed the frame of the truck bed and held him in place by hugging him tightly. Margaret had swung around to the door and gotten into the cab with Henry.

Ben grinned back at Curtis and said, "If you kiss me, I'm going to kill you when we get back."

Curtis smiled back and said, "Only way I'm kissing you, Mr. Ben, is if'n you put on dat dress Miss Kendra wears sometimes."

They both had a slight chuckle as they sped down the rutted road back to Green Cove Springs. Henry finally pulled up outside of the doctor's office, where they found him sitting on a bench outside of his office, with his bag. Henry assumed that

Delores had gotten through to him on the phone. Doc Bradley groaned as he climbed up into the truck bed with his bag. At his age, he didn't do much climbing. The sky was overcast, so it wasn't as hot as it could be.

It was obvious where Ben had been snake bit and the doctor gently touched the affected areas, then reached into his bag and pulled out a syringe and vile.

"This was a good sized snake, wasn't it?" he asked.

"Yessah," Curtis said. "Bout a five or six footer."

"Didja kill it?"

"Yessah," Curtis replied. "It had already bit Mr. Ben, but when he fell, the snake was right by his face, fixin' to strike again. When I gots there, I kilt it with my long handled hacked blade."

"Weren't *you* scared?" the doctor asked, making conversation to keep everyone calm. "Most coloreds I know would run from a snake, even a foot long."

"Yessah, Doc Bradley. I was plenty scared, but I was more scairt for Mr. Ben. I really din't think bout it much, I reckon."

"I see," Doc said mindlessly.

He filled up the syringe and gave Ben four anti-venom shots. One on the inside of each leg and one under each arm, close to the lymph nodes.

"Henry, pull this truck under that big live oak tree in back of the hospital." he ordered then looked down to Ben. "I hope you're comfortable, Ben, cuz that's where you're sleeping tonight. I ain't moving you any more than I have to."

Henry slowly pulled the truck around the back of the clinic and under a large Live Oak tree. Ben's leg was swelling up almost double its size. The pain a snake bite victim endures is usually intense because of the swelling of the flesh, and not so much the bite itself. Ben began to squirm with the pain. An hour after the anti-venom shots were administered, the doctor gave Ben two strong pain killers. Very soon, Ben quieted down and became groggy.

"Well," the doctor said. "You guys may as well head

home. He's pretty much done for the night."

The doctor wasn't sure if Ben would survive, but wasn't telling them that. A big snake meant a lot of venom. He wasn't sure how much venom Curtis was able to suck out of the fang wounds, but doubted if he had gotten enough.

"Alrighty, Doc," Henry said. "When will he be able to come home?"

"It's gonna be several days, anyways," Doc said. "Well move him to a bed in the morning, after the anti-venom has worked its magic. Tomorrow or the next day, we'll know if he's going to lose that leg or not. After that, we'll keep him here until the poison has run its course."

"Henry, I'll have an intern drive ya'll back in my car. Your truck just became a hospital bed for tonight. I don't want to move him...not in the slightest."

"Okay," Henry said. "Let's head on back, everyone."

Curtis stared at Henry. Henry saw the concern in his eyes and thought he knew why.

"Curtis, you coming with us?" he asked.

"Mr. Henry, can I stay here the night...make sure Mr. Ben is alright? Tomorrow is Saturday and only a half-day work. I'll catch up next week.

"Now wait a minute, "the doctor objected. "We don't need no nig..." he stopped, then restated, "We have nurses here that will check on him from time-to-time."

Henry looked at Curtis, then replied. "Curtis, if you want to stay here tonight, then so be it. We'll see you in the morning."

Henry then looked over at the doc, who sighed and then told a nurse to get an orderly who could drive Henry and Margaret home. Before the orderly arrived, Henry walked across the street to the café at the train station. He came back with two bags and handed one to Curtis.

"There's two sandwiches in there, Curtis," he said. "That ought to tide ya over 'til morning. I'm guessing you can get water from that faucet on the side, over there. There's a cup in the cab."

"Thank ya Mr. Henry," Curtis said quietly.

"You're welcome," Henry said. Then, looking over at the doctor, "Doc, could you see that these two have blankets tonight?'

"We'll take care of them," the doctor said quietly.

Margaret smiled and waved at Curtis as she and Mr. Henry climbed into the doctor's Pontiac for the ride back to the camp. As they rode, Margaret and Henry ate their sandwich. Henry offered the intern half of his sandwich, who politely accepted.

Back at the camp, the intern dropped them off then headed back. Tomorrow they would return in a wagon to check on Ben and retrieve the truck. Claire had calmed down somewhat after Delores had called the doctor's office for an update, but wanted to see her husband as soon a physically possible. Henry promised they would return in the morning.

During the night, Ben woke up and opened his eyes to see Curtis sitting next to him, wrapped in a blanket.

"Curtis," he whispered. "I think I done pissed my pants."

"It's aright, Mr. Ben," he said, then lied, "I done the same thing m'self 'bout half hour ago."

They both chuckled quietly, then went back to sleep.

The next morning Claire rang the morning cant, in her husband's absence, then went back inside to fix breakfast. She was going with Henry back to the clinic to be with Ben at nine a.m. Across the road, Henry went out back of the cinder block house. He saw Willy and motioned for him to come over. Willy complied.

"Willy, I have a problem and I need to talk with you about it." he said.

"Yessah, Mr. Henry," Willy replied. "You know I will help you if'n I can. You've been good to me and Stella, and I does whatever I needs to help yall."

"Can you ride a horse?" Henry asked. He watched Willy's reaction. He was looking for weakness.

"Yessah, I can ride a horse as good as the next man, I

66

reckon."

"Can you kick ass if you need to?" Henry asked in a loud voice.

"I suppose I could if'n I nee..." Willy stopped midsentence. He understood what Mr. Henry was getting around to asking. "Whatchya gonna ast me Mr. Henry?"

"I think you know, Willy." He said.

"Yessah, I do." Willy replied. "You wantin' me to be your woodsrider, is that it?"

"Yes, Willy. I need you as my woodsrider," Henry said. "What are you going to tell me?"

"Mr. Henry...BossM..." he said. "You treat me as a man. You given your Negroes the right to feel a little pride about themselves and you've never beaten any of us, that I knows of. I truly respect that, I truly do. I told you befo' that I'd give you my best and my best is what you get. If you need a woodsrider until Mr. Ben gets better, I will do the job as best I can, all day, every day."

Henry smiled then held out his hand to Willy who shook it firmly. "Thank you Willy. I knew you wouldn't disappoint me. You start Monday."

"Yessah."

"Now I need you to go pass the word we're having a meeting this morning and you're gonna hold it."

"Yessah, Mr. Henry."

"I want you to send everyone home, there'll be no work today. I need to catch up on the tally sheets and have them zeroed out by the time you take over as woodsrider on Monday. Tell everyone they'll get paid fifty cents for today, even though they didn't work. Also tell them there will be a meeting Monday before work starts."

"I'll surely do that, Mr. Henry."

Everyone was happy not to have to work today and headed for the pond to stay cool and splash around. It was one of the adult's only form of entertainment not involving alcohol. Many of the women made up sacks of pot-lickers and corn cakes left over from last night's supper.

Henry went over to where the new well had been installed. It sure made a racket, he thought! He tried the faucet and let some deep well water run across his hands. He recognized the sulfur smell of Florida well water and cupped his hand to catch some to drink. It was cold and the taste was better than the sewage they drank from the shallow water well. Delores had told him the well company said they would be back next week to run pipes from the well to the cinder block house just ten yards away, and over to their house. He would be glad when that happened. A foreman's quarters deserved indoor plumbing.

At nine he took Claire back to Green Cove to visit Ben. They had moved him to one of the beds inside the clinic. He was one of three patients in a small room with six beds. Curtis sat in a chair next to his bed and seemed happy to see them. Claire walked over to Curtis as he stood respectfully. To his surprise, she wrapped her arms around him and hugged him tightly. He was afraid he didn't smell good enough to be this close to a white lady, but she hadn't noticed.

"Thank you for what you did for Ben," she whispered.

"Yes ma'am," was all he could think to say. "He's a good Bossm."

She smiled up at him then sat next to her husband as Henry and Curtis left the clinic. Henry made sure Claire had enough money to buy something to eat and told her he would be back to pick her up around two. Today was Saturday, but work had been cancelled.

Henry and Curtis rode home in relative silence. Once they left the town of Green Cove Springs, Henry looked over at Curtis.

"Curtis, you saved Ben's life, you know," he said.

Curtis looked ahead, then over to Henry.

"Mr. Henry, I jus done what any man would'a done. I jes' happen to be close when he got bit and knowed what to do. My sister got herself bit when we was kids."

"Is she okay?" Henry asked.

"No sah," Curtis said quietly. "She died."

68

Henry was immediately sorry he had asked the question. "I'm very sorry, Curtis."

"It's alright, Mr. Henry. You didn't know," he said solemnly. "She's with Jesus now. I might not know a whole lot of things, but I know Helen is with Jesus."

Henry reached over and patted Curtis on the shoulder. He really didn't know what else to do. There were no words left, not now.

The next day, the preacher rode up from Bostwick to deliver the Sunday message at the jook. He reported that God has made it possible for a single room building to be constructed just twelve, short miles down the road. It would be used as a school room and a church on Sundays! He said that everyone would be welcome! Most everyone looked at each other with the same sarcastic look. They knew the camp would never provide enough wagons to take them all to church, so if they wanted to worship the Lord in his brand new church room, they would have to walk the twenty-mile, round trip on their only day of rest. They felt the jook would do them just fine.

That night was one of the hottest that folks could remember. Even the quarters for the foreman and woodsrider, who were afforded the luxury of electricity and oscillating fans, were blistering hot and sleep was next to impossible.

For the less fortunate, which was *everyone* else, mosquitoes feasted on semi-nude bodies desperately trying to stay cool. Many placed pails of water next to their bedding, so they could soak rags to drape over their bodies. Some mixed the water with turpentine to ward off insects, while trying to stay cool.

In one of the cinder block rooms, a single candle remained lit longer than any of the others. Fourteen-year-old Margaret Floyd drew on a wall that her brothers had painted white for her. She used sticks that had been burned at the tips, allowing her to draw with the blackened ends. Her mother slept on the mat against the far wall and was used to her daughter staying up late at night to draw on the wall. She felt that if you

69

take away a child's dream, you suffocate their soul. Margaret drew image after image, with her latest being the truck Mr. Henry was given. It was drawn with the detail that only the eyes of a young woman could capture, as they still possessed a hunger for exactness. She embellished her images with the purity of youth.

At last, she could hold her eyes open no longer. She laid down on her mat, next to her mother's and fell instantly asleep. She curled up and pulled her dress down to cover her legs to keep the mosquitoes away. The images of her work faded in and out of her consciousness.

Very few in the camp received more than a couple hours sleep this night, as they slapped at the constant bites of insects and fanned their children as best as they could. Even the roaches and rats were particularly active as they too, seemed to suffer the heat of this night.

In the morning Margaret's mother gazed upon her daughter's latest artwork. A single tear rolled down her cheek. How can a person draw such a picture? It was so detailed, it looked more like a photograph. She knew Margaret always loved to draw. She also knew her skills were a gift from God and felt blessed to have such a child in her life.

That morning, Claire rang the morning cant, informing residents that another day in hell was about to begin. Wives were always the first to rise, pushing themselves into the kitchen to cook breakfast for their husbands and whomever else they were responsible for. It was the routine of the camp.

Claire made herself busy around the kitchen. Looking out the kitchen window of their house, she saw Willy over by the stables. Henry told her he had assigned Willy as woodsrider. He had gotten School Duster out and was brushing her down before putting on her blanket and saddle. Her bridle was already on and he handled her like an experienced equestrian. She wondered where Willy had learned so much about horses. Then she noticed something that didn't look right. Turning, she grabbed the shotgun off the wall, a box of shells from the shelf, and then headed out the back door. Ben usually carried a Henry Rifle, but she knew better than to grab that. That was *his* baby. Willy noticed Claire headed in his direction with a shotgun and stopped what he was doing. He knew a white person didn't generally approach a Negro with a shotgun unless they wanted your attention.

"Something wrong, Ms. Claire?" he asked nervously.

"If you're gonna be woodsrider today, you may need this," she said as she handed him the shotgun. "If you run across any more snakes, you should have something to take care of them."

"Yes ma'am," he said as he slide the gun into its holder, strapped to the saddle. "I'll take good care of her."

"I know you will, Willy. Make sure you drink a lot of water today. It's gonna be another hot one."

"I'll do that, Ms. Claire," he smiled. "The heat's gonna be bad, but the turp will be flowing quick!"

"People are a lot more important than that sap!" Claire said sharply. "Don't you drive them too hard, Willy!"

""Yessum," Willy said. He was determined to do a good job, but didn't want to upset Ms. Claire doing it. "I do the best I can."

"I know you will," she said. She smiled at Willy then headed back into the house.

Willy felt a little confused, but hurried getting the horse ready to head across the road for a quick meet-up with the workers before they went out.

CHAPTER SIX

"Now it's gonna get mighty hot today," Willy said as he stood next to the woodsrider's horse, "so we need to make sure we drink plenty of water, but not enough to make you sick."

Henry watched from the back as his temporary woodsrider said a few words to the workers before they started rolling out. He was curious how a Negro would handle being the boss for the other Negroes. He never had to place one in charge before.

"We all knows Mr. Ben got hisself snake bit and we wish him to get well," he continued. "So let's show Mr. Ben we can still get the work done by working smart. The turp is warmed up and will be flowing today!"

Willy smiled and looked around, trying to read the workers reaction to his temporary position. "Any questions?" he asked.

"I gots one," Daniel asked. "What makes you think we's gonna work for your dumb, nigger ass?"

Daniel had always been a smart alec and trouble maker. He had no sooner gotten his question out when the back of Willy's hand leveled him flat with a thunderous blow against the side of his head.

"Dayum," a worker in the crowd exclaimed. Everyone just stood there. Willy stepped forward and stared down at Daniel.

"Because if you don't work, we's all look bad." Willy said. "And I hereby give every one of ya'll my permission to stick your foot right up Danny's ass if he even slows down for one second!"

Henry was more than amused. He had suspected Willy would make a stronger leader than the others. Daniel had forced his hand and challenged his authority in front of the other workers. His only response had to be a reaction equal in intensity and delivery. Henry felt that Willy's response had been appropriate. He also now felt that Daniel would have to go. There were too many good people out of work for someone like Daniel to be a constant nuisance.

"Now let's have a good day turpentinin." Willy said. "Everyone will be exactly where they left off, except Justin, Wilson and Lester. I need you men dippin' today. The turp is gonna flow well today, and we gots a lot of cups needing scraping and barrels to fill. Tallymen, keep good tallies today. Let me know if'n anyone calls out quicker than they has before. Water wagons, keep 'em running. Okay, let's go bleed us some trees!"

Everyone turned and headed out to their assignments. Daniel picked himself up and brushed off. The only sounds you heard were the tools clacking together in everyone's bag and people climbing up in wagons for rides to outlying crops. The camp was still working two crops with one about finished for this season. Henry was pleased with the meeting and looked forward to reviewing the evening tally sheets. He turned and headed back to his house, where his wife would be putting breakfast on the table.

He read the weekly paper as he ate. His face became a mask of concern as he read about the depression and of the thousands of homeless folks drifting across the country. He read about the hundreds of "shanty towns" appearing in American and how citizens were struggling to feed their families. He thought it was odd that a newspaper made such a fuss over a way of life that was commonplace in the turpentine camps. It seemed like God was allowing white people to see how Negroes had been living their lives ever since they were born.

Later, after breakfast, Henry tallied up Friday's numbers. Ben getting bitten by a snake certainly had an effect on production, but not as much as he had expected. He will still need to speak with Larry Larson about current events and numbers. He was mapping out the next crop of 10,000 trees to be worked when Delores came up and put her arms around his neck.

"Are you coming with me over to the commissary

73

today?" she asked.

"A little later, I suspect. I need to get my thoughts together on a couple issues."

"Oh? What's going on?" she asked.

Henry sighed, then said, "We're going to have to fire Daniel. That nigger ain't nothing but trouble and we've had too many other people come through here looking for work. I want you to get ahold of me the next time we have anyone wander through, lookin' for work."

"Well, that's just about every day," Delores said. "What are you looking for? Single or family?"

"Get me a family," he said. "Man, wife and one child if something like that shows up. The extra mouths won't be too bad if the buck's a hard worker. The men are usually more motivated to take care of their families."

"Okay, if any come in today, I'll call for you," she said. "I need to show you something."

"Shit, something bad?" he asked. He didn't need any more bad news right now.

"Well, let's get it out of the way," he said.

Delores smiled at her grumpy old man and took his hand. She lead him out the door and over to the front of the cinder block house. The commissary was closest to them, but she walked on by, down the front walk of the building.

"Where ya taking me?"

"Shush," Delores said. "You'll see when we get there."

At the third apartment down from the commissary, Delores stopped and knocked on the door frame. All the workers had already gone out to the field. Agnes Floyd, Margaret's mom, came up to the front, drying her hands on an old tattered wash towel.

"Mr. Henry...Ms. Delores! What a nice surprise!"

"Morning," Henry mumbled. He wasn't sure what this was about, but exchanged a greeting nonetheless.

Delores stepped forward and said, "Agnes, would it be alright if we showed Mr. Henry, your drawings?"

"Why yes ma'am," Agnes said. "I wasn't 'specting

74

company so early, so you'll have to 'scuse the mess."

"Oh that's alright," Delores said.

Agnes led her and Henry back through the front two apartments to the room in the back. It served as their kitchen and bedroom for her and Margaret. The stench was almost overwhelming as heavy odors of sweat, fried food and urine made the air thick and hard to breathe. Agnes didn't seem to notice. In the back room, Agnes stood in the doorway and motioned for her guests to enter.

Henry was getting annoyed at this point. He couldn't quite imagine what had gotten over his wife for her to want to bring him over to this filth. He saw one of the walls to the side and stopped walking. He stood there, completely still, staring at drawings on the wall that he had only ever seen in magazines. Images of the family boys, with such detail, Henry could read every emotion they felt as they posed to be drawn. Ben's house across the road showed every crack in the wood, the chickens in the yard and even a lone branch on the roof, which had fallen from a wind storm the day before. Henry remembered that day last month.

Further down, Henry saw a twelve inch square of white cardboard baring an image of his truck. The tire company name could be read on the side and the back fender was scratched exactly where he had scraped the Live Oak tree as he backed in to give Ben shade last week. Everywhere were images of almost everyone in the camp, showing about every emotion there was to feel. Anger, joy, sadness and excitement were all depicted with such exactness you knew right away how they were feeling.

"Agnes," he stammered. "I never knew you could draw like this."

Agnes chuckled softly. "Mr. Henry, I didn't do this. It's Margaret, Mr. Henry... Margaret." She wiped a tear from her eye and said, "She's a child of God, Mr. Henry. She's our gift."

"Well, it looks nice," Henry said as he hurriedly left. He walked away at such a pace, he confused the two woman he left standing there.

"Ms. Delores, he ain't mad is he?"

"Of course not," Delores smile. "It's just for once in his mean ol' manly world, he don't know what to say. He'll be alright...I promise."

Henry walked. He walked past their house, into the woods and kept on walking. He walked until he knew he was far away from other people. He wanted to be far away from other people. He placed his hand on a longleaf pine tree and looked down at the ground. His arm shook as it supported his weight.

He had fought some of the meanest, strongest son-of-a-bitches on the face of the planet. He had scars on his arm where he had stood the pain of a burning cigarette longer than another man as they drank themselves stupid and sought to prove who was the toughest. He had dug buckshot from his own leg with his hunting knife. He had done all those things, yet the drawing of a fourteen-year-old child had made him feel so...small. He couldn't understand it right now.

Finally, he composed himself enough to return. He found his wife at the commissary, looking through a catalogue. She smiled up at him when he entered.

"You okay?" she asked.

"Yeah, I'll be alright," he said. "I just wasn't expecting that. Margaret's drawings are incredible. I've never seen anything like them."

"What do you think about this?" Delores said as she turned the catalogue around for Henry to see.

It was artist kit. It contained paints, colored pencils, sketch pads and charcoal. It was priced at $7.20.

"My God, honey! Can we afford something like this?"

"Henry, I've been thinking about this for a while now," Delores said as her eyes teared up. "Did you know she did all of that drawing with the burnt end of a stick?"

"What?" Henry asked.

"It's true. Her momma showed them to me. Her brothers hold them in the fire until they burn, then scrape them into a point." She held Henry's arms. "I know it's a lot of money, but I've saved up $12 from my pay, over the months. I believe God

76

has shown us what gifts he has given that child. I believe he expects us to help her achieve whatever potential she is capable of."

Henry held up his hand for her to stop talking. She started to protest when he said, "Do it."

"What?" she asked. She wanted to be sure she understood exactly what he was saying.

"You're right," he said. "Do it."

Delores wrapped her arms around her husband and squeezed him hard.

"My Dear God," she said. "I'm so lucky to have a man like you for a husband."

"I know…" Henry grinned.

That evening, as the sun slowly dropped down below the tops of the pines, the workers and wagons begin their slow drift back into camp. Everyone was dripping with sweat and aching. Willy looked over and saw Henry and Delores sitting on their back porch. He rode over and leaned forward to hand Henry that day's tally sheets. Henry took them and began looking them over.

"I don't knows what a reglar day will show, but I made sure everyone kept up the pace," he said. "I'm hoping they's okay, but figured they may be a little short with Mr. Ben out of it."

"Mr. Ben don't do any turpentinin," Henry said.

"I knows that sir, but he's gone and I tooks his place. That took me away from chipping."

Henry felt stupid for not realizing that himself. Looking at the tally sheet he noticed that it was about one man's tally short for a normal day, maybe a little less. Ben's longer experience at being the woodsrider may account for some of the deficit. Delores excused herself to go start cleaning the kitchen.

"I believe you done yerself proud, Willy." Henry said. "I don't see anything wrong with these numbers, but I don't want you working anybody to death either."

"Oh. No suh, Mr. Henry," he said. "I hardly hat to whup

anybody, 'ceptin for this morning. I had to get Daniel's attention real quick."

"I saw that," Henry said. "You did what you needed to do, which reminds me…we need to talk about that buck."

"I think I knows what yer gonna say, BossM. You want me to handle it or let Mr. Ben take care of it when he's well again."

"Ben don't get home until tomorrow night," Henry said. "After that, he'll probably need another day or two to get back up on his horse. I don't think we have that much time, Willy. If we don't take care of Daniel right now, someone is gonna kill him."

I believe yer right, Mr. Henry. "I'll go take care of it right now."

"Tell him he can stay the night here and settle his debt in the morning. At that time, we'll have Eric run him down to the steamboat dock and place him on a steamer for Jacksonville." Henry said, then added, "If he goes quietly, tell him he is square with the company. If he starts any shit, he'll still owe this mill whatever he has on the books."

"I'll tell him, suh."

Willy stopped by and told Stella he would still be a while before he could sit down to dinner. Stella told him she would keep his food warm, but to hurry. He then went over to the jook where he knew Daniel would either be eating or drinking (which wasn't allowed when there was work the next day). He saw Daniel against the back table as soon as he went in. When Daniel saw him, he tried to slide a glass to the center of the table. Willy approached the table and sat down. The entire room went silent.

"No use trying to hide that anymore," Willy said. "Pack your shit and get out. This camp is tired of the shit you do and your attitude. You make us all look bad."

"You can't fire me, nigger," Daniel hissed. "You ain't got the authority."

"You knows I do," Willy replied. "Now pack your shit and leave quietly. If I have to throw you out, I will."

Daniel, true to his nature, was defiant until the end.

"You and what army is gonna send me packin'?" he asked.

Willy sat there, staring Daniel down. He hadn't wanted it to come to this, but he would do his job and if that meant throwing this young punk out on his ass, then so be it.

After a short while, Willy rose to his feet. To his surprise, another worker stood also, then a second, a third and so on. Soon, the entire room was on its feet, staring down at Daniel, who was completely caught off guard. He had wrongly assumed he was far more popular than he was.

"You talking to The Man," Barry said, who lived in the same shanty as Daniel. "Mr. Willy, I'll excort this piece of shit back to his shanty and makes sure he goes quietly."

"So will I," said another.

"Me too," said a third.

"Sounds good, boys," Willy said.

Daniel stood and glared about the room. He walked towards the door, then turned around.

"I'll get ya'll for this," he threatened. Several jumped up and headed for where he was standing, but Wilson stepped out in front of Daniel.

"We can't let this man make us do anything we might regret," he said. "If we let our anger guide what we do, then we're no better than he is."

Wilson looked over at Daniel's escorts and nodded for them to go. The room watched as Daniel was lead away, back to his shanty. Daniel packed everything he owned into a canvas bag and left with his two escorts right behind. As he walked by the bonfire that some workers had gathered around, he casually dropped his sack into the flames. Those around the fire stared at him in disbelief, but stayed quiet, not wanting to antagonize him any further. At the road in front of the camp, Daniel turned and headed south, alone. Away from earshot, he began to sob. He hated his life and he hated himself.

It was a moonless, dark night. He cried most of the way

79

down to the West Tocoi steamboat dock and train terminal. Once there, he walked out on the dock, oblivious to everyone and they, him. About the only steamers that stop by this pier now, was the one picking up turpentine for transport to the Jacksonville still. The pier was in disrepair and in serious need of attention. At the end of the dock, he looked around for a moment. Making sure nobody had seen him, he walked over to one of the heavy sandbags use to stabilize cargo unloaded from the steamboats during the day. He took off his belt and strapped the sandbag to his leg. After one more glance around, he stepped off the end of the dock.

The next night Doc Bradley said Ben was healthy enough to make the trip home. He was shocked at how fast he recovered, but was glad to get back to his normal routine by sending him home. His leg was still swollen, but should heal fine. Henry had the truck outside with Ben's wife and Curtis to carry him home, but the doctor insisted he would ride back in the county ambulance. He gave Claire enough pain medication to keep Ben comfortable for the next two weeks.

Before they left, the doctor called Henry into his office as Claire sat next to Ben, in the back of the ambulance, holding his hand. Curtis was waiting in the truck.

"I want to tell you something before you left," the doctor said.

"Yessir," Henry said. He figured this would be a serious talk.

"That nigger that found Ben and killed the snake?"

"Yes, Curtis, yes."

"There is absolutely no question in my mind, that he saved Ben's life," the doctor said. "His quick action in dealing with a very large rattlesnake, not only saved Ben's leg, but saved his life as well. I guarantee it. I don't know how he knew what to do, but he sucked a good deal of the poison out of Ben before it had a chance to spread too much."

"I figured as much and I appreciate it Doctor Bradley. And you've done quite an amazing job yourself, sir."

"Well, I appreciate the nod," he said. "But that boy's savior is sitting out in the cab of your truck."

"Thanks, Doc," Henry said. "Do you have an invoice for your services?"

"Sure do, right here," he said, as he handed an envelope over to Henry. "Now you need to get those people home. They need a couple weeks of routine and Ben needs at least a week flat on his back.

"Thanks , Doc. We'll be headed out now. We appreciate your service."

"Your welcome. Keep me posted on his recovery."

"I'll do that, Doc. Goodbye."

Henry went out to the truck and waved to the ambulance as it pulled away. Curtis sat up front and Henry had to drive faster than he normally did to keep up with the ambulance. He had called Delores before they left the hospital, to let her know they would be returning soon. The two drove on in silence.

Twenty minutes later they saw the ambulance slow down and stop. Henry thought it was odd to stop a half mile away from turpentine camp, so took the truck out of gear and got out to see what was the matter. The ambulance driver and assistant were just getting out as well.

"What's the problem?" Henry asked.

"You got any clan activity in this area?" the driver asked as he stared straight ahead.

Up ahead, Henry saw the reason for their concern. There were torches on both sides of the road, about six or seven in all. They looked to be down by the camp.

"What in God's name is going on?" Henry muttered. "Tell ya what. You guys stay here while I drive down to check it out. If it's okay, I'll turn around and flash my brights at ya. If I turn my lights off, turn around, head back to town and take Curtis with you."

"We ain't allowed to take any more than…"

"Just do it!" Henry screamed.

The ambulance driver stepped back. He understood that

to argue would be useless and possibly, dangerous.

"Yes sir," he replied.

Back at the truck, Henry told Curtis to get out and stay here with the ambulance until he got back. Curtis did what he was told. He knew better than to question Mr. Henry.

Henry drove off towards the torches. The driver and assistant saw his brake lights as the truck stopped. After what seemed like several minutes, the truck turned around flashed its high beams at them.

"Curtis, get in," the driver said. Since the assistant was already in the back with Ben, who seemed oblivious to the whole thing, Curtis climbed into the front seat. The driver pulled ahead slowly.

"Jesus H. Christ!" Henry said loudly to the thirty or so people who gathered to welcome back Ben. "You guys scairt the shit out of us! We thought you was the clan."

"I'm sorry, it was my fault," Delores said. "They asked me if I thought it would be alright and I said 'yes'."

"Well, ya still scared us," he said as he gave his wife a hug.

As the ambulance drove closer to the camp, the driver asked Curtis if he knew what was going on. Curtis smiled and told him it was a welcome home gathering. The driver smiled, then reached down and turned on the emergency lights, causing the crowd to cheer even louder.

Backing up to Ben's quarters, the driver and assistant brought Ben out and those nearby were cheering him and wishing him well. Henry and Curtis helped carry the stretcher. Ben smiled and patted Curtis on the hand. He waved groggily as they took him inside and put him into his own bed. He needed the rest. The rest of the crowd began to dissipate after a few minutes. Everyone had to work tomorrow and that first cant came awfully early.

Before Curtis had a chance to return across the road to the workers quarters, Claire asked him to wait a minute. She went into the kitchen and returned with a large paper bag filled with three dozen blueberry muffins. Curtis automatically took the bag, but after looking inside, tried to return them.

"Aw, no Ms. Claire," he protested. "You ain't gotta do this."

"Mister Curtis," Claire replied. "You saved my husband's life. There is no way I could ever thank you enough for what you did. Please accept these. It would make me so very happy if you did."

There was no way Curtis could refuse her kind gesture. He smiled politely at her, then said, "Thank you, missus. I'll make sure these get extra special attention."

Claire smile back at him, then squeezed his hand.

"Thank you, Curtis."

Claire slept curled up next to her husband that night. She thought she might have lost him forever and thanked God she had him back. For once, the night was mercifully cool and the mosquitoes weren't so bad. It wasn't quite yet the end of September, so there was plenty of heat left in the year, but days were slowly getting a couple degrees cooler. Only two more months until the end of turpentinin for the season, but as anyone who had ever worked turpentine before knew, months could drag on for years.

CHAPTER SEVEN

At one time, the St. John's Railroad connected Jacksonville with St. Augustine and West Tocoi. It was in a sense, the lifeline of the community. In 1892 Henry Flagler built the Flagler Railroad on the East side of the St. John's River, which promoted the decline of much of Clay County. This was especially true in areas south of Green Cove Springs. Tourists and real estate investors saw more opportunity in areas closer to St. Augustine and the Flagler Railroad. Especially hard hit was West Tocoi.

Because of the steamboat docks, residents along the road still received mail service, but little else most communities enjoyed. The West Tocoi Turpentine Camp, however, was relatively immune to the state of the local economy. Being self-sufficient and operating a forest-related business, they benefitted from isolation with the exception of supplies.

Oliver whistled merrily as he negotiated the ruts in the grassy, dirt road, connecting Green Cove Springs and West Tocoi. He had been driving a mail truck for Clay County, Florida for over eighteen years and loved his job, especially along this route. Most of the houses were well off the road, so Oliver parked the mail truck at the beginning of their driveway and *ran* their mail up to their front door. He estimated he ran nearly ten to fifteen miles a day.

On this humid September morning, he stopped in front of the cinder block building and carried a package into the commissary. He walked in looking down at the package with a confused look. Inside he saw Delores and Claire separating canned goods and placing them in boxes on the shelf.

"Can you ladies tell me where "Turpentown" is?" he asked.

"Turpentown?" Delores asked. "Never heard of it."

"Well, that's what it says right here," he said. "I have

three packages for "West Tocoi Turpentown: Attention Delores."
That's you, right?"

"Oh, I know what that is," Delores said. "It's from an art
supply mail order?"

"Yup," Oliver said. "If you sign here, I'll get the other
two packages."

"Sure will."

She took the clipboard and signed on the "received by"
line. Oliver returned and handed her the other two packages.

"Thank you," she said.

As the mailman drove off, Delores anxiously opened the
largest of the three packages. In it were sketch pads and a copy
of the order form. Claire was looking on with idle curiosity.

"Well, here's why," Delores said.

"What are you talking about?" Claire asked.

"It's a long story, but bottom line is that I ordered some
art supplies a couple weeks ago. On the order form, where you
print your name and company, I wrote in "West Tocoi
Turpentine." The word "Turpentine" was smudged and looks
like "Turpentown," she explained. "See?"

Looking at the form, Claire saw that it did indeed look
like "Turpentown."

"I like it," she said. "It sounds more distinguished. Are
you taking up art?"

"No, it's for one of the workers," Delores said. "You
know who Margaret is, right?"

"Of course! She's the tallyman who helped Ben. She
came and got Henry."

"That's her," Delores said. "Well, you should see some
of her drawings. They are remarkable!"

"Oh really? I knew she was a pretty smart girl," Claire
said. "You taught her to read, right?"

"Yes and she reads really well." Delores said as she got
up then added, "You stay here, I'll be right back."

Delores hurried next door. She returned with the drawing
of Henry's truck that Margaret had brought over for Henry after
her mother had told her how much he liked it. She said it was for

85

Ms. Delores for being so kind to her and teaching her how to read. Claire looked at the drawing as her mouth dropped open in amazement.

"This is incredible," she said.

"I told you so!" Delores exclaimed. "Henry is so proud of this."

"Well, I didn't know we had so much talent in *Turpentown*," Claire said, smiling.

"This is why we bought Margaret these art supplies. It coast me over half of my savings, but she drew this with the end of a burnt stick! Can you imagine what she can do with drawing supplies?"

"Well keep me posted!" Claire said. "I wished I had of known you were doing this. I could have given you a couple dollars."

"Aw, that's okay," Delores smiled. "It was kind of spontaneous. Now I got to get this drawing back home. Henry was none too thrilled that I brought it over here. He said it might rain!"

Since it was Wednesday, Margaret came over that evening for her reading lessons. When she arrived, Delores asked her to run get her momma and come back. She thought she had done something wrong, until Delores assured her that everything was alright.

After returning with her mother, Delores had them sit at the kitchen table. Agnes looked worried. She thought they had done something wrong as well.

"Margaret," Delores said as Henry and Agnes looked on. "We have something for you."

"Yes ma'am," Margaret said.

"We received some supplies for "Turpentown" and since you're the Turpentown Artist, these are for you," Henry said. He could barely contain himself as Delores set three boxes down on the table.

"See," she pointed. "It says "Turpentown right there."

Margaret looked with wide eyes at the three boxes sitting

in front of her. She wasn't quite sure what to do.

"Go ahead," Henry said. "They're your supplies."

Margaret looked from Henry over to her mom. "They says it okay, chil. Open them."

Margaret started opening the first box very carefully. As the paper came off the first package, Margaret saw that it contained colored pencils, pens and chalks. Her hands began to shake and her eyes tear up. The second box revealed an assortment of paints, while the third was sketch pads.

"Momma?" Margaret asked.

"It a'right, child" Agnes managed through teary eyes.

Even Henry's eyes were watering. He mumbled something about his allergies, but fooled nobody.

Margaret handled each article in the packages with delicate care, as if they were all made of glass and could shatter. Her eyes roamed over every inch of every pen, pad, pencil and jar of paint. There were even brushes in the larger box. Such a simply gift, but the most important gift of her life.

"When can I draw?" Margaret asked.

"Any time you like," Delores said. Agnes stood up, not wanting to take up too much of Mr. and Mrs. Clayton's time.

"We best be going," she said. She looked around one more time as if to memorize how white folks live or perhaps, to cherish this moment, and remember it forever. "I'm gonna make sure her brother's knows to leave her art things alone."

"Stop by the commissary and show me your work, when you finish some," Delores said.

"Yessum," Margaret said shyly.

After everyone exchanged departing smiles, Agnes and Margaret went back to the cinder block building. Agnes beamed with pride as she held her daughter close. If only her pa could see her now...

Margaret began drawing right away. Agnes had to insist she stop long enough to eat her supper, but then went right back to drawing after dishes were done. She was obsessed by her new world of drawing with pointy tips and colors, allowing her drawing to be even more detailed than before.

She drew for several hours with her colored pencils after most had gone to bed. Her first drawing was a rendition of the cinder block house, with many of its residents standing in front. Some were leaning against a pole holding up the walkway roof, while others stood upright or to the side. Its details were exact and the colors, true. Above it in bold, block letters she drew "Turpentown." She held the stiff board drawing up to the candle to look for anything she may have missed, then placed it in the corner, satisfied with her work.

After morning cant the next morning, she was only a little slow getting up. Momma was already melting some lard to fry up some corn cakes. She freshened herself up with a couple splashes of soapy water from the washing pail, then dried herself off, got dressed and grabbed her drawing as she headed out the front door. Her brothers barked at her for cutting through their room, before they had time to get dressed. She barely heard them. Privacy was a luxury ill-afforded to those who worked the turpentine camps.

Down at the commissary, she propped up her drawing by the side door, so Delores would see it, coming to work. She made sure it was leaning in to the door, so the morning dew couldn't dampen her art. She then turned and hurried back to her own apartment to ready herself for work that day.

The following week, Larry Larson stopped by, while making his regular rounds. Henry was talking with Eric about keeping the tools sharp, when he heard the truck coming down the road. He went out front to meet Larry as he shut off the truck on the road in front of the cinder block house.

"Greetings, Larry." Henry said. "I was wondering when you would be back around this way."

"Howdy, Henry," he said. "Heard you've been a little busy down here."

"We try not to let things get boring," Henry smiled.

"I've been watching your numbers. They seem to have dipped a little, since Ben got bit."

"Yeah, but just a tad," Henry said. "I had to take Willy off production a put him as woodsrider and we lost a buck, but he was replaced within a couple days with a married couple."

"Wait. Who is "Willy?" Larry asked. "I thought it was just you, Ben and Eric."

"Willy was one of the group I brought back from North Carolina. He was the one with the wife." Henry said.

"You put a *Negro* in as woodsrider?" Larry asked.

"Sure did. He can ride a horse as well as any man, knows what to look for and he is popular with all the other niggers." Henry explained. "Besides, Ben will be back in the saddle tomorrow or the next day. I need Willy back to hacking. You heard about the run of malaria we had right after you left last time? We had three adults with malaria and two were bucks. That cut production a bit as well."

"Well shit, you've had a run of bad luck, I reckon. Still, your numbers ain't gone down that much. I understand you had to have a deep water well drilled and pump put in. We should have done that when we opened this place. Did you say Ben will be back in a couple?"

"Yup," Henry said. "By Friday anyways."

"Okay," Larry said. "The turpentine industry won't be around forever, you know. The National Holdings Company may get into the trucking industry. They're shipping more and more goods by truck, nowadays. We're gonna be looking at becoming a carrier or start selling trucks. We may even get into training, so when that time comes, I'll keep you posted."

"But we still have thousands of acres of trees," Henry said.

"We both know that turpentinin is a death sentence for any forest, but it's not the trees drying up that's the problem. The problem is the *industry* is drying up. Since most ships are now being made of metal, pitch ain't in that big a demand. Luckily, most ships still have wooden decks and some walls, but more and more, it's metal and metal don't need the pitch to make it water-proof. The demand for turp is not what it used to be either."

"I see," Henry said. He had not realized the situation was becoming so dire. "How long does the industry have?'

"Oh, another seven to ten years tops, I'd say."

"What will all these workers do?"

"That depends on the economy," Larry sighed. "This depression is kicking everyone's ass. I guess they'll be struggling to survive just like everyone else. I know turpentinin is rough, hard work and Lord knows some of these people have been through pure Hell on Earth. But, at least they've had steady work, a place to live and food to eat, all provided by turpentine."

"Well, we will just keep on doing the best we can," Henry conceded. "Pardon my manners, but can I get you a glass of water?"

"Sure can!" Larry said. "I was wondering if I was gonna get to taste that new water you got."

Larry and Henry walked over to the commissary and greeted Delores. Henry brought down the two stools that were upside-down on the top shelf, so they all could sit.

"It's good to see you again, Larry," Delores said. "How have you been?"

"Just fine," Larry said. "Thanks for the water."

"You're welcome."

"Where's Claire?"

"She's across the street with Ben," Delores said. "He's getting ready to get back on that horse, so Claire has been working his leg to loosen it up a bit."

"How is she working his leg…nevermind." Larry said. He realized the question may sound different from how he meant to ask it.

Larry relaxed a little as he looked around. He always admired how neat Delores and Claire kept this place. This was probably the best kept commissary of all the camps he managed.

"The place sure looks well kept," he said. "You must spend a lot of time…" He saw something that caught his attention and stopped him speaking, mid-sentence. He was looking at the drawing of Turpentown Margaret had done.

90

"Is that a photograph?" he asked.

Henry looked over to where he was staring then smiled. "Nope," he replied. "That's a drawing by a local artist."

"Wow," Larry said. He noticed the name given the cinder block house. "Turpentown, huh? How much did that run ya?"

Delores and Henry both chuckled a little.

"It was drawn by one of the workers," Henry said.

"What?" Larry said. "You have someone working *here* who drew that?"

"Yes," Delores replied, "She's one of our tallymen and only fourteen years old."

"Oh, my God! That's fantastic!"

"Want to see more of her work?" Delores asked.

"Sure," Larry said.

"Okay, give me one second and I'll go down there and see if it's okay. Be right back."

Delores walked down to the third apartment where Margaret and her family dwelled. Agnes was sitting on the bench out front.

"Hello, Agnes."

"Hello, Ms. Delores. How are you today?"

"I'm fine, Agnes. I have a question. Would you mind if I brought someone down here to look at Margaret's drawing on your wall?"

"Not at all," Agnes smiled. "I jes' cleaned up and I'm always proud to show off Maggie's pictures."

"Thanks," Delores said. "We'll be right back."

"Yes ma'am."

Larry was just as impressed with Margaret's work as everyone else had been. He stood and stared, looking at one drawing, then another. Delores noticed Margaret had added more work since the last time. There were now colored pictures of several scenes and workers around the camp. There was also picture of School Duster and of the pit bulls, Pete and Bonnie. Each drawing was more spectacular than the last. Larry shook his head silently as he admired each drawing.

91

"When does she have time to do this," Larry asked Agnes.

"She usually has a candle lit after everyone has gone to bed," Agnes replied. "She ain't been drawing when she spose to be working."

"She sure does a good job," Larry said, then looked at his watch. "Welp, I got to get going. Still have one more stop before I head back to Jacksonville. Henry, I have something in the truck for you, before I leave."

"Okay," Henry said. "Agnes, thank you for showing Mr. Larry, Margaret's work."

"You're welcome," she said as they left. "Mr. Larry, I'll have Maggie draw one up for you!"

"Why, thank you, Agnes. I'd like that!"

Larry retrieved something from his truck then met Henry and Delores back at the store. About that time, Claire was coming over from their house across the road. Inside the store, Larry handed Henry two rolls of heavy mesh fabric.

"Whatcha got here?" Henry asked.

"It's skeeter cloth. Cut in one-yard squares, it has eyelets so you can hang them on a nail above the window to keep the skeeters out. It will let cool air in, but not much of a breeze." Larry said. "It keeps the skeeters out, though."

"Really?" Delores exclaimed. "That stuff will sure come in handy. Are we going to be selling this in the commissary?"

"Nope. This here is on the company. Fifty per roll, so there's one-hundred total. That should cover about every window in the camp and then some."

"Fantastic!" Delores said. "Thank you, Larry. This sure will help."

"You're a hell of a man," Henry said.

"Aw, it ain't nothing, Larry said. "Every now and then we come across something that would make life a little easier for these folks living out here. Now, I really got to go. Still got some running around to do."

They all said their goodbyes as Larry drove back up the

92

road towards Green Cove Springs. Henry, Delores and Claire began sorting through the skeeter nets and placing them in groups of threes and fours.

"Are we placing them on the inside windows of the rooms in the cinder block house?" Claire asked.

"I was thinking about that," Delores said. "I think we should since each room could contain one family. If the families in the outer rooms don't put their skeeter nets up, the family in the middle can still cover their windows and be protected."

"Good idea," Henry said. "So it's four per three-room unit, correct?"

"Yep."

"I got five windows, do I get five?'

Everyone turned to see Ben standing at the counter.

"Ben!" Henry said. "How's the leg?

"Should you be up?" Claire asked, walking over to his side.

"The leg's a little stiff, but I can walk on it," he replied. I was up on School Duster when Willy was saddling her up earlier and it's less painful for me to ride than it is to walk. I should be able to start back tomorrow."

"Are you sure?" Claire asked.

"Yeah," he said. "It's the being in one spot that gets my leg to start hurting again. Once Willy gets back at evening cant with School Duster, I'll walk her around for a bit."

"Well, if you're absolutely sure you're ready, I'd be proud to have you back," Henry said. "Willy needs to get back to chipping. He's done okay as woodsrider, but his skill is bleeding the trees."

"I'll have a quick meet up with the workers in the morning and let em' know I'm back," Ben said. "I'll find out from Willy if he's got a drift ready for hacking or some streaks already needing chipping."

"I believe he's got both, according to his tally sheets." Henry said. "Just so your know, Marcus is now a tallyman. He took Michael's place who has moved up to hacking or chipping. William, Margaret's little brother will move up to take over as

93

water hauler. They both already know what they're doing."

"Sounds good," Ben said. "Won't be much of a transition."

"You just watch that leg," Claire said. "If it gives you problems, come get me and I'll be the woodsrider."

Ben and Henry started snickering and were immediately in trouble.

"You men don't think that women can be woodsriders?" Delores asked.

Henry looked over at Ben and exchanged glances that only men-in-the-know could exchange.

"You know," he said. "We need to go down and talk with Eric about what method he uses to sharpen the hacks and chippers."

They both exited in a hurry through the side commissary door. As they passed Claire, she said, "Look Delores. Now we got us a chicken race."

They both started clucking as they hurried away. Real men knew their limitations.

Down the walk, Henry spoke. "Hey, did you know we are now called "Turpentown? We got a package last week with that on it."

"Yeah, that's what Claire was telling me. I like it. Claire said everyone seemed to like it too."

"Yeah, it fits," Henry said. "Even Larry liked it. Now we need to get a sign made."

"If you're serious," Ben said, "I'll bet the coopers can come up with one."

"That's fine," Henry said. "Just make sure they're caught up with the barrel making."

"You got it, Henry."

That evening, Ben waited for the workers to come in from the pines. Soon, as the sun started its daily dip down behind the tree line, the workers slowly began to make their way into camp. They came from different distances and different parts of the property, some as far out as a mile and a half. Then, the one he sought came into view.

"Curtis," he said. "Can I have a minute?"

Curtis looked over, saw Ben and smiled.

"Evening, Bosm," he smiled. "Sho is good to see you up and about."

"Good to be here," Ben said. "Look, Curtis, I wanted to tell you man-to-man that I appreciate what you did for me. You gave me my wife, you gave me all the food I eat, you gave me the sunshine on my face. Curtis, you gave me everything that I would have lost if you hadn't have done what you did. Thank you Curtis…my friend."

"Mr. Ben, we…all of us, we're all men and we's on the same team." Curtis said. "When one of us stumbles, the rest of the team helps him up. Dat's all it is."

"I understand," Ben said. "Thanks for catching me," he whispered.

"Yessah."

That night was cooler than it had been in quite a while. Most everyone slept better than they had in months…and hardly any mosquitos were able to get past the skeeter nets.

CHAPTER EIGHT

During a typical late October mid-morning, Curtis and Louis were calling out their scrapes as William marked their progress from a distance.

"Curtis!" one yelled.

"Curtis!" William replied, as he placed a dot by Curtis' name.

After a short pause;

"Louis!" came the yell.

"Louder! Louder! Louis," William replied, as he placed a dot by Louis' name.

Ben came riding along to check scrapes.

"Looking good boys," he said after examining their work.

"The best for you Bossm. Only the best for you," Louis replied. "It's good having you back, Capm."

"Good to be back," Ben yelled over his should. "Now get you skinny little asses back to work!"

Ben stopped, then turned around in his saddle, "Oh, and Curtis, no more biting me on the leg!"

Curtis smiled broadly, "I only bit you on the leg cuz' you have such purdy legs."

Ben rode on and they all smiled as Curtis began to chant, "Werken for the Bosm, werken for the Bosm."

As Curtis and Lewis turned their focus back on their work, an evil presence crept up behind them.

"Well, what have we here?" a voice called from behind.

Curtis and Lewis turned around and saw three men on horseback approaching them. The pine needles had padded the hoof beats of the horses and muffled the sound. Leading the three was a short, stocky man in his early twenties with a wild look in his eyes. His name was Wesley and was followed by Richard and Shorty. They all carried rifles. Wesley was impatient and hungry for trouble.

"What are you boys doing out here," he asked.

Curtis saw a wild cockiness in his eyes. He had seen that look far too many times before.

"You heard him, nigger!" Shorty screamed. "What are ya'll doing out here?"

"Now hold on," Louis started, but Curtis grabbed his arm.

"We werk for the Wes Tocoi Turpentine Company, suh," Curtis said. "We're tapping the tree for sap."

"Ya'll look like escaped convicts to me," Wesley said. "Maybe we need to tie ya'll up until we can find out for sure."

"That won't be necessary," Ben said from behind the riders. The three jerked around to see Ben on his horse behind them, with his Henry rifle cradled across his arms. "These bucks are workers for the West Tocoi Turpentine Corporation. They're on company property and ya'll are trespassing."

"We're hunting deer," Richard said. He was the only one of the three, who appeared *not* to be looking for trouble. "We didn't know we were on anyone's property."

"Shut up, Richard, you dick head," Shorty said. "I think we need to walk these bucks back to town and see if they're wanted for anything."

The loudest noise that any of them heard that day was Ben cocking his Henry rifle and pointing it directly at Shorty.

"I'll tell you what, asshole," he yelled. "If you punks want to stand your shooting skills up against mine, I'll be happy to accommodate you. Now, one more time…you're on West Tocoi Turpentine Company property, you're interrupting production and you're pissing me off!" Ben then shot a round a few feet above Shorty's head. All three ducked down in their saddles.

"Shit!" Richard said. Acting like a tough punk was one thing, but staring down the barrel of a Henry rifle was something they hadn't bargained for when they left to go deer hunting that morning. "Take is easy, mister!"

"Now, I know you boys want to go deer hunting today and that's fine," Ben growled. "But we have work to do here and you are holding up production. Get off this property and we all will be just fine. That gunshot will bring a lot of people coming and I'm sure someone has already called the Sheriff."

"Wesley, I'm getting out of here," Richard said. He turned his horse around and headed back the way they came. Shorty followed him, but Wesley stared at Ben for a short time.

"You'll hear from us," he said as he turned his horse.

"That would be fine, Wesley. Just make sure it isn't on a work day."

After the three had left, Curtis looked at Ben and said, "Thank ya, suh. I reckon we's even now."

"That's what you think," Ben grinned. "You cut up the leg of one of my best pair of trousers."

They all three started laughing and Ben headed back to the camp. He was fairly certain Henry would have heard the gunshot and was headed back their way. He met Henry headed their way in the truck.

"Is everything alright?" he asked. "I thought I heard a shot."

"You did," Ben said. "We had three men approach Curtis and Louis. They had guns and were harassing them."

"They had guns?" Henry asked. "Why the hell would they come out here to start trouble?"

"They said they were hunting," Ben replied. "That could be, but when they came upon Curtis and Louis, they figured to have a little fun."

"Assholes," Henry mumbled. "Well, okay. Let me get on the phone with the sheriff. Did you get any names?"

"Yeah. I heard them use "Wesley" and "Richard." I'm not sure who was who."

"Okay. I'll let the sheriff know."

Henry turned to go back to the commissary to use the phone as Ben headed back out to ride the crops. The sheriff recognized the names and told Henry they were trouble makers. He said Wesley Porter's dad owned a feed store in Orange Park and had often gotten his son out of trouble. He said the other two young men were Richard Harrell and Steve "Shorty" Lovett, whose dad was on the Town Council. The sheriff also reported that both Wes and Shorty were suspected as having ties to the clan.

That night, after supper many of the workers sat on the walkway in front of the cinder block house, enjoying the cool, night air. More were in the back, either in the jook or around the fire. They talked about most anything, but mostly about how their day went and if any of them had experienced any problems. Mr. Ben, the woodsrider, was a popular topic, and how he had stood up against outsiders looking to start trouble at a chance meeting of turpentine workers.

In the distance and south of the camp, some truck engines could be heard and a low rumble of voices. Soon, about a mile away, light could be seen by those standing up close to the road. Most everyone heard the approaching crowd well before they could see them. Ben came across the street and met Henry out front, midway between Henry's house and the cinder block house. The lit torches of the mob grew brighter.

"Everyone get inside and close your window boards! Stay inside and don't look out!" Henry yelled as he turned towards the quarters. Everyone jumped up and headed in, closing their doors and windows behind them.

"Wilson," Henry continued. "Run back to the shanties and tell everyone to stay inside and close their windows. Ben, I'm calling the sheriff. You might want to go be with Claire."

Okay," Ben said. He ran back across the road and told Claire to close all the windows and doors, and lock them. Claire was worried, but did what Ben wanted. Ben handed her the shotgun, then grabbed his Henry and went to stand out by the road. By that time it was clear the gang of rowdy people coming were clan.

Many were dressed in white robes and carried torches. Some just had hoods on, hiding their face. There were four trucks and about as many horses, with many carrying guns and

99

one member in the back of a truck holding a long pole with a burning cross held up high. As they neared, many of them shouted out obscenities. One of them looked over at Ben standing there with his rifle.

"Hey, boy. You better run inside and hide," he said in a young man's voice."

"I'll stand here if I feel like it," Ben said.

The hooded youth, started walking toward him as Ben cocked his rifle. Another member grabbed the youth by the arm and said, "Simmer down, now! We came out here to march and nothing more!"

As the two turned around to rejoin the mob, the second member's robe flipped up a little. In the torch light, Ben could see the two pinstripes down the pant leg of a law enforcement officer's uniform. It was either the sheriff or one of his deputies!

"Thanks, Sheriff," Ben yelled out as he waved.

The hooded sheriff looked over at Ben and pointed his finger at him. He continued to point until they had walked past him and further down the road. The sheriff pointed at Ben for some time, even while turned around backwards, but keeping up with the mob. Finally, he turned around and kept walking with the rest. Ben stared at him until he was out of sight.

There were thirty-four members in this group with two of the trucks bringing up the rear. Finally, they were all past and started fading away down the road. About a half-mile away, the crowd turned left on the cross-over road, which went back to Highway 17. As the last of them disappeared down that road, Henry and Delores came from across the street and Claire came outside. They all stood by Ben.

Henry looked over at Ben, who was still staring down the road with the others. "Why the hell were you standing out here?"

"Because," Ben said. "If they start scaring us into our houses, then they'll get the upper hand. The more they take away from people, the more they'll want."

"What the hell was that all about?" Delores cried.

"It was a message," Henry said. "It was the clan leaving their calling card, and probably a warning."

"What was the warning?" Claire asked.

"It was meant to tell our workers they should stay here at the camp and not wonder into town."

"But our workers don't go into town. It's against the rules," Delores said. "They know that. They only time any of them have ventured into town was to save a *white man* and they were with us."

"Yeah," Ben said. "But with that incident today with those hunters, they're just being assholes and wanted to everyone to know they're still here."

"Honey, did you get ahold of the sheriff," Delores asked.

"No. He wasn't at the office and his wife said he was out."

"I know where he was," Ben said.

"What? Where?" Henry asked. He had a feeling he was going to be sorry that he asked.

"He or one of his deputies was one of the clan. I saw the double pin-striped trouser legs. It *may* have been one of his deputies."

"Nope, it was him," Henry said. "His deputy's trousers have a solid lighter blue stripe down the side. Only *he* wears the double pin, gold stripes."

"That's not good."

"I'll have a talk with him in the morning. I need to go to town anyways to get more gas.

"I'm going with you, Henry," Delores said.

"No you ain't," he said. "I'll take care if it, so just relax. Ben, will you go over to the quarters and let everyone know it's safe to come out. Explain to them it was just a show and that we expect no problems."

"Will do," Ben said.

Ben walked over to the cinder block house and banged on the first door.

"It's over," he shouted. "you can come out now! Everyone meet out back by the old well for a talk!"

The first person he saw come out of a front in the units

101

was Wilson.

"Wilson," Ben said. "Run get everyone in the shanties. Tell them we're having a meeting by the old well."

"Okay, CapM," Wilson replied, before taking off around the end of the building.

Ben walked around the commissary side of the quarters and over to the old well. People started showing up immediately and chatted nervously amongst themselves. During the time the clan marched in front of the camp, many of the workers had gathered in the jook, as most of them drank. They all walked back to the old well, which had become a meeting place after it was filled in. The cinder blocks that had surrounded it, now served as a place to sit, with several more blocks placed randomly around. There was talk of hollowing it out a few feet for community fires, but that was the last thing on folks mind at the moment.

"Listen up, here," Ben shouted above the chatter. "Listen up and gather round."

Everyone crowded in as close as they could and stood silently, waiting for Ben to speak. By that time, the mob was miles away.

"As ya'll know, about an hour ago, we had the clan march down the road in front of our camp," he began. "We believe it was because we ran off some hunters earlier today, who were thinking about starting some trouble with our workers."

"You sho took care of them, Mr. Ben!" somebody yelled, giving way to cheers throughout the crowd. Ben held up his hand.

"Quiet, please!" Ben said. "We will not tolerate anyone coming on Turpentown property and disrupt production."

Ben felt "Turpentown" was far easier to say than "West Tocoi Turpentine Corporation." What he didn't know was, although a few had referenced the camp as "Turpentown" since Margaret's drawing, he had just inadvertently officiated the new nickname for the camp.

"We are fairly certain that tonight's march was just a calling by the clan, to make sure we still know they exist." he continued. "I don't think any of us niggers will forget about the existence of the clan!"

There was a momentary silence. It was something Ben had not meant to say, and found it frightening how quiet it became and how quickly. But then, with equal speed and intensity, the entire crowd began shaking their head in approval. What Ben had said in an unscripted deliverance of dialogue had done more to promote trust and dedication between turpentine workers and their company, than at any other camp or any other time before.

An intensely racial term when used in conjunction with "us" had done more to bridge a racial divide than anyone could possibly understand at the time of that meeting.

The crowd quietly cheered on, followed by chants of "The Man." Finally, Ben had to raise his hand again, to quiet everyone down. The crowd quieted immediately. Most everyone there no longer saw Ben as the woodsrider who would take a cane across their back if they slacked up or did not work to their potential. They now saw Ben as their leader, whom they would follow, respect and give their absolute best to.

"We will continue to work those trees over yonder and I will continue to whup yer ass when you go and get lazy on me." Ben said. Some in the crowd smile at this statement. They knew he was just saying words; words he was *supposed* to say. "Do not go into town and stay on this property, as the law says. If we keep away from trouble, hopefully, it will keep away from us. We will work together and do our jobs."

Ben looked around to make sure everyone had heard and understood him. He saw Margaret in the back, smiling through the crowd at him. Since no one raised their hand, he said, "Okay, that's all I have to say."

Slowly, everyone wondered away. To Ben's surprise, many stopped by to shake his hand, before returning to their quarters. The last to say good night was Margaret. She handed

103

Ben a squared twenty-four inch, colored drawing on compressed canvas board. It was of him, on School Duster with Bonnie next to them. They were surrounded by longleaf pine trees. All of the trees were catfaced and oozing resin. The picture was perfectly detailed like all of Margaret's drawings.

"Why thank you, Margaret!" Ben said. "This is beautiful! Did you do this today?"

"I finished it two days ago," she smiled shyly. "I have one for Ms. Delores too, but I jes' started it. I'm gonna do one for Mr. Henry and Ms. Claire too."

"I'm sure they will be every bit as beautiful as mine," Ben said. "Thank you so much, Margaret. This means so much to me."

"Yer welcome, Mr. Ben. Now I have to git to bed. See you in the trees tomorrah." She smiled and hurried away.

Ben watched her as she went back into the concrete hell of the cinder block house, knowing that soon, the place she called home would change from a heated sweat box to a frozen cell, with the coming of winter. He made a mental note to himself to make sure every worker's residence had a fire bucket and plenty of wood to keep warm that winter. He couldn't understand why the comfort of the workers was never important to him before.

The next day, Henry placed all his four empty gas cans in the bed of the truck and drove into town. He didn't feel the need to retrieve any spring water from town since they now had a deep water well. In town, he parked across from the sheriff's office and went inside. Carolyn, the sheriff's clerk had just gotten off the phone and greeted him as he walked in.

"Good morning, Mr. Clayton. How may I help you today?" she said cheerfully.

"I'd like to speak with the sheriff."

"Just a moment, I'll let him know you're here," she said. She rose and went down the hall.

Henry looked around the office and at the pictures on the wall in much the same manner as anyone sitting alone in a

104

waiting room would do. He saw portraits of past sheriffs and an entire wall of police officers killed in the line of duty.

"He'll see you now," Carolyn said. "Please come with me."

Henry knew exactly where the sheriff's office was located, but followed protocol.

"Henry!" Sheriff Morgan exclaimed, as he held out his hand. "What brings you into town?"

Henry endured the obligatory handshake, then replied, "I think you know what brings me into town, Howard."

The smile on the sheriff's face transformed into a serious mask of concern.

"Why, no Henry. I'm sure I don't know what you're talking about," he replied.

"Cut the shit, Howard," Henry said. "I know you were in that March last night."

The sheriff leaned forward.

"I heard about some sort of a walk that took place last night," he said, "and let's say for the sake of argument, I was walking as well. How are you gonna prove it?"

"I don't have to prove anything," Henry said. "I just want to talk about it."

"You have my attention," the sheriff said. "Now talk."

"Why the march? What did those people do to you?"

"Nobody said they did anything," he said. "Now I don't know for a fact, but from what I've heard around town, a couple of your niggers came into town a couple months ago. I also heard your woodsrider was harassing some local boys who were out for a pleasant day of hunting. Maybe, just maybe, the community was just reminding your folks of the boundaries we have around here."

"First of all Sheriff Morgan, the niggers you speak of who came into town, saved a white man's life. If it hadn't been for them, Ben Carter would be dead right now!" Henry said. His face was red and he was more than a little bit riled. "Secondly, your "local boys" as you call them, were *not* being harassed. It

105

was them who were doing the harassing, on company property! And I'll tell you right now…if they come back on company property to harass our workers, I'll shoot them myself."

"Calm down, Henry," Sheriff Morgan said. "You just make sure your workers don't come into town and I'll make sure none of the local punks stray out to your company's property. There ain't no deer out in that area anyways."

"That has always been the agreement, sheriff," Henry said. "But emergencies happen and they can't be helped. I will make sure none of our workers stray into town, unless it's a medical emergency. They've already been talked to. You and me got plenty of other things to worry about, so let's just get on with life."

"Sounds like a plan," he said. "Now if you'll excuse me, I have a few things I need to do around here."

Henry stood, but didn't bother with a departing handshake. Henry grabbed his hat off the rack and as he was walking out the door, said, "By the way, Sheriff Morgan, the next time you attend a clan rally, you may want to get out of uniform first."

The sheriff smiled, "You know how my schedule is, Henry. Sometimes I don't have the time to wipe my ass."

Before leaving town, Henry filled up the four gas cans, then stopped and picked up four more fire buckets. Ben had asked him to get some more since they had four more residences being occupied. He wasn't sure why Ben wanted these all of a sudden.

When he arrived back home, he called Larry and updated him on everything that had transpired over the past couple days. After his call to Larry, he felt tired and decided to lay down for a nap. He walked over to the commissary to let Delores know, then returned home and lay down. Soon, he was dreaming.

He saw himself as a young man, standing in the middle of the road. The sky was dark and a crowd was coming from up the road. They had torches. He tried to move to the side, but

106

couldn't. They drew near, yet Henry couldn't move a muscle. Finally, they were standing right in front of him. They all had on white robes. The leader of the crowd approached Henry and removed his hood. It was his father. He had a wicked glare in his eyes, filled with hate and contempt. He started to lower his torch, so that Henry could see his face better, but quite unexpectedly, it began to rain. It rained harder than Henry could ever remember. Soon, all of the torches the crowd carried were extinguished. The crowd turned and left. As they were leaving, Henry's father turned around and whispered, "Son, I'm sorry."

Henry lay there, sleeping. "Son, there's a truck coming. Henry, there's a truck coming. Henry?"

Henry was awakened by his wife's gentle shaking.

"Henry?" she whispered. "There's a truck coming."

"Wha?" Henry mumbled. He sat up.

"There's a truck coming."

"Okay," Henry said groggily. "I'll be right there. Let me get my pants on."

Henry got up to get himself ready for visitors. He put on his pants and splashed water in his face. He then went outside to see who was coming. It was Larry. He was just pulling up in front of the camp cinder block house, just past his house. Larry smiled broadly when he saw a makeshift sign in front, declaring the site as "Turpentown." It was the first time Henry had seen it as well. They must have put it up last night.

"Greetings," Larry said as he climbed out of his truck. "I like your sign."

"Howdy," Henry replied. "They must have put that up last night. It's the first I've seen it."

"Looks pretty good. Who did the chisel work?"

"I don't know," Henry said. "It must have been one of the Floyd boys. They're pretty good at coopering. That must have been what they were doing out there last night. I heard the racket."

"I may have them build me a bench," Larry said. "Can they do that?"

107

"Of course they can," Henry smiled. "My cooper is a Master Carpenter and is second to nobody. I made sure I had me the best when it came to carpentry. It's more of the turpentine industry than people realize. There's always something to build. I suspect the Floyd brothers probably built the sign, though. Those are Margaret's brothers."

"She's one of the reasons I came out here," Larry said.

"Oh?" Henry said.

"Yes, but first let me tell you about the *other* reason I'm here. As you know, the National Holdings Company has many business interests. As you know, we're active in the turpentine industry, but we're also invested in trucking, warehousing, rental properties and retail investments."

"Okay," Henry said. He didn't know where Larry was going with this, but didn't want to appear rude.

"Anyways," Larry continued. "One of our franchised retail outlets has finally buckled. We were trying to keep them afloat, but when you're retail and in the middle of a depression, there ain't much you can do to get folks to buy more appliances or household goods. To make a long story short, we now have in our possession, two GE refrigerators. They're floor models, but they haven't been used and should work fine. They're yours if you want them."

"Refrigerators?" Henry smiled. "Really? Thank you, Larry."

Henry had never had the luxury of a refrigerator before. He had seen them from time to time, but never had one in his residence. Delores was going to be excited!

"I figured," Larry said, "that you could put one in your house and one over ta Ben's, since they require electricity to operate. Like I said, they aren't really new, but they're in good shape and have a freezer for two trays of ice."

"I can't tell you how much we appreciate you thinking about us." Henry said.

"That's okay," Larry said. "We had eight of them and needed to get rid of the last two, so I thought about ya'll. Now I have a favor to ask you."

"You just name it," Henry said. He couldn't think of much he wouldn't do for Larry right now.

"I'd like to borrow Margaret." Larry said simply.

"What?" Henry almost yelled. He was clearly not expecting Larry to ask that question. He had always considered Larry a decent, God fearing Christian.

"My God, Larry! She's only fourteen years old!"

At first, Larry didn't realize how remarkable his request sounded until Henry reminded him of her age.

"Wait a minute, Henry!" he said. "I would like her to draw a picture for me, nothing immoral or anything!"

That calmed Henry down considerably.

"Shit, Larry," he said. "You had me going for a minute there. When did you want to *borrow* Margaret?"

"I was thinking about tomorrow," Larry said. "My wife and I would like to take her to Green Cove Springs and have her draw our portrait in front of the springs. We'll even pay her for doing it."

"Tomorrow?" Henry asked. "Okay, tomorrow is Thursday, so I'll have William running her tallies. He could use the practice anyway. Yeah, tomorrow would be good."

"Great! We'll come tomorrow and pick her up around ten o'clock. I got those refers in the bed of the truck. You want to get someone to unload them? They're a might heavy."

"I'll get a couple workers to unload them," Henry said.

"Sounds good!" Larry replied. "I'll see you tomorrow."

Henry went down and spoke with Agnes about Margaret going to town with Larry and his wife. She gave her permission, but asked that they keep a good eye on her daughter. Henry assured her they would.

At evening cant, Henry told Ben he had a surprise waiting for him over at his house. Claire showed Ben the refrigerator and had already placed food items inside. She said tomorrow, she would boil some tea and have him a tall glass of iced tea waiting for him when he came home. Ben was as excited as Claire at having a new luxury in the house.

CHAPTER NINE

Margaret was a little excited about going to Green Cove Springs with Mr. and Mrs. Larson. This was her first ride in a car and she thought it was quite an adventure. Mrs. Larson was a nice lady who brought her candy for the trip. She had tasted chocolate before, but it had been a long time since anyone in her family could afford such a luxury.

Faye Larson thought Margaret was a delightful soul. She was well mannered and had a smile that would light up a room. Margaret had brought her art supplies, but Faye had a surprise for her in the trunk. She and Larry had decided on the Springs Park as a backdrop for their drawing. Also known as the "watering hole for the rich," many wealthy northerners who weren't ravaged by the effects of the great depression, traveled down to the springs for health and rejuvenation. When the Larson's and Margaret arrived, it was crowded to capacity.

They parked the car well away from the springs and proceeded to walk in its direction. Occasionally, someone would stare because they were surprised to see a Negro, especially this closed to the spring. Both the Larsons and Margaret were too focused on looking for a good spot to pose, for them to notice.

"Oh dear," Faye said. "Where will we have our portrait done?"

"I don't know, honey," Larry said. "Let's look around a bit."

Margaret was amazed at the sight of all the people crowded around a clear spring. She looked around, taking it all in. When she had come into town when Mr. Ben was snake bitten, they had gone to the other side of the main road and she had not seen the springs. She knew Mr. Henry brought many barrels of spring water to the camp, but she had never seen the source of the water.

"Ms. Faye," she said. "I brought two boards. I can draw one of you and Mr. Larry standing next to that tree and another one down by the spring after some people leave."

Faye looked over at the huge Live Oak tree and liked the idea immediately. Larry smiled at her to let her know it was okay with him as well.

"Why Margaret, that's a grand idea," Faye said. "You just tell me and Larry where you want us to be."

"If it's okay with you and Mr. Larry, can we head over to the tree? There's nobody by it right now and I can draw you with the tree behind you and the spring below you."

"Let's go," Larry said, as they all walked over by the tree.

Margaret had Larry stand a little to the right of the tree, with Faye on his left, holding his arm. Past her, you could see the spring down the hill. Margaret stood fifteen yards away and began to draw. Initially, she shaded the various colors of the their bodies, then the tree behind them and lastly, the springs down below. Although she had never had a single lesson, her colors blended magnificently and the proportions were exact.

At one point a man who worked for the Spring Maintenance came over to ask what they were doing there. Specifically, he wanted to know what *Margaret* was doing there. Negroes were not all that uncommon in the area, but usually as servants and kept out of sight. He came within six feet of her and stopped in his tracks. He couldn't believe what he was seeing on the drawing Margaret was creating. He had never seen such talent in action before. Somehow, it seemed that a skill like hers justified her presence in a mostly white area.

After another twenty minutes Margaret announced she was almost done, and that Ms. Faye and Mr. Larry could move around now. She went over and sat close to them on a bench. She looked into her canvas bag and took out three finely sharpened black pencils. She had her basic colors laid out and now began detailing her drawing in black. Larry and Faye walked quietly up behind her and peered down over her shoulder. Faye let out a faint gasp. She had never seen an exactness of her image as she was now observing. It was stunning. She was pleased at how well she looked and glad she had started eating more vegetables and less fried foods last year.

By now, curiosity had drawn four people around, also stunned by what they were observing. Margaret added the detail, rendering her drawing into a likeness many had never witnessed before. She did not use a ruler, yet her lines were straight. Larry was a little concerned at the attention she was attracting, but was equally impressed as everyone else. Margaret looked up and was surprised that so many people were watching her draw.

"Oh, goodness," she exclaimed. "I didn't know ya'll were here! Mr. Larry, this is done and there's a bench over there by the spring."

"Ok, let's go!" Faye said. "I could use a seat."

The three of them headed down to the spring and the bench awaiting them there. They were followed by a small group of people.

"What company are ya'll with," a person in the group asked.

"The National Holdings Company," Larry replied. "If ya'll will let us finish this, I'll give everyone a card when we are done."

The clear, sulfur springs were beautiful. You could see at least forty feet down and the water was cool. Larry and Faye sat on a bench halfway up one of the hills surrounding this historical site, while Margaret sat a bit further up and began drawing. Eight people sat behind her to watch her draw. The air was cool and the day was perfect for being outdoors. Although Larry wore a smile the entire time they were being sketched, he was preoccupied with new concerns about their newfound talent, living at the camp. There was much to think about.

Another forty-five minutes passed as Margaret finished up her second drawing. It was every bit as remarkable as the first. Even more people began to gather round, so Larry handed out what business cards he had, then ushered everyone back to the car. He needed to speak with Henry about Margaret, so was eager to get back.

Back at Turpentown, Faye opened the trunk of the car and took out her surprise for Margaret. It was another twenty sketch boards of various sizes, four more boxes of colored pencils and even a pencil sharpener. Margaret was thrilled! She still had two sketch pads with paper, but was almost out of the drawing boards, which made much better presentations.

"Thank you Miss Faye!" she said. "I was about out of these!"

"You're welcome," Faye replied. Then reaching into her purse and taking out four quarters, she placed them into Margaret's hand. "And don't tell anyone I gave you this."

"But, Miss Faye," she objected. "You don't have to give me any mon..."

"Shhh..." Faye interrupted. "It's our secret, okay?"

Tears welled up in Margaret's eyes. She had never owned this much money. "Okay, Miss Faye."

"You be sure and hide that really well," Faye said. "And let me tell you something. If someone wants to pay you for your drawings, you just go ahead and take it. You're a very talented young lady and artists get paid for their work, just like anyone else!"

Faye then leaned over and kissed Margaret on the forehead. She had never been kissed by a white woman before. Margaret could almost sense her life was changing, but didn't quite understand it.

"Thank you, ma'am."

Faye smiled, and then walked over to the commissary to drop off a couple boxes Larry had picked up in town. Delores greeted her and offered her a glass of *cold* sweet tea from her new refrigerator next door, to which she accepted. As Delores hurried next door, Faye spotted Henry and Larry talking out back.

"Yes, that's exactly what I'm saying," Larry said. "We can make more off that little girl's drawing than we could off her tallying. People get paid good money for drawing like that! I had at least twelve people ask me about her in the short time we were at the springs!"

"Well, you're the boss," Henry said. "I know you're right about the girl, too. Before the depression hit, I've seen Delores spend three times what a worker makes on something that hangs on the damn wall!"

"That's what I'm talking about," Larry said. "In fact, I don't want Margaret out in the crops any more. I'll see what I need to do to set up some appointments for her. I handed out the last eight business cards I had."

"How are you going to pay her?" Henry asked. "She makes a eighty-cents a day working as a tallyman."

"About the same thing she's making now." Larry said. "On days that she's drawing, we'll pay her a buck-fifty. When she's not working, she can sit around the apartment all day, making a buck a day. Better yet, she can help Delores and Claire in the commissary, as long as it doesn't strain her drawing hand."

"Sounds fair to me," Henry said. "William did real good tallying today, so it won't be too big a deal for him to tally from here on out. We got a couple worker children ready to start haulin' water, so we're good."

"Okay," Larry said. "Well, I want to get back to town before it starts to get dark."

Um, before you go I wanted to ask you something," Henry said. "Since we're almost into the holiday season, what do you say we butcher up two of the hogs for Thanksgiving. As you know, we've had a pretty good year, production wise and we had two good litters of pigs."

"Sounds good to me," Larry said. "We *have* had a good year, but keep in mind, the industry is slowing down. There's still a demand for pitch in the housing industry, but the wooden ship building is almost done, except for small vessels. Turp is still needed for medication, soap and paint products, but I don't know how much longer it will be profitable either."

"Well, we still got plenty of trees," Henry said. "So we'll bleed them as long as there's demand."

"Oh and something else," Larry said. "Ben ain't whipping any of them anymore, is he?"

114

"Hell no," Henry said. "I asked him a few months back and he said he ain't needed to whup anyone since last year or the year before."

"Good," Larry said. "There's now a law against hitting anyone who works for you."

"I don't think we've anything to worry about. Ben is almost like one of the boys now, and besides, most of the workers here know that there ain't shit for work anywhere else. They've seen too many vagrants passing through."

"Sounds good. I'll keep you posted on what's going on. See you next trip."

Okay," Henry said.

Larry went to the commissary, finished Faye's iced tea, and then drove back to Jacksonville with his wife. Henry went down to speak with Margaret and her mother before evening cant. Agnes was thrilled that her daughter wouldn't be out in the woods anymore. She was proud of her artistic talents and looked forward to seeing what the future held for her. She had always wanted to provide the best for her children after her husband was killed six years earlier, but could never pull her family out of the disparity of the turpentine industry.

In the morning, Margaret went down to the commissary to help Delores. She wasn't sure what to do, but Mr. Henry made it clear that she was not to be out in the forest. Delores and Claire were happy to have her help. It gave them the opportunity to play word games as they worked.

Larry called before lunch and told them he would be picking Margaret up at ten o'clock the following morning. He had already received two people wanting portraits drawn. One was a family and the other, a couple. He told Claire to let Margaret know that because it was Saturday, she would be paid for a full day, even though she probably wouldn't work that long. He also said that lunch was included. Margaret was happy for the opportunity to draw again.

"Are your pencils all sharpened up for tomorrow? Claire asked her.

115

"Oh, yes ma'am," she replied.

As the three woman sorted through boxes of canned beans and cigarettes, Delores asked Claire what twenty four times twelve cents was. Margaret answered immediately.

"Two dollars and eighty-eight cents," she said, then thought about it. "I'm sorry Miss Claire. I interrupted."

Claire finished the math on paper then stared up at Margaret.

"Margaret, that was very good!" she said. "Where did you learn to do math in your head so fast?"

"Miss Delores taught me arithmetic," she replied. "And English and spelling."

"I didn't teach you to do it in your head like that," Delores replied.

"I just did the twenty-four times ten, then twenty-four times two and added them together."

Delores smiled, then asked Margaret, "Maggie, why doesn't more children come over to learn like you?"

Margaret stared at the floor, then looked up at Delores.

"Because," she said. "I think they are a little afraid of your house...because the Boss Man lives there."

Delores looked at Claire. It had never occurred to her that children may be a little intimidated at the notion of coming to her house.

"Miss Delores?" Margaret asked.

"Yes, dear?"

"I think if you were to teach schoolin' in one of the empty shanties, you would have many children come and learn."

Delores' face lit up. She had thought about how nice it would be to let the workers use one of the shanties for a church, as they did in other camps, but a school? That would justify the usage, especially if there were no plans on moving any more workers in any time soon. There were currently seven children who don't work the crops. She could teach them for a couple hours on weekdays and the others on Saturday afternoon.

"Margaret, why didn't you tell me this sooner?" Delores

asked.

"I'm sorry, Miss Delores. I didn't want to tell you, your business." she replied.

Delores could see the concern in her eyes and was sorry she made her feel that way. She went over and put her arm around her.

"Aw, it's alright," she said. "If I fixed up one of the shanties, would you help me decorate it? I won't be able to pay you, but we'll have more children coming to school."

"Yes ma'am!" Margaret exclaimed. "I would like that very much!"

"Good! I'm going to need an artist like you!" Delores said. "Now, would you take this box down to Stella? She ordered a couple things for cooking."

"Yes, ma'am," Margaret said. She grabbed the box and headed out the door.

Delores looked over ay Claire and winked.

"Looks like we have a project coming up," she smiled. "All we have to do now is convince our husbands."

"Honestly, I think they'd both love the idea," Claire said. "Teaching a soul is God's work and I'm sure they will both see that it would only improve things around here."

That evening, Delores and Claire spoke with their husbands and, as predicted, neither man had a problem with converting one of the unused shanties into a church and school. They knew Delores wouldn't take any child away from their duties if they were workers. She only planned on some classes at night, after evening cant, then maybe one on Saturday afternoon. Church services would be held on Sunday as they always were.

The next day Margaret and her mother rode with Mr. and Mrs. Larson into Green Cove Springs, where Margaret sketched three couples, two family and six single portraits. She made the National Holdings Company over a hundred dollars. One of the families she sketched was the Mayor's.

Word soon spread about the plans to convert one of the empty shanties into a schoolroom and church. Every worker in

117

camp was excited. Larry Larson heard about their efforts and stopped by to speak with Henry that following Friday.

"It won't affect production and only serve to raise the spirits of those working here," Henry explained.

"I agree one-hundred percent," Larry replied. "Ten years ago these turp workers were accused of being "Godless creatures." We can't very well accuse them of being Godless if we deny them access to God."

"So you're okay with our own church and school on company property?"

"Of course! What else am I going to do with the twenty gallons of paint out in the back of my truck?"

Henry smiled at Larry. He had worked with him for the past twenty years, through the darkest of times and knew him to be a good businessman and keeping his mills productive, even though they were in the middle of a depression. Over the years, he had come to realize that even though he tried to hide it, he was he was also a very compassionate, decent human being.

"I'll get it unloaded right away. What color did ya get?" Henry asked.

"A lot of white and about five other assorted colors."

"You're a good man," Henry said.

"Hell, we got half a warehouse full of stuff like that. Let me know if they need any more." Larry said.

"I'll do that."

"There is one thing I'll need from you," Larry continued.

"What's that?" Henry asked.

"Your vote," Larry smiled.

"What?" Henry exclaimed. "What are you running for?"

"County Commissioner," Larry said. "A year from this month."

"County Commissioner?" Henry exclaimed. "But I thought you lived in Jacksonville."

"We bought a house on the river in Orange Park last year," he replied.

"Well, of course you'll get my vote," Henry smiled. He

118

honestly thought Larry would make an outstanding commissioner.

After the paint and twenty-two brushes had been unloaded, Henry watched as Larry's truck disappear down the dusty road headed back to Green Cove Springs. The air was cool and mosquitos weren't as thick this time of the year. Thanksgiving was in twenty more days, so there may be enough time to have the schoolhouse done by then. They would start immediately.

Henry spoke to Ernest Floyd, their master cooper. He told him about the plans for the church and that they would need five rows of benches for folks to sit on and a pulpit. He said he would like to get them in before Thanksgiving, but he must be caught up with barrel making for pine sap before he did any work on the benches. Ernest assured Henry it would be taken care of.

The outside of the shanty was painted white with brown trim by Sunday evening, and the interior was completed the following Sunday. Many workers helped paint after evening cant, using lanterns to help them see. Margaret began painting murals of both church and school themes that Claire and Delores had drawn rough sketches of. Her paintings were of the usual detailed exactness and a sight to behold. Alternating sections of wall were painted as a religious depiction or school scene, with children sitting at their desk or writing on a chalkboard.

Having plenty of lumber from a load shipped down from Georgia, Ernest finished up the benches for the church. Since the benches would also serve as desks for the school children during classes, some mothers had sewn cushions from empty burlap feed sacks and stuffed them with moss. This would allow the children to sit on the floor in relative comfort and place their supplies on the bench to work. Both Claire and Delores would adjust their schedules and take turns teaching.

Until a couple months ago, they had a traveling preacher

119

who would visit on occasions. He stopped visiting when a one-room church was built closer to his area.

Claire had spoken with the head of the Episcopal church earlier in the year to see about having another man ordained. Basically, all he would need is a Certificate of Ordination issued by the Clay County Council of Churches after meeting and interviewing the candidate. Turpentown now had a preacher who was not ordained, but preached the gospel at the camp jook joint. That man was Alonzo "Catface" Demmers.

Catface received his nickname because of the two rows of slanted scars he had on his chest. He first started working at Brownhill Turpentine Camp, outside of Bakers Bend, North Carolina twelve years ago. He had been warned that the catfaces he had cut were too horizontal, thereby restricting the flow of sap. After the third warning, the camp foreman beat him, and then carved an example on his chest. He recovered from his beating, but the infection from the catface on his chest almost killed him. He became better at slanting his hacks and firmly believed it had been the hand of God that had kept him alive when his employers did not think him important enough to waste antibiotics on.

"I don't understand how God could be so loving as to allow me a pulpit from where I can express to you what a joy it is to share His word," Catface said as he stood in front of the congregation of their new church. "We look at life and feel somehow, we've been left behind. But if we stepped back and truly looked at what we have, we realize that we're all children of God and share equally in all the joys and treasures that we have if we would only reach out to them.

We have food to eat, we have our jobs, we have shelter from the storms, we have clothes to wear and most important, we have each other. Consider the souls which pass by our camp almost every day. Many have no homes, most have little to eat and few have money on which to live. And now we have this beautiful new church and schoolroom!"

Catface gave every time to gaze around the room and

take it all in. The room was larger than any other room at the camp. The interior load-bearing walls had been removed and six-by-six inch beams put in to support the weight of the roof and accommodate a larger gathering of people.

"This morning," he continued, "Our message is one of thanks. Thanks to God for all that he has provided for us. And thanks to Mr. Henry and Miss Delores and everyone else who helped us to have our own church and our own school. We must work hard to show them we care and appreciate everything they do for us."

After the morning sermon, most gathered at an outside grill that was set up to cook some chicken. Stella had used the cinder block kitchen to boil up a big pot of black beans and greens. After eating, many went to swim in the nearby creek, while others stood around to socialize. Larry had driven down to see the church and pay his respects. He, Henry, Ben and a handful of the workers stood under the shade of an oak tree to smoke cigarettes, and talk about things men talk about at such gatherings.

"Henry, have you been keeping up with world news?" Larry asked.

"A little bit," he responded. "Are you talking about all the trouble going on over in Germany?"

"Yes. It's looking pretty scary over there. It wouldn't surprise me if it didn't erupt into a war of some kind. That guy, Hitler, is pretty crazy if you ask me."

"Yes, I agree," Henry said. "Let's just hope he keeps all that trouble over there on his side of the pond."

"I certainly hope so."

"Say, how's your bid for County Commissioner coming?" Henry asked.

"Had to forget it," Larry said. "I have too many business endeavors, which could be viewed as a conflict of interest."

"Sorry to hear that," Henry said. "I think you would have made a fine County Commissioner."

121

"Well, thanks, but I just don't have the time to sort through all the processes in getting elected."

"Gotcha," Henry said.

About that time, Willy walked up with something in his hand.

"Whatchya got here," Larry asked.

"It's some kind of a belt buckle, I think." Willy said.

"Mind if I look at it?"

"Yessah, Mr. Larry," Willy said as he handed it over.

Larry took the old, corroded buckle and looked it.

"It looks like an old Civil War belt buckle, but I can't quite make out any of the symbols," he said. "Where did you get this, Willy?"

"I found it out in crop two. A couple hundred yards out that way," he said, pointing.

Larry gave the souvenir back to Willy.

"The closest skirmishes around here were over at Oloustee," he said. "Some soldier probably dropped it along the way."

"Can I keep it, Mr. Larry?"

"Willy," Larry smiled. "You can keep anything you find out in them pines that ain't belonging to the National Holding Company, used for the extraction of pine sap to make turpentine."

The other men smiled.

"Thank ya suh," Willy said. "Can I get any of you some coffee or sweet tea?"

"I believe I'll have some, thank you," Henry replied.

"Me too!" said Ben and Larry.

"Coming right up," Willy said as he headed over to the side window of the commissary where Claire had a pitcher of ice-cold tea. He brought the men back their tea then excused himself politely to go for a swim. He ran the short distance from the quarters over to the creek one hundred yards away. He saw Stella standing by the creek side, watching the others swim. He came up behind her, slipped his arm around her waist and kissed

122

her on the back of the neck.

"That better be my man behin' me," she purred. "If you ain't, you better be ready to have your ass whupped by my husband."

"Now does this feel like any other man in the camp," Willy asked as he pressed his body closer to hers.

Stella turned to face him and said, "Now if you're going to press that sexy body against me, I'd prefer you do it so I can look into those brown eyes of yours."

She had her face turned up to him and he kissed her gently, then wrapped his arms around her. At this time, there were no problems in the world. There was no hunger or poverty or injustice or suffering. There was only one man and one woman, very much in love.

"Willy," Stella said. "I wanted to tell you I'm sorry."

"You're sorry?" he asked. "What are you sorry for?"

"For all the sleep you'll be losing."

Willy's expression took on a look of bewilderment. Stella was not making any sense at all. He held her at arm's length and looked into her face.

"Stella, what the heck are you talking about?" he asked.

"Our baby will sometimes wake up at three or four in the morning," she said. "I'll be getting up to feed her, but she may fuss a little until she's been fed."

Willy noticed the very faintest signs of a grin at the corners of her mouth as it occurred to him what she was saying. His eyes filled with tears as he screamed at the top of his lungs!

"Aaaaaaaaaaaaa!"

The entire camp heard him as most everyone jumped and turned to the two standing on the creek bank. Many came running, thinking one of them was hurt.

"We're going to have a baby!" Willy wept as astonished onlookers joined in the moment. There were hugs and handshakes all around. It was a very confusing site for Larry, Henry and their group as they came running through the woods.

"What happened," Henry shouted. "Who's hurt?"

"Nobody's hurt, Mr. Henry," Louis smiled. "Willy jus

123

found out he's gonna be a daddy."

Henry and the others stopped, when they realized what the occasion was. One-by-one they made their way over to Stella and Willy to offer their congratulations. The two were elated. They weren't actually trying to have a baby, but they both had been hoping for one for the past nine years. Stella was afraid she may be getting too old to bear children, but those feelings had all but disappeared now. Soon, most of the group had wondered over to the jook joint for some hoecakes, pinto beans and a glass of shine to toast the soon-to-be-parents. Since tomorrow was a work day, they knew it would be a short celebration.

CHAPTER TEN

On Thanksgiving Day of 1935, Henry and Ben sat with their wives on Henry's back porch after a magnificent country-cooked dinner. Even their dogs Bonnie and Pete, enjoyed an occasional scrap tossed off the porch. They had not only finished their own dinner, but had visited the workers feast at the jook to wish them a Happy Thanksgiving as well. While there, Stella, Agnes and the others, had insisted they have a piece of pumpkin pie, made from the pumpkins they had grown in their gardens on the opposite side of the shanties. They all agreed the pie was delicious.

The air had turned cool and breezy as the sun crawled down into the pine trees occasionally peeking through, casting golden silhouettes on Ben's house across the road.

"I sure am happy for Willy and Stella," Delores sighed. "Stella told me months ago they would be thrilled if she got pregnant. Henry, will we still be using the same midwife that delivered that baby earlier this year?"

"I don't see why not," Henry said. "She seemed to have done alright when she delivered Nathan and Rachel's baby in their shanty, earlier this year."

"Well, we'll be going through Doc Bradley," Ben said. As soon as the last words were out of his mouth, his face turned serious and Claire's face turned red. Delores looked from Ben to Henry, and finally over to Claire.

"Claire?" she asked.

"Oh, shit," Ben said. He realized he had let the cat out of the bag before they had officially announced that Claire may be pregnant as well.

"What?" Henry asked, staring at Claire's stomach.

"We were going to tell you when we were absolutely sure," Claire said as she glared at Ben. "We have a doctor's appointment next Tuesday and will know for sure then. I'm pretty sure, though."

125

Delores rose and stepped over and gave Claire a hug as Henry rose to shake Ben's hand.

"That's great news," Henry said.

"I'm so happy for ya'll," Delores said. "How far along are ya?"

"Well," Claire said. "Almost three months, as far as we can figure."

"That's wonderful news!"

"I suppose you're gonna want a day off when the baby is born," Henry said.

Claire's face looked shocked, but Ben knew Henry's humor and responded.

"No, you slave-driving sumbitch," he laughed. "I'm gonna want *two* days off."

The mood had turned joyous as they opened a bottle of wine and took turns toasting the day and each other. Soon, the telephone rang.

"I'll get that," Delores said. "It's probably my sister from Ohio, wanting to wish us Happy Thanksgiving."

Delores rose and went inside as Henry, Ben and Claire started discussing boys and girls baby names.

"Henry, it's for you," Delores said through the back door. "It's Larry."

"Be right back," Henry said to his guests.

Delores placed their small, bright red Zenith AM radio on the kitchen window ledge pointing outwards, but waited for Henry to go finish his phone call and return to the porch before turning it on.

Ben and Claire saw a look of concern on Henry's face as he sat back down.

"What is it?" Ben asked.

"Shhh…listen." Henry said as Delores turned the radio on.

"…asked about one coming ashore so late in the season, Robert Higgins, Chief Meteorologist for the State of Florida said that although hurricane season officially doesn't end until the thirtieth of November, it was extremely unlikely for a hurricane

126

to hit a coastline this late in the season. Furthermore, he continued, one of this magnitude, being a category-four, was even more unlikely. As we know, a category-four hurricane is capable of generating sustained winds from one hundred and thirty miles-per-hour, up to one hundred and fifty-six miles-per-hour!

Repeat Alert! The Weather Bureau has issued an emergency alert for all Florida's East Coast, especially Northern Florida and Southern Georgia. This hurricane is expected to move inland just above Jacksonville, tomorrow evening at approximately seven o'clock, but could come inland as far south as St. Augustine. Residents are advised to board up windows if possible and seek shelter in secure locations. Those in low-lying terrain should seek shelter on higher ground and prepare for high winds and possible flooding!"

"Oh Dear God," Delores said.

"Delores, how are we doing in groceries?" Henry asked as he looked up at the sky.

"We're good," she replied.

"Good! Now will you get me some paper and something to write with? We need to start taking notes and write down whatever we can think of to prepare for this storm. We have almost twenty-four hours. We don't know how hard it will hit us, but we can expect one hell of a storm blowing through. Ben, do you want to go tell the workers that there is a hurricane gonna hit tomorrow and there will be no work? I'll go rattle the cinder block folks."

"Will do," Ben said as he rose. "I'll have them pick up any loose tubs or other stuff laying around."

"Good idea!" Henry said. "You and Claire should plan on staying with us. You've got all that crawlspace under your house. I'm thinking a heavy wind might blow it off its foundations."

"The worker's shanties are the same design," Ben said. "Maybe they should stay in the cinder block quarters."

"That may be a good idea, too," Henry said.

"Okay, we can figure that out as we go along," Ben said.

"I'll go back and let them know about the storm."

"Okay."

Ben headed to the back of shanty row just as it was almost completely dark, but still light enough to see some very mean-looking, dark clouds looming in the distance. An occasional flash of brilliant white light was proof positive this storm meant business. He saw a small crowd standing by the fire.

"We got us a hurricane coming in folks! Spread the word quickly and let's get the windows shuttered and any loose pails or tubs picked up," he yelled. "After everything is secured, everyone head over to the cinder block quarters. It will be much safer for you there, than in these shanties."

Just about everyone heard him in the area and soon, the place was a beehive of activity. Several women began taking down clothes hanging on the clothesline stretched across several side yards. Others began picking up pails, bucks, washboards and anything else that could be blown away.

Up front by the cinder block quarters, Henry was spreading the same news and the workers were frantically closing their shutters and nailing them where they could. Those without latches, Henry instructed to nail boards across the frames. He went inside the commissary and was disappointed they hadn't taken the time to install metal clips securing the roof trusses down to the top-plate of the external walls. They were called "hurricane clips" for a good reason. Too late now, he thought.

Back outside he walked down the front walk and told each unit to expect workers from the shanties seeking shelter in the block structure. They all agreed the block building was far sturdier than the wooden structures, and would welcome those seeking shelter.

Ernest rushed over to the cooperage and chained the large stacks of old-growth pine boards together. If these started flying around, he thought, they would surely cause a lot of damage.

128

By three a.m. the camp was as close to being storm-ready as they were going to get. There was nothing left to do, but wait. Everyone was encouraged to try and get some sleep, but most knew there would be no sleep this night. The wind had picked up slightly and the shuttered windows rattled on occasion. The cinder block quarters were packed with most of the shanty dwellers, except those who chose to ride the storm out in their shanty quarters.

By six a.m. the wind was howling, but not like they had expected. Henry and Ben monitored the radio for every detail. They learned the hurricane had turned north and that they would avoid a full force storm. At this point, the most irritating characteristic of the storm was boredom. Some brave souls even ventured outside to feel the strength of the storm and check on the condition of the camp.

That evening, the winds increased to near sixty-two - miles per hour and the camp hunkered down. As the winds subsided, most of the camp was able to finally get some sleep. By six the next morning, the air was calm, but still overcast. Henry and Ben went outside to survey the damage and formulate a plan of action. One of the shanties and a corner of the cinder block building had roof damage, but nothing serious. The pines had buffered the wind, before reaching the shanties.

"Come on," Henry said. "Let's go check out the crops."

"Let's go," Ben said. He knew Henry wanted to check the trees to see if there was any damage or uprooted trees. Henry took a scrape bucket and turned it upside-down. He stood on the bucket and peered down inside the quart-sized Herty cup. He then stepped down, away from the tree and looked at the bottom catface.

"When was this crop chipped?" he asked.

"Um, most on these streaks was only 'bout two days," Ben said. "Should be close to half-full."

"Are you sure," Henry asked?

"Course, I'm sure," Ben said. "Why you ask?"

"Ring the morning cant for a meeting," Henry said. "We're working today."

"Right away, Henry," Ben replied. "What's going on?"

Henry looked over at Ben as they walked back to the camp.

"Have you ever heard of the process known as a "tube squeeze'?"

""I think so," Ben replied. "Isn't that where they tried to sap early trees by tying a rope at the top and pulling it back and forth to *squeeze* the sap out?"

"Yup," Henry said. "The storm did it for us. Those cups are full. We didn't get all that much rain, but got plenty of wind action."

"Full?" Ben asked. "Well hell, we got a shitload more streaks that are further along than those! Their cups will be overflowing!"

"Exactly," Henry said. "And did you see the lower catface of those same trees?

"No."

"Bleeding sap." Henry said. "All that swooshing around that those pines were doing freed up the lower streaks as well. Now, we can scrape all that after it starts getting cold, but the new drips need to be dipped or we're gonna play hell getting that gum outta there. Now, I don't know how cold it's gonna get and how fast, but I suspect that storm changed the game a bit."

Ben was beginning to understand the sense of urgency Henry was feeling. Dipping was a whole lot easier than scraping, which took twice as long. There was work to be done and a lot of it. The sooner it was completed prior to cold weather setting in, the easier and faster it would be to work the sap. Once cold weather set in, sap turned to gum and stopped flowing almost completely.

A typical wake up was one ring, followed by two rings, which meant get up, get ready and get to work. The morning cant, which signaled a meeting prior to work, was three pairs of two rings. This told everyone there was information to be put out. After cant was rung, people began showing up at the well, behind the cinder block quarters.

"Good morning, everyone," Henry said in a loud voice.

130

"I hope everyone made it through the storm okay. Is everyone alright?"

Most everyone mumbled they were okay as Ben did a head count. Everyone was there as far as he could tell.

"We've had quite a night," Henry continued. "The wind really worked the sap and the cups are full. Today, being Saturday, we'll work a full day dipping. We need to collect all the sap the storm has brought out, so everyone will be dipping. Tallymen, I'll need good counts today and you're gonna be busy! Tomorrow, after churches services, we'll be working as well. Everyone will be getting a full day's pay for today and tomorrow. That will give everyone a little extra money for the holiday season coming up."

The crowd mumbled approval at the prospect of making an extra two dollars for Christmas. In the past, when camps added extra hours the workers sometimes did not get paid for their efforts.

"Also," Henry continued. "The bottom faces have flow pretty good, so we'll have lots of scraping to keep us busy as the weather turns cold. Are there any questions?"

Everyone looked around, but nobody had anything to ask. Most were anxious to get started.

"Okay, let's get to dipping!" Ben said.

Ben was on horseback, so Henry hurried over before he rode off.

"Ben, I need you to have Margaret tallying today. Whoever took her place needs to be dipping. We need all the dippers we got," he said. "I'll go let Margaret know she'll be tallying today."

"Will do," Ben said. He then turned around and rode back towards the workers walking away. "Hey, William! Wait up!"

Henry went down to where Margaret stayed with her family to let her know she would be tallying today. She was thrilled to be back out in the pines and told Henry she would be ready shortly. She found her old pair of shoes, put them on and went down to the commissary to get the tally sheets.

Those working nearby crops started walking out to their drifts, while others climbed aboard the wagons heading out. They would all be dipping today. That involved emptying the Herty cups into a four gallon bucket. Once that was full, they would carry the bucket to the closest barrel and pour it in. At that time, they would call out their name for the tallyman to record. Each name called out represented four gallons of sap being poured into a barrel by a dipper.

The day was as active as anyone could remember. Names were being tallied rapidly and the barrels were filling up fast. Ben rode around as Bonnie followed close by. He instructed the barrel wagons to store the barrels in a field next to the road for transport to the steamer in West Tocoi starting Monday. By the end of the day, there were sixty-four full barrels in the field, representing one of the best days every. The next day, after church, another fifty-four barrels were collected.

On Monday, as Henry and Larry went over the tally sheets for that weekend, they were both impressed with the volume of sap that was collected.

"Nice tally," Larry said. "How many wagons do you have running the barrels to West Tocoi?"

"Two," Henry said. "The other large wagon is being used to transport workers. This weekend's barrels are stored just down the road, waiting for pick up."

"You may want to use the truck to transport as well."

"I was thinking that too," Henry replied. "I'll get Curtis to start driving."

"Alright," Larry said. "There's something else we need to talk about as well."

"Oh?" Henry said. "What would that be?"

"Margaret."

"Margaret?"

"Yes," Larry said. "I had a guy come to me last week. Apparently, there's city group up in Riverside that's wanting to have some historical images drawn on the side of some of their

132

buildings. They heard about Margaret from somewhere and ask to see some of her work. I showed them the sketches she had done for me, and so they want to hire her to do the artwork on the buildings."

"When would this take place?" Henry asked.

"They want to get started as soon as possible," Larry said. "It would require Margaret to move to Jacksonville, at least temporarily."

"Her momma wouldn't like that too much, I'm guessing."

Larry sat down at the table with Henry and looked him in the face.

"I know," he said. "I was thinking Margaret and her momma could move up there."

Henry frowned and looked down at the table. He already had enough on his mind and this was just one more thing to worry about.

"What about Margaret's three brothers?" he asked. "Ernest, the oldest, is our cooper, the youngest our water boy, and all three of them can dip."

"Henry, look at me," Larry said. "I know your main concern at this camp is operations and making sure every single detail is taken care of to ensure the turpentine flows. Margaret's brothers will be taken care of here and I know they'll have to separate for a spell. But, it's a chance. It's a chance for a better life for Margaret and her mom. They'll still see each other occasionally."

"I know," Henry said quietly. "I know it would be a shot for them and I want them to have the best possible chance at life. I just didn't want to lose them. They're some of my favorites."

And then, after a pause, "Of course it's the best, so you take good care of them and make sure they have a clean place to stay."

Larry smiled and reached across the table and grabbed Henry's hand.

"They'll be taken care of," he smiled. "I don't suspect

this job will last more than a couple months or so. Besides, the plan is to start in March, after the cold months and before operations get back in full swing."

"Sounds good," Henry said. "Have you spoken with the transport people about the docks down in West Tocoi? They're in pretty bad shape."

"Yes, glad you brought that up," Larry said. "We're going to send a couple coopers from this camp and our Decoy Road camp. We have a cold front moving in, so that ought to make scraping of the drifts we just dipped a whole lot easier. After we finish up scraping the resin from the trees, we should be caught up enough to send a couple workers over that way. Do you still have a lot of the old-growth pine boards available?"

"Yup," Henry said. "Still have about two or three bundles. I'm having the coopers build a small smoke shed to smoke us up a few pork butts for Christmas dinner."

"Outstanding idea," Larry said, as he stood up. "I'll mention that to the other camps. Maybe they can do something similar."

"Thanks, Larry," Henry said as he stood to shake his hand. "Twenty-three more days until Christmas. Got any plans?"

"Gonna sleep in," Larry said. "The wife's gonna cook up her usual Christmas feast and I'll probably take my traditional nap after dinner."

Henry walked Larry back to his truck then joined his wife back in the commissary. Delores was placing new orders on the shelf under the counter. Since some of them were modest Christmas presents, she kept them out of sight until their owners came to pick them up.

"Where's Claire?" Henry asked.

"It's her turn to teach math." Delores said. "I think she may have five students today."

"Oh? How many do you usually have?"

"Oh, about six or seven. I think one of the children is starting to learn the tally sheets."

"Then the math she learned will help her out," Henry

134

said.

A worker appeared at the side window of the commissary.

"Hello," Delores said. "How may we help you?"

"Hello, Miss Delores, Bosm Henry." he said. "Starting to get a little cold, today."

Henry smiled. "Yup, outta harden that resin right up."

He recognized him as Charles, one of the new bucks from up north. "How can we help you?"

"Mr. Henry, I wanted to ask you," he started off. "How do we go about ordering a new guitar for Memphis? Me and a bunch of others want to surprise him fo' Chrissmas. He's always doing something for one of us. He's a good person and his guitar is all cracked around the neck."

"Well," Delores said. "Let me see what I can find in our catalog."

She rose and went over to where she kept the thick mail-order book. She started flipping through the pages until she found the section she was looking for. She took it to the window ledge and placed it so Charles could look at the pages. Henry looked on in interest.

"You see," Delores said. "There's about five models you can choose from, with the price right next to each one."

"How bout that one?" Charles asked, pointing to one of the cheaper models. "That one's purty."

"That one is nine dollars and eighteen cents," Delores said. "How are you going to pay for this?"

"Well," Charles said. "We got this much in scrip."

He placed a handful of coins on the counter. Delores counted out two dollars and forty cents.

"You're about seven dollars short," she said.

"Yes ma'am," he said shyly. "We was wondering if'n we could put the rest on company credit. We have about twelve people who all want to chip in."

Delores looked over at Henry, who stood there expressionless. She took a pencil and wrote some numbers done to do the math.

135

"That would be fifty-seven cents each, if you have twelve people. They will all need to come in and sign the ledger."

"Yes, ma'am." Charles began to smile. He didn't know if they would be allowed to use credit to make up the difference. "Will this be here befo' Chrissmas?"

"Well, I don't know for sure," Delores said. "But I think it would only take a couple weeks if we hurried it."

"Okay," Charles said. "Can they come in after evening cant?"

"They sure can, Charles," Delores said. "I'll stay an extra hour, but not much later than that, okay?"

"Thanks you, Miss Delores. And can we keep this a secret?"

"We won't tell anyone," Henry said.

"Thank you Bosm," Charles said, happily. "And I'll gits back to work. I'll work doubly hard to make up for my time. There's lots of scraping to be done!"

After Charles left, Henry looked over at Delores, then down at the catalogue.

"How much profit do we make off the commissary purchases?" he asked.

"Well Henry, you know everything is marked up three hundred percent," she said. "That's company standard."

"Well, just this once, why don't we cut our profit margin and get them this one," he said, pointing at the second best model. "After all, it's Christmas."

"Henry Clayton!" Delores smiled. "Have I told you today how much I love you?"

She wrapped her arms around him and hugged him tightly.

That evening, after cant, not twelve, but fourteen workers stopped by to sign for store credit, and contribute to the gift they were getting Memphis. Henry and Delores decided to order the best model in the catalogue. It was a beautiful Gibson acoustic guitar with pearl inlay. Delores called the distribution center to ensure they had it before Christmas. It would be there in ten days.

On Decembe14, 1935, the postman dropped off a box at Turpentown. That evening, after evening cant, Henry sent word for Charles to stop by the commissary. When Charles arrived, Delores washed her hands, then opened the box containing the guitar. She took it out and handed it to Charles. As Henry and Claire looked on, Charles looked at the guitar but did not take it.

"Miss Delores, I's shakin' too much to take that. My hands are sappy and I might get it dirty," he said. "I've never seen anything so beautiful in my whole life."

His voice was shaky and eyes watering.

"Well, that's okay Charles," Delores smiled. "I know how you feel. Did you want us to store it here or did you want to take it?"

Charles seemed to think about this. Delores saw his uncertainty.

"Tell you what," she continued. "We'll hide it at our house until you need it and even gift wrap it for you."

"That's a wonderful idea," Claire said. "We still have a lot of wrapping paper!"

"Thank you, Miss Delores and Miss Claire," Charles stammered. "That would be mighty kind of you."

On Christmas Day of that year, the camp was just finishing up their meals of smoked pork, pinto beans, collards, corn-on-the-cob and hoecakes. It had turned cold and the workers were taking turns eating at the seven long tables set up in the jook joint. Several had gathered around outside around the bonfire they had started to keep warm.

At around 7:00 pm Charles, Willy and Louis held their hands up for everyone to listen up. Over half of the workers knew what was going on, but many did not, including Memphis. Charles had made sure Henry and Ben had received an invitation of the presentation, along with their wives.

"Friends," Charles said. "On this joyous occasion, when we celebrate the birth of our Lord, Jesus Christ, we have the opportunity to come together to express our faith, embrace the brotherhood of our people and show gratitude.

We have many things to be grateful for. We have the opportunity to work, we have food to eat and we have friends in both the hard times and good times as well. One man has always been there to help, whenever and whoever needed it. We would like to take the time this day, to thank this man for all that he has done and for being the friend whenever we needed one. Johnny "Memphis" Waters, please come on up here!"

The room erupted in applause. Memphis sat over in the corner with his old, cracked and worn guitar still in his hands. His expression was one of total shock. At the urging of those seated around him, he slowly rose and walked up to the front of the room. There he received handshakes and manly hugs from those close.

"Memphis," Charles began, "We would like to take this time to thank you for everything you've done for everyone, and for the fine music you play for us when it's time to relax and enjoy life's pleasures."

Memphis smiled shyly as Willy continued where Charles left off.

"Memphis, when the wagon broke its axle, you made time to help me fix it after church, even though it wasn't your job and you shoulda been relaxin' at the time. I don't know of a single person in this turpentinin camp, that you haven't help at one time or another. You're always smilin' and cheerin folks up, even when times are the hardest."

The entire room was nodding in agreement and occasionally uttering "yessah" to verify the words Willy was speaking.

"Because of everything you have done for us, it is now time for us to do something for you," Charles smiled.

At those words, Stella came around the corner carrying a Christmas wrapped package. She handed it to Willy, who in turn, handed it to Memphis.

"A thousand thanks to you, brother," he said.

Memphis accepted the gift humbly and turned to face the room.

138

"I can't thank ya'll enough," he said with tears in his eyes. "Ya'll are the family I never knew."

"Open the package!" the whole room shouted.

Memphis blushed then did as he was instructed. As he pulled the Gibson acoustic guitar from its box, the entire room gasped. Only six people had seen it up until that point, and even they were stunned by the beauty and sheen of the new instrument as it reflected a whole room full of lanterns. Memphis, one of the hardest, toughest individuals present, broke down in tears. He was joined by half the room. Even Henry and Ben feigned coughs to mask their emotions.

"Ya'll," Memphis stammered, after a few seconds, "This is the most wunnerful thing anyone has ever done for me in my life."

The room once again, erupted in applause. Many stood up to get a closer look, but none dared touched the elaborate treasure. Many broke out in a chorus, urging Memphis to play something.

"Play us a song, play us a song," they chanted.

Finally, Memphis lifted it and pulled the strap up over his head. His fingertips ginger skimmed across the surface of the body and the shiny guitar strings. He tested the tone of the strings and adjusted them until the sound was right. Finally, he started strumming his guitar and fell into a melody.

He sang Silent Night. The room became completely still as the workers and management of one of the hardest assignments of life, all fell silent and came together in the spirit of Christmas. There were no bosses or workers, no niggers or CapMs…they were all children of God. They listened to one of the most remarkable presentations of Silent Night ever rendered.

After Memphis had presented a flawless performance and the crowd had regained its composure, Henry went to the front of the room and held up his hand to speak. He told everyone that there would be no work tomorrow, and that the season was over. As Henry and Delores Clayton, and Ben and Claire Carter left the jook, every worker who could, reached out and touched their arm as they passed by. It was a simple gesture of both respect and farewell. No words were necessary.

CHAPTER ELEVEN

It was a mild winter, with temperatures only reaching freezing on three occasions. Some workers still scraped trees to collect the hardened sap. They used two-wheeled half barrels instead of Herty cups to collect the hardened resin at the base of the tree. Production was usually down during the winter months, but after the storm a few months back, many barrels were filled and transported to Jacksonville for boiling and distilling.

Other workers replaced planks and support beams on the pier, which occasionally docked a steamboat from the St. Johns River Transportation Company. Larry Larson made sure the steamboats still maintained a scheduled stop there to collect the barrels from Turpentown and two other turpentine camps in the area. Other camps in Florida either routed resin straight to Jacksonville via the railroad or carried it there directly with trucks or wooden wagons.

Delores and Claire stepped up their school teaching, providing math and English courses for nine of the camp youth and three adults. They were amazed at how fast some of their students learned written English and mathematical problem solving. Next year they planned on adding science and geography to the curriculum, using second hand books that had been donated by the Clay County Board of Education.

Margaret showed incredible potential and was always eager to learn more. She read to her brothers at night and convinced two of them to start attending school as well. Occasionally, she still made trips to Green Cove Springs to sketch portraits of couples and families who had seen one of Larry's posters. One time a wealthy couple even showed up at the turpentine camp, wanting a portrait drawn of them sitting in front of the cinder block quarters.

On May 9, 1936, at 4:00 am, Claire woke up to mild cramps and gently woke Ben up, sleeping next to her.

"Ben, it's time," she said quietly.

Ben lifted his head and looked over at the clock next to the table on the bed.

"We still got a half hour," he said half asleep.

"No, Ben. It's *time*."

"OH SHIT!" Ben said jumping up out of bed. "How far apart are they? Has your water broke? I'll go call the doctor!"

"Ben," Claire smiled as she reached for his arm. "My water hasn't broke, yet. I only had a cramp. We have time. Be calm."

"Okay, okay," Ben said. "What do we need to do?"

"I could be in labor for hours. When the contractions become longer and more frequent, then we call the doctor."

After Ben calmed down he reached over and held Claire's hand as he smiled at her.

"Honey, can I get you anything?" he asked.

Claire squeezed his hand back. "You could get me a nice cool glass of water. Also, a warm towel for my back, please."

Ben smiled, then got up and went into the kitchen. Pete, their pit bull, lay in the corner and watched Claire intensely. He sensed something was different.

"It's okay, Pete," Claire said softly.

Pete rose, walked over to the side of the bed and licked Claire's hand. Ben returned with Claire's water and a warm towel, which he gently placed under her back.

"What next?" he asked.

"We wait."

At 9:25 am, the doctor had arrived with a nurse and examined Claire. He told her he foresaw no complications and gave Claire the option of traveling to the hospital or delivering her baby in the comfort of her own home. She asked that she stay home.

Delores had arrived to provide moral support as Ben and Henry stood out back to smoke. Henry didn't smoke very often,

142

but this was a special occasion. It was Saturday, which meant a half day, so Henry had placed Willy in charge of operations.

"So, have ya'll decided on a name yet?" Henry asked.

"Carolyn Michele, if it's a girl," Ben smiled. "and Jacob Michael, if it's a boy."

"Beautiful names."

"Thanks, Henry."

They both stared out at the trees in Ben's back yard, as they finished their cigarettes. The majestic white oaks, which graced the back property behind the stable next to Ben's house, were pleasant to look at. Henry thought back to the time they had tried to have their own baby, only to find out Delores was unable to bear children due to a medical disorder. He knew how much she loved children and how disappointed they had been. She felt bad she was unable to bear him and son, but he had assured her that, with her at his side, his world was complete.

Soon the silence was broken by the high-pitch squeal of a newborn baby. They looked at each other as Ben's smile expressed the absolute joy he was feeling.

"Well, papa," Henry grinned. "You best git in there and meet your kid."

Ben let out a yelp then rushed inside. There he saw his lovely wife, soaked in sweat, exhausted and smiling broadly.

"Claire?" he asked.

"It's a boy, Ben!" Claire said with tears streaming down her cheeks. "Jacob Michael Carter, welcome to the world."

Doctor Bradley cradled the newborn bundle in his arms and smiled at Ben.

"Well, daddy," he smiled. "Come hold your son."

Ben took his son into his arms and gazed down into a tiny face peeking back up at him between the edges of a soften baby blanket. Ben immediately saw Claire's features as he cuddled the bundle lovingly.

"He looks just like you, honey."

"Don't be silly, Ben," Claire said. "He has your eyes and your smile."

"I'll have to agree with Claire on that," Delores said. She sat by Claire and occasionally dabbed her head with a cool, dampened cloth.

"Okay, daddy," Doctor Bradley intervened as he gently took the baby from Ben's arms and laid it on Claire's chest. "Let's let that baby get something to eat and his mommy get some rest. After checking mommy and baby one more time, I need to get back to town. I may have another mommy-to-be come and see me today."

Ben handed his newborn son back to the doctor then sat next to Claire on the other side of the bed. He smiled at her and held her hand tenderly. Her face was a little swollen from the strain of pushing so hard, but Ben thought she looked like and angel.

"Woman, I love you," he said tenderly. "You're made me the proudest daddy on the planet."

"And I love you," she replied sleepily. "Now you go tell Henry the good news and I'm gonna take me a short nap. What do you want for dinner tonight?"

Ben smiled and whispered softly, "Woman, you ain't cooking tonight. I'm gonna whup up some of my world-famous biscuits and gravy."

"Well, in that case, you got a deal."

Outside, Ben gave Henry the good news. Henry smiled and shook his hand.

"Congratulations, daddy," Henry said as he reached into his top pocket. "Now I've got something I've been saving for this day."

Henry extracted two Cuban cigars he bought the last time he was in town. They had cost him forty cents each, but felt the occasion justified the expense. He gave one to Ben then struck a match against the porch rail.

"Aw, thanks, Henry," Ben said as he puffed against the flame Henry held to the end of his cigar.

Henry took a long draw on his own cigar and exhaled a plume of bluish smoke.

144

"You're a good man," he said. "We go back a few years and, even though I've had to whup yer ass on a few occasions, I consider you my best friend."

"Back at you, ya dadburn slave driver."

Before Doc Bradley headed back to town, he stopped by the commissary to check on Stella, who was minding the store in Delores and Claire's absence.

"So," he asked her. "When is your due date again?"

"Next month, I reckon," she replied.

"And how much kicking is your baby doing?"

"Heck, he sleeps mostly," she said.

Doc Bradley smiled as he felt her pulse. He kept from frowning, not wanting to alarm her.

"Can I feel your belly?"

"Yessah," Stella said as she lifted her blouse.

The doctor felt her stomach and pushed gently in search of the baby's head. He probed a bit longer and then smiled at her.

"Okay, things look good," he said. "You have Delores call me if you see any blood or anything unusual. This is your first child, am I right?"

"Yessah."

"Okay. I got to get back. Don't do no heavy lifting."

"Oh, I won't," she lied. She had already lifted a good deal of boxes today. She made a mental note not to do any more lifting. This was her first baby and had never been told she shouldn't lift things when pregnant.

As the doctor left, he wondered if he should have insisted that she make the trip into town so he could examine her better. He shrugged it off as his mind focused on the patient he had waiting for him back in town. The female worker that served as the camp's midwife had only delivered three babies and was not familiar with the signs which indicated a baby was in the breech position.

The next day after church, several men sat around a fire as two pork roasts sat searing on a grill. They had butchered a hog yesterday, with most of it hanging in their newly built smokehouse.

"That was a good sermon today, preacher," one of the men remarked.

"Thank you, Memphis," Catface replied. "And that was some nice pickin' on the geetar las' night."

"Yessah, you was rockin' it las' night!" another worker named Joe said.

"Ya'll can thank yo selves," Memphis said. "That new guitar sings like the choir."

"Hell, our choir don't sound *near* that good." Joe said.

"Watch yo mouth," Catface laughed. "They all has good hearts."

They all chuckled as they gazed into the fire cooking their meat. Joe poked the pork roasts with a grilling fork and watched as the red juices dripped down into the fire.

"That's what the trees do," Joe said. "They bleed. They bleed for us...and we bleed for them."

"All of God's children bleed," Catface said. "All living things bleed. It's the circle of life."

"Circle of life?" a relatively new worker asked. "What does "life" have to do with turpentinin?"

"What are you talking 'bout, boy?" Catface asked. "What did you do befo' you got work here?"

"I worked a turpentine still up in Georgia," he said.

"And why did you leave that place?"

"Because the sap runned out, you old fool." the young buck replied.

Catface stood up, then walked over and sat on the log next to him and looked into his face.

"Son, what do you know about life?" he asked. "What's yo name?"

"Dwayne."

"Dwayne, you only been here a couple weeks. How long you been working turp?"

"Bout two years now, why?"

"Because you don't know shit about what you're talking

146

about," Catface said as he opened his shirt.

Dwayne looked down at the catfaced scars on his chest.

"Son, I've been turpentinin for twenty-two years now," Catface said quietly. "This was what they did to you if your work wasn't good enough not too many years ago. What would you be doing if they hadn't hired you here?"

"I guess I'd still be lookin' fo work."

"That's what I'm talking about," he said. "Boy, the work here is hard, I ain't saying it ain't. But it's *life,* boy. It's our *life.* Look at all the poor souls walking by here every single day, lookin' fo work. They can't even feed their families. Some of them have even starved to deaf, son. Turpentinin is life."

"Yessah," Dwayne said. "I see where yer comin' from."

Catface went back over to where he was and sat back down. The group stayed quiet for a few minutes before Memphis pulled out a small bottle of cheap whiskey.

"I was saving this for next weekend, but I reckon now would be a nice time to have a taste," he said. "Everybody gets a tug."

Memphis took a drink from the bottle then passed it to the next man. They all had a drink and finished grilling the meat. Each of them felt a little more grateful they had a means of feeding their family and enjoyed the remainder of the night.

The next morning Dwayne found Henry speaking with Ben at the edge of a crop, and walked up to them. Henry was acting woodsrider today as Ben spent some time with his wife and newborn.

"Suh, kin I says sumthin?" he said.

"Go ahead, Dwayne," Ben said.

"I wanted to thank ya'll for giving me a job here. I haven't been doing real well, because of my shoulder, but I promise startin' today, I'm gonna be one of yo hardest werkin bucks."

"Sounds good Dwayne. How's the turp flowing today," Henry asked.

"She's flowing real well, suh! Now I gots ta git back.

147

Don't want to git behind," he said.

"Okay, Dwayne," Ben said.

Dwayne turned and hurried off as Ben looked over at Henry.

"What the hell was *that* all about?" he asked.

"I don't have a clue," Henry said. "I'll check the tally sheets tonight and see how he compares to last Friday. If he's more productive then good for us!"

"I hear ya."

"Now you get back to that baby," Henry said. "I'm gonna go make the rounds. I'm sure you'll be having some housework to do as well."

"You have no idea," Ben said as he walked away. "Claire should have been a dadburn foreman!"

Henry smiled as he rode out to the crops.

The following month, Stella stood as she stirred a pot of black beans, when she suddenly cramped up and felt warm fluid gushing. She clutched her stomach and dropped to her knees. She knew her baby was coming.

"Miss Delores!" she yelled. "Miss Delores!"

Delores was in the commissary, putting up groceries that Henry had just brought in. The space between the roof rafters and the top of the internal walls allowed for sound to pass through easily. They both heard Stella yelling and dropped the cans as they both headed out the back door. Delores ran down to Stella's unit, where she found her curled up on the floor. Henry ran further down to where the midwife stayed.

"Stella?" she said as she kneeled next to her. "Is it time?"

"Yes ma'am!" Stella said.

"Henry went to get the midwife, hold on, girl!"

"I is tryin," she said. "It hurts terrible Miss Delores."

"Can you stand to get back to your bed?"

"I can try, Miss Delores."

With an incredible effort, Delores help Stella stand and walk back to her bed in the next room, where she laid down. It was a thin matt with little padding, but only a few of the workers

had the luxury of a mattress.

Henry returned with Donna, the midwife. She asked Stella how close the contractions were, but Stella said it was a constant pain and couldn't tell one contraction from the next. Donna washed her hands then kneeled next to Stella. Henry took that as his cue to leave the room. He told Delores he would be outside if they needed him. After he left, Delores turned to Donna and asked her what she needed her to do.

"We're gonna need some warm water and some towels," Donna said.

"She has the stove hot. I'll put on some water," Delores replied as she rushed into the kitchen.

In the kitchen, she took the pot of black beans off the stove, found a different pot and placed it on the stove filled with water. Then she found Stella's towel shelf, grabbed two and took them into the kitchen. Stella let out another loud moan.

"I can feel the head," Donna exclaimed loudly. "Wait! Oh no! It's not the head, it's her bottom!"

A breech birth, Delores thought!

"Henry, call the doctor!" she yelled out to her husband. "Tell him she's having a breech birth and is gonna need stitchin' up!"

"Okay!" Henry said, as he ran back to the commissary.

"A breech?" Doc Bradley asked over the phone. "Are they sure?"

"How the fuck would I know?" Henry asked. "I was just told to come call you and tell you that!"

"Well shit," he said. "I was gonna play golf at Ponte Vedra today."

Henry couldn't believe what he was hearing.

"Jesus Christ, doc," Henry said angrily. "We wouldn't want to interrupt your golf game just because a woman could bleed to death!"

"Now hold on, Henry! I didn't say I wasn't coming," he protested. "I just said…"

"Then get your ass down here," Henry snapped then

slammed down the phone.

"Geez, what an asshole," he muttered to himself.

Back behind Willy and Stella's unit, Henry stood by the back door and called for Delores. She came out, her face, a mask of concern.

"Is the doctor coming?" she asked.

"I think so," Henry said.

"You think so?" Delores asked incredulously.

After Henry described his conversation with the doctor, Delores face turned red.

"Why that son-of-a-bitch!" she said. This was the first time Henry had ever heard his wife curse, other than "darn."

"I heard there's a black doctor that just moved to town," Henry sighed. "After we get through this, I'll go pay him a visit and see if we can get him to take care of the workers here."

""I think that's a wonderful idea," Delores said, just as Stella let out a scream.

"Gotta go," she said, as she rushed back inside the building.

There, she found Donna with both of her hands wrapped around the baby's waist as its butt was protruding. Only half of the baby was out and blood was everywhere. Donna glanced up as Delores reentered the room.

"Miss Delores, I'm gonna need a fresh, wet towel," she said. Delores noticed that Donna looked exhausted.

"Right away," she said.

"I'm gonna need something to cut with, too! A knife or some scissors," Donna said loudly. "Oh, and some string or twine."

Delores grabbed a knife in the kitchen then grabbed the wet towel from the pot. It wasn't as warm as she had wanted, but would have to do.

Back in the bedroom, she was surprised to find the baby completely delivered. Donna turned around quickly and reached out to Delores.

"Quick, Miss Delores! I need some string or maybe a

150

shoelace. Please, hand me the knife," she panted.

Delores handed her the knife, then picked up a shoe next to the wall. She hurriedly removed the shoelace and handed it to Donna.

"Could you cut it in two for me?"

"Sure," Delores said.

She handed Donna one half at a time and she tied both around the umbilical cord about two inches down, then took the knife and cut the cord in two. Delores noticed that Stella appeared to have lost consciousness, as Donna picked up the baby. Delores noticed it was a girl as she began to wipe her down with a warm, wet towel.

After the doctor arrived, he treated Stella then examined the baby.

"Both baby and momma look fine," he said. "Stella is going to need plenty of rest for the next several days. Keep putting this ointment on her and she'll heal up just fine. Donna, you have done a fine job."

Donna managed to smile as she sat to the side. Stella began to moan and Delores handed the baby to her.

"Here Donna, you can hand Stella her baby," she said.

As Stella opened her eyes, Donna placed the newborn baby girl on Stella's chest.

"Momma, here's your newborn baby girl!"

"Aw, thank you Donna," Stella said weakly. She stared down at her baby as the tears started rolling down her cheeks.

"Shania," Stella whispered. Donna and Delores smiled at each other.

"That's a pretty name," Delores said.

About that time, Willy entered the room. Henry had sent a worker out to the crop where he was working to let him know it was time and to return to the camp.

"Stella, baby," he said. "Are you alright?"

"Willy?" Stella replied. "See your daughter? The doctor says she's healthy. You can hold her when she gets done feeding. She's powerful hungry."

"You just let her feed," Willy said. "There's plenty of time for me to hold her later."

Outside, Doc Bradley spoke with Henry for a few minutes before he left.

"Henry, I'm sorry I came off sounding like that," he said. "I know it sounded cold, and you're right, delivering a baby is far more important than playing golf."

"Well, hell doc," Henry grumbled. "I reckon we all gotta set our priorities. We're probably gonna start getting the new Negro doctor in town, to start taking care of the workers. He may have a little more compassion with these folks."

"That's your choice," he said, frowning. "I'll be billing your insurance company for the delivery of Claire's baby and this visit."

Henry walked the good doctor out to his car and watched as he drove off. After the car had disappeared down the road, Henry went back into Willy and Stella's apartment. Inside he found Willy, holding his newborn daughter with a broad smile on his face.

"Is it okay to come in," Henry asked.

"Sho can," Willy smiled up at him. "Mr. Henry, would you like to hold Shania?"

Henry started to say something, but Willy rose and placed the newborn in his arms. Henry gazed down at the tiny black face as she stared back up at him. He was surprised at the alertness in her big, green eyes.

"She a beauty," Henry said. Both Willy and Stella smiled over at him.

"Thank you," they said.

Henry continued to stare down at the tiny face, until finally, she blinked a few times then fell off into a baby nap.

"This young-un looks to be pretty tired, Stella," he grinned. "Better give her back to you."

Henry gently handed the baby back over to Stella then said he needed to get back to work. He patted Delores on the shoulder as he rose.

152

"Honey, I've got to get back to work," he said. "Willy, can I see you outside for a second?"

"Yessah," Willy said.

Outside Henry turned and smiled at Willy as he came out.

"Willy, I'm afraid I can't use you the rest of the day. There's only three hours left to evening cant and we have too many people out there already," he said in a serious tone.

"Is something wrong, Bosm?" Willy asked. He thought he had done something wrong.

"Nothing's wrong, Willy! I want you to spend the rest of the day with your *family*."

It finally occurred to Willy what Henry was saying.

"Oh! Thank ya, Mr. Henry!" he smiled.

"Now you get in there and enjoy that pretty little baby," Henry said. "Tomorrow's Saturday, so take it off as well."

"Yessah, Mr. Henry!" Willy said. "And thank ya, suh!"

Henry turned and walked away, before he heard a voice behind him.

"Hold on, there Henry Clayton," Delores said. "You don't mind if I walk with you, do ya?"

Henry smiled and put his arm around her as they walked together.

"Woman," he said. "I'm proud to have such a purty lady walking at my side."

They both walked on smiling. They both were also thinking about how beautiful Stella and Willy's baby was, and reminisced about the times they had tried to have their own.

The following day, Henry drove the truck into town and paid a visit to the Negro doctor who had recently set up practice close to one of the town's poorest communities. He agreed to start providing medical attention to the most serious cases of illness and injuries at Turpentown. He said he would pay them a visit the following month to check up on Stella and her baby. Claire would continue to use Doc Bradley.

Nights were a bit different for the next several months

around the camp. Occasionally, the sounds of bullfrogs and crickets were joined by the squeal of a newborn baby wanting to be fed. No one was bothered, however. Everyone knew that babies were a part of life and required feeding on occasions.

On the north part of Jacksonville, in the Riverside District, Margaret had just finished painting a mural on an inner wall of an historical building. She had been given an old photograph by the business owner, which she replicated with infinite detail. So far, she had painted historical scenes on the sides of three buildings in the area. Soon, local business owners began asking her to adorn the inside brick walls of their buildings, after seeing her creativity on the other building's exteriors. Both Margaret and her mother stayed in an apartment above one of the businesses.

Margaret was cleaning up her art supplies in her last building when a middle-aged African American lady stepped in the door and gazed upon Margaret's work.

"Hello, ma'am," Margaret said politely.

"Hello child," the lady replied. "You must be the girl that has been painting all the beautiful scenes on the walls around here."

"I guess, ma'am," Margaret blushed. "I've done a few."

"How old are you, honey?"

"I'm fifteen, ma'am."

The stranger walked over to Margaret and looked into her eyes. There she saw both the innocence of her youth and the confidence of a skilled artist.

"Child, you have an amazing gift," the lady said. "Don't let anyone ever hold you back. Make sure you get some education when you can, and always remember the gifts you have were given to you by Jesus. Hold his name in high regard."

"I do, ma'am. My daddy is with Jesus," Margaret said.

"And he knows how well you have been doing. He watches you from heaven every day."

The lady bent slightly to give Margaret a hug, then turned and walked away.

"Ma'am?" Margaret called after her.

"Yes, child?" the stranger replied.

"What's your name?"

"Augusta," the lady replied.

"My name is Margaret."

"I know, Margaret." Augusta said. "Now I got to scoot and catch a train. Goodbye, Miss Margaret."

"Goodbye, Miss Augusta."

Larry drove Agnes and Margaret back to Turpentown that evening. Everyone was happy to see them and had prepared a nice dinner for their reception. Delores had even baked a huge batch of brownies for everyone to enjoy. Margaret was thrilled to meet and hold both of the newborn babies.

Her oldest brother, Ernest walked up, holding the hand of a young black girl, whom Margaret had not seen before.

"Margaret, this here is LuAnn," he smiled.

Margaret smiled at the young lady and held out her hand.

"Please to meet you, LuAnn," she said.

"My pleasure," the young girl smiled shyly. "I've seen your pretty pictures. I wish I could draw like you."

"We can draw some things together, if you like...maybe on Sunday after church."

"I'd like that very much."

"Are you getting some schoolin' here?" Margaret asked.

"Yes, ma'am," LuAnn replied. "Both Miss Delores and Miss Claire are teaching me to read! I almost have my first book finished, but I still have a ways to go before I catch up with some of the other students."

Delores smiled after overhearing their conversation. Having passed a written test, she had gotten her teaching certificate transferred to Clay County. She had also spoken with the Clay County Board of Education about the process of issuing diplomas, when she felt a student had learned enough to pass a written exam. The board agreed to discuss it at their next meeting, since Turpentown's schoolroom was not officially recognized as a public school.

On June 15, 1936, the Clay County School Board of Education officially recognized the West Tocoi Private School for African Americans. They had considered requiring them to attend the newly built Clay High School in Green Cove Springs, but decided to certify their schoolroom instead of dealing with the logistics of trying to provide a bus route for only a few students. They even agreed to issue diplomas for students passing final exams.

After hearing about their efforts, Larry Larson offered to pay the forty-six dollar filing fee required for certification. He had come to recognize that workers were far more productive if you kept them motivated and was more than happy with the productivity of Turpentown compared to the other camps he managed. He encouraged other foreman to improve worker-to-management relations by engaging in morale improving methods.

Delores continued to teach through what was typically the designated "summer break," because none of those attending her classes wanted any such delay and were eager to learn as much as they could. Most of her students became proud of their achievements and felt themselves a better person by the education they received. Delores could only pray that her efforts would in some way, benefit those who sought to better themselves.

By August, Delores had received word that a sum of eight-hundred dollars had been placed in escrow by the Rosenwald Fund, which contributes to improving education among African Americans. Delores used a portion of the money to buy six desks for her students to sit in. Since her and Claire taught three separate classes, everyone would have a comfortable place to sit while learning, writing and reading. Claire taught grades one-through-six and Delores taught those designated as grades seven through twelve, and for the adults wanting an education, on Saturdays and Sundays. The adults would be issued "diploma equivalency certificates."

1936 was also a Presidential Election year, but none of the workers from the turpentine camp registered or even considered it. In 1870, African Americans were given the right to vote under the 15th Amendment. The South placed literacy tests, polling taxes and other obstacles, to unfairly keep blacks from voting. Additionally, those who *had* met the requirements were often severely beaten if they tried to vote.

CHAPTER TWELVE

In March of 1937, two new crops of ten-thousand trees were started. A sawmill was constructed adjacent to the turpentine camp, and much to the delight of local residents, white workers from surrounding areas were hired. Larry Larson saw the move as an arrangement which would benefit both his company and many out-of-work men, still struggling to feed their families. Twenty-four men would be hired, depending on their skills and transportation. If needed, some could carpool with those still fortunate to have a vehicle or wagon. Some would even ride horseback to get to work. Most of the equipment had arrived the week before and was sitting on the lot, awaiting assembly.

A properly run sawmill required many skills. Men who ran the band and circular saws were referred to as "sawyers." The men who handled the logs on the saw carriage were "doggers." They turned the log after each cut and *dogged* the log in place to expose a different side for cutting. Planers ran the plane, which made the sides of the boards smooth, and the chippers threw random pieces of wood onto the conveyor belt leading up and into the mulcher.

A man named Chuck Murray was the fifth and final applicant to interview for the position of sawmill foreman. He had worked mills most of his life and had the skills required to both manage the mill and the workers. Henry interviewed him for the position and was relieved they were hiring a foreman for the lumber operations. Henry had experience with sawmill operations as well, but had his hands full with the turpentine camp. He was impressed with Chuck's experience and the answers to some of the questions he asked.

"If hired, what would be your number-one priority?" he asked during the interview.

"To cut as many trees into old-growth pine boards as

possible, without gittin' anyone hurt or kilt." Chuck replied with a heavy southern drawl.

Henry was impressed with his acknowledgement of the importance of safety requirements. Working at a sawmill was dangerous work, so strict safety precautions were needed to prevent anyone from getting hurt.

"Have you ever seen anyone hurt in the yards?"

"I seen a man git half his face cut off when the band saw blade shattered. He was hit with a two-foot piece of the blade," Chuck replied. "Wasn't a purty sight."

"What caused the blade to shatter?"

"Started out with a cracked blade," Chuck said. "You could hear it was cracked as it sawed through the cypress logs, but the yard boss wanted two more logs finished up before they changed the blades. It didn't last."

"What saws are you familiar with?" Henry asked.

"A linebar bandsaw and carriage-fed circular saw," he replied. "Also worked planers, edgers, chippers and all that."

"Where you ever the sawyer?"

"Shoot," Chuck smiled. "I spent more years as sawyer than I did as foreman. I was a foreman for the past six years."

"Why'd you leave your last job?" Henry asked.

"I ain't never been fired from a job," Chuck said. "Last job was Sanderson until they sapped out."

"Okay," Henry said. "Where you living now?"

"I live over t' Middleburg," he said.

"Alright," Henry said. "How can we get ahold of you after a decision is made?"

"Mr. Clayton? I sawed your ad in the county newspaper. Ain't nobody in my area has a phone and just about everone is looking for work. You tell me when to check back and I'll drive back over here. When ya' gonna be choosing?"

"Let's see," Henry said. "Today is Tuesday. Can you come back on Thursday and help me pick out your new crew?"

It took a second for Chuck to realize that he had just been hired. He smiled broadly as he understood."

"Yessir!" he beamed. "Can I ask just one question?"

"Shoot," Henry said. He really liked this guy.

"What will you be paying?"

"For the first ninety days, you'll be on probation, getting twenty-five a week," Henry said. "After your probation, we'll bump you up to thirty bucks a week. And since we'll both be "foremen," I want you to understand that you'll be reporting to me."

"Sounds good to me!" Chuck said.

"Now, I need you to help me put together a kick-ass crew," Henry said seriously. "We're gonna need lumberjacks, two or three sawyers, doggers, edgers and laborers. I want the best and we're gonna hand-pick the best."

"We'll pick us out some good-uns," Chuck said. He was beginning to take his new position seriously.

"Okay, then," Henry said as he stood up and extended his hand. "We'll see you about seven on Thursday. We'll be working seven-to-five. Oh, and how are you for cash?"

"Sir?" Chuck asked.

Henry knew that Sanderson had closed down six months ago and suspected Chuck may be in need of some money .

"Do you need any cash until your first paycheck?" he asked. "Tell you what, I'll give you fifteen dollars for Thursday and Friday. We'll start fresh on Monday. Paydays are the second Friday of the month."

"Why thank ya, sir." Chuck stammered.

Henry gave Chuck three of the four, five-dollar bills he had in his wallet. Chuck thanked him then left. Henry stepped outside and watched Chuck drive off in an old, beat up Ford pickup. He looked forward to working with him.

When Chuck arrived back at his house he told his wife about the day. He said for her to get ready for a trip to the grocery store. She cried the entire way there. For the past ten days, they had survived off of corn from the field next store, and whatever fish Chuck could pull out of Black Creek.

Initially, Henry and Chuck interviewed sixty men and would start twelve of them on Monday to set up the saw mill.

For the weeks leading up until now, Henry and Larry had discussed what type of equipment they would need, and decided on the timeline of installation and eventually, operation. The sawmill would consist of three areas on a three acre clearing they had created. The head saw would cut two sides off the pine logs, leaving them flat so they would roll smoothly down the rollers toward the line bar. It was then flipped over on the second side to travel up the conveyor chains to the linebar bandsaw, which would saw off a board from the log. Then, through a series of rollers and lifts, the board would continue down the line and the log would be looped back around to go through the bandsaw again. This continued until the entire log had been cut into boards.

On Thursday, Henry and Chuck began interviewing the men who had seen the ad in the county paper. Chuck knew of a few out-of-work mill workers and told them of the openings as well. Several of them showed up. By the end of Friday, they had selected all the men they needed. Twelve men would start on Monday to set up the assortment of saws, rollers, conveyors and steam engines to power the two saws. Three of these men began cutting down sapped-out trees on the first two crops, and trimming them into logs. By April 5th, the mill was ready for operation and work began.

Initially, both the turpentine and sawmill workers eyed each other with idle curiosity. They all had jobs to do and focused on their responsibilities. The layout of the new and worked crops were not in close proximity with each other, so there were few encounters of the white men with the black workers. Since the white workers of the sawmill expected and received a lunch break, Henry initiated a noon ringing of the lunch bell and told the turpentine workers to take lunch then. There were no objections since they only took long enough to eat, before returning to work. Ben said it would be easier for him to monitor them that way as well.

After two weeks, the sawmill had acquired its rhythm as bundles of boards began to stack up. Larry purchased and sent down a 1932 Studebaker semi-truck, with a flatbed trailer to transport the lumber to Jacksonville. He also hired a driver and was surprised at the difficulty in finding one with the proper credentials to drive a big rig.

On the third week of operation, a group of the sawmill and turpentine workers were eating lunch in close proximity of each other. One of the sawmill workers peered over at the black workers on break. He was in his mid-twenties, and was known to be both a smart alec and carried little regard for any race of man, except his.

Hey boy," he shouted over. "What they got you guys doin' over there, climbing trees?"

Only one or two of his fellow workers felt his actions were amusing. The turpentine workers simply ignored his babbling. They had heard far worse than this barnyard bully, so went on to finish their lunch and enjoy the break.

"Hey! Monkies!" the punk shouted. He then raised both arms above his head, with his hands dangling limp in a weak imitation of a chimpanzee. Soon, even his coworkers grew tired of his antics.

"Come on, Bert," a fellow worker said. "Leave them niggers alone."

"Aw, hell," Bert replied. "I was just havin' a little fun."

Henry watched from behind the tree line with a concerned look on his face. He then turned and walked around to where he and Chuck had been sitting and spoke with him briefly. Chuck stood up and walked with Henry back to where his workers were finishing up their lunch.

"Hold up, men!" Chuck said to his crew. "The boss has something to say to you."

Henry stepped forward. To say he was not smiling would have been an understatement. His face was crimson red and a mask of anger.

"Men, my name is Henry and as most of you know, I'm the foreman of this entire operation," he started out. "Let's be perfectly clear about something. Both the sawmill and the turpentine mill are owned by the same company, a company that depends on its workers for production."

Henry walked over and stood directly above Bert and looked down at him. Bert stared back up nervously.

"If the workers can't get along," he continued, "it impedes production. If production is not good, profits are not good and the company loses money. If the company loses money, it will do whatever necessary to ensure continued operation.

The turpentine half of this operation is the *primary* half of the operation. Without the trees being drained of their sap, you mother-fuckers wouldn't have any lumber to cut, so the company would shut down this fucking sawmill, long before it closed the turpentine camp, if at all."

That was all Henry had to say. That was it. He turned and walked away.

Chuck waited until Henry was well out of earshot before speaking.

"Way to go, cocksucker," he said as he pointed a finger in Bert's face. "If you cause me or any one of us to lose our jobs, you will be hurt and, as Jesus is my witness, you will be hurt bad! You got me, punk?"

The whole group was glaring at Bert. All of them knew how lucky they were to have a job, especially considering the thousands of others they knew were out of work.

"I gotcha," Bert finally said. "I was just having some fun."

"Being scairt to death about how yer gonna feed yer family is *not* fun, ya little fuck!"

Chuck let that set in for a few seconds, then turned to the rest of the group.

"Men, starting tomorrow, both camps will be eating lunch together," Chuck said. "Now, if any of you have problems with working with coloreds, you'd best leave your pride at home when you come to work, cause that kind of behavior will **not** be tolerated. Not here! Does everybody understand?"

"Yessir," the group acknowledged.

"Now that we know the policy, anymore talking in a

163

disrespectful manner towards any employee of the National Holdings Company will be terminated immediately! If there's anyone who doesn't understand this policy, please raise your hand."

No hands were raised. Chuck smiled and added, "Men, this is work. This is a job! Let's thank the Lord we have this opportunity while there's so many people out there, goin' hungry. Okay, now…back to work everyone!"

More than one person had something to say to Bert as they passed him. More than one person could not afford to lose their job.

The turpentine workers had been told about the combined lunch break that would start tomorrow. Many were not happy with the development, but said nothing. They had understood the importance of steady work and food to eat long before the white men started working next door. That evening, Willy talked with Stella about the incident and his worries for the future.

"I thought someone was going to say somethin', but everyone kept their yap shut," he sighed as he held their baby. "Damn, dis chil' is getting' big!"

"She sho is," Stella said. "And watch yo' mouth around the chilren."

Willy smiled as he bounced his daughter on his lap. He loved the way she giggled and the joy in her eyes. Stella handed out tin plates to other blockhouse dwellers as they came to the back window. She brought Willy's plate over and took the baby. As Willy looked down at the fried catfish, collards and corn bread, he realized how hungry he was and began eating voraciously. Stella smiled as she breast fed the baby. Her plate was sitting on the shelf by the window and she would eat when Shania had finished feeding.

Margaret appeared in the window and set her family's tin plate on the ledge. She smiled down at Stella feeding her baby.

"Aw, Miss Stella," Margaret said. "You n' Shania sure is beautiful. Here's our supper dishes, all clean and ready for tomorrow."

"Thank you, Margaret," Stella replied. "My Lord, child,

164

you sho' is getting tall. Growing like a pretty flower!"

"Thank you, Miss Stella!" Margaret blushed. "Did Miss Delores tell you? I might be getting my diploma in June!"

"That's what I heard!" Stella smiled. "We're all so very proud of you! I'm getting pretty good at reading and arithmetic, but I don't know about no diploma."

"You can do it, Miss Stella! I know how smart you are."

"We'll see child."

The next day, a quickly constructed tin roof had been placed on six pine logs, stuck in the ground, bordering the two camps. It would provide shade for most of the workers during noon lunchbreak. All workers were told a noon bell would be rung to signal lunch break. Henry had the bell moved from the woodsrider's shanty and remounted on the side of the blockhouse, by the commissary. At noon, the bell was rung for lunch.

The workers slowly gathered under the shelter. The whites sat on one side and the blacks on the other. Not much was said until both Henry and Chuck arrived. Ben stood by and sat on his horse. Each of the workers brought their own lunch. When all had gathered, Henry held up his hand.

"Men," he began in a monotone voice. "Before everyone starts eating, I want half of you white men, to get up and trade places with a black man. I want black, white, black, white."

One man stood up immediately and said, "I ain't sittin' with no nigger," he announced. "Who's with me?"

As he walked away, he turned to see who was joining him and saw that he was alone.

"Are you shitting me?" he asked incredulously. "You boys gonna put up with that?"

"Keep walking," Chuck said. "You can pick up your paycheck tomorrow."

"Fine then!" the man said, walking away. Ben followed him to the front and watched as he got in his pickup and drove away. Henry looked over at Chuck and nodded his approval.

Henry turned back to the group and asked, "Anyone

165

else?"

Slowly, many of the white men stood up and walked to the other side of the gathering, where a black man would stand and trade places with him.

"Okay, then," Henry continued. "We'll take our lunch break like this every day. As I said yesterday, we all work for the same company. At times, we will be working side-by-side, when we needed. Does anyone have any problem with this?"

Bert, the trouble-maker from yesterday raised his hand.

"What is it, Danny?" Henry asked, frowning. He was prepared to terminate him on the spot. He was already treading on mighty thin ice.

Bert stood up slowly. He seemed to gather his thoughts before speaking.

"Boys," he said in a shaky voice. "I mean, *men*. I wanted to apologize for the way I acted yesterday. I only say stupid shit to try and be funny. I reckon I don't always think about what I'm saying until after I say it. I'm sorry."

His statement surprised most everyone sitting there. Henry looked over at Chuck, who grinned back slightly.

"Very good, Danny," Henry said.

Several of the black workers nodded their acceptance of his apology. The tension seemed to dissipate the longer they sat there.

"Going forward," Henry continued. "We'll have a place to cook and we'll be providing lunches for those who want them. We were going to charge you ten-cents a day, for this service, but if ya'll bust yer asses to get work done, we'll take care of the cost. Now, I don't know how soon we can start this. A lot will depend on production and how we're looking after two or three weeks, but it's in the works."

As Ben rode back up, Henry nodded towards him.

"This here is Ben Carter. He's the woodsrider for the Turpentine operations."

Ben tipped his hat sat on his horse, outside the circle.

"Ben," Henry continued, "Carries a rifle. He does so to take care of snakes and other unwanted critters that may wander

166

into camp, up to no good. If you see a snake, a wolf or any other critter that could cause harm to any of our workers, you yell for Ben. Other than that, no guns will be brought into either camp. You leave your weapons in your truck."

Henry paused for a second then said, "That's about all I have for now. Chuck? You got anything you want to say?"

"Just a couple words, boss," he said, turning to the group. "Men! Are we ready to work?"

A few "yes sir's" were heard, but that wasn't the response Chuck was looking for.

"I said," he screamed. "Are we ready to work?"

This time, both crews yelled. "Yes sir!"

"All right, then," Chuck yelled. "We all know times are hard, but we have to work to feed our families! Now we're gonna finish our lunches, then we're gonna kick some ass, cuz we're the hardest workin' sons-of-bitches in the south! Are you with me?"

This time, the whole group jumped up and shouted at the top of their lungs, "Hell yeah!!"

Many workers shook hands with the man next to them. The spirits soared and the camaraderie became contagious. Soon, everyone went back to finishing their lunches, but conversations broke out among the men, as Henry and Chuck walked back to the front.

"Good job, Chuck," Henry said.

"Thanks, boss," he replied. "I might be wrong, but I don't think we're gonna have too much problems with any of the workers here on out."

"I believe you're right," Henry smiled. "Specially with a hard-ass like you calling the shots."

Chuck smiled, as Henry offered his hand. They shook hands and Henry turned toward the blockhouse, while Chuck turned and headed back to the break area.

The next morning, after workers had headed out, a man appeared at the side window of the commissary. Henry looked up from the tally sheets he was working and recognized the man as the one who had walked out from the lunch gathering yesterday.

"Chuck says I should come and speak to you." he said.

"Yes," Henry said as he stood. "I have your check for you. You're Dennis Hamm, is that correct?"

"Yessir, but I wanted to talk with you a spell, if I could," he said. "Mr. Henry, I'm really sorry about the way I acted yesterday. It's just that times are changin' and I'm trying my best to change with them."

Henry stared down at his work and said nothing. He wanted the man to consider what he had done.

"Mr. Henry, please…I'm beggin' you," he almost cried. "I'm thirty-five years old and been out of work for over a year. I got so much frustrations built up inside me. Please, Mr. Henry, I got three kids to feed."

"*Everyone* has kids to feed, Dennis," Henry told him. "Even them coloreds out there."

I know that, sir…and I'm real sorry."

Henry scratched his chin for a moment, as he thought about the situation. Finally, he had a thought.

"Have you ever worked turpentinin?" he asked Dennis.

"No sir," he replied. "But I can learn. I swear to you, I can learn!"

"Okay," Henry said. "Now listen, you little asshole. I'm going to give you a second chance, but you'll be working turpentine with the coloreds. If you work out with them, after two or three months, we'll shift you back over to the saw mill. Do you understand?"

"Yessir," he said. "I'll work hard, I'll work real hard."

Okay, then…we'll see," Henry said. He then turned to his wife. "Delores, ring for Ben, will you? Dennis, you can go stand out there by the well. We'll talk about your pay later."

"Yessir!" Dennis exclaimed, and walked away.

"Okay, Henry," Delores said, as the worker walked out back. She went to the side and rang Ben's call sign on the bell. A few minutes later, Ben showed up, got off his horse and tied her to a branch.

"Somebody rang me?" he asked.

"Yeah, I did," Henry said. "Let's talk out front."

Henry explained the situation with Dennis. He told Ben to lead him out to where Willy was working. He said to have Willy teach Dennis turpentinin as best he could, and that he could use him for any type labor he needed. Ben smiled as he listened, until Henry finished.

"Jesus, Henry," Ben said. "Yer a genius."

"Why, Ben," Henry said, acting surprised. "You're just *now* beginning to realize that? Oh, also, watch them real close at lunch break, okay?"

"Gotcha," Ben said as he mounted back up on School Duster. He led the new turpentine worker away.

Henry walked over to the sawmill and told Chuck what was going on. Chuck agreed with his decision and gained new respect for the wisdom his boss had shown. Lunch that day, further cemented the bond between the two groups. It was a new working atmosphere for all involved.

At five p.m., the saw mill shut down and its workers went home. Dennis continued to work until the evening cant, as darkness fell. Willy told Ben that the new man was working out real well, and that he had taught him the techniques of dipping. He also said tomorrow, he would teach him scrapping, but wanted to keep him dipping for the time being. Ben said he would relay the information to Henry.

Just as Henry was helping Delores bring in supplies through the side door, a black man appeared at the window. Henry looked over and noticed he was dressed much better than the usual drifters they had wandering by, looking for work.

"Can I help you?" he asked.

"Yessir," the man said. "I hope so. My name is Booker Benson. Do you have a young lady living here by the name of "Margaret Floyd?"

Henry became suspicious and wondered why he was looking for her.

"Why do you want to know?" he asked.

"Let me explain," he said. "I'm from the Tuskegee University in Alabama. We received word about an artistic prodigy who has exhibited her works of art on the sides of buildings and interior walls, up in an historical section of Jacksonville. I had the pleasure of viewing these paintings yesterday. Would you happen to know if she is in possession of her high school diploma? We'd like to speak with her about an art scholarship."

Delores' jaw dropped as she looked over at Henry, who looked shocked as well.

"Can I see some sort of identification," Henry asked. He wanted to make sure this man was who he said he was.

"Surely," Booker replied, as he pulled out his wallet and showed Henry, then Delores his identity card from the university.

"Delores," Henry said. "How far along is she?"

"She's one of the smartest girls I've ever met," Delores said. She could barely contain her enthusiasm. "She only needs two more weeks of class, then take her finals. She should be ready for graduation by June 1st!"

"Excellent," Booker said. "I have a room at the Powers Inn, in Green Cove Springs. Could we set up an interview for maybe sometime tomorrow? I'm in room 12."

"We'll have to check the schedule..." Henry started.

"She'll be there," Delores interrupted.

"Yes, we will be there," Henry said. He knew Delores was right. This was a huge opportunity for a special worker. "What say, 10 a.m.?"

"Sounds perfect," Booker smiled. "We'll see you tomorrow."

The gentleman from Tuskegee University, one of the most prestigious African American Institutes of higher learning, left the window. Outside, they heard his car start up and drive away. Henry looked over at Delores. She was crying.

"Oh, Henry," she sobbed as she placed her head on his shoulder. "I don't know what I'm feeling, right now."

Henry pulled her head back to look into her eyes. His

170

eyes where watering as well, but it didn't matter.

"You should be proud, woman," Henry said. "All of your hard work and faith in people have paid off."

"Not yet," she said. "But let's see how it goes, tomorrow. Let's go down and speak with Agnes and Margaret."

"Alright," he replied. "Then afterwards, I'm taking you into town for some bar-b-que."

"Woo," Delores smiled. "Big spender!"

"My baby gonna go to college?" Agnes cried. "My baby Margaret, gonna be a college student?"

"We'll know more tomorrow," Delores said as she hugged Agnes. Margaret sat on the bench with her brother, not knowing what to make of what they were saying.

"Mama," she sobbed. "I don't want to leave you."

Agnes turned to Margaret and smiled.

"Oh, honey, she said slowly. "You knowed you would have to go away someday. That's what life is. But, don't you worry, child. We'll be waiting for you when you get back."

Ernest, Margaret's oldest brother, kneeled before her and took her hands into his.

"Maggie," he said, looking into her eyes. "Dis your chance. You know we ain't as smart as you. You has to go. You has to go for yourself and you has to go for us."

Margaret pulled him up and gave him a hug. Her other two brothers joined in.

"I'll go, mama," Margaret said as tears streamed down her cheeks." I'll go for us."

Agnes turned toward Delores and Henry. "What time you needs her ready?"

"We need to be there by 10 a.m., so we'll leave here at about nine," Henry said.

"She'll be ready."

Henry and Delores turned and left, giving the family some privacy and time to talk. Delores held Henry's hand as they walked back to their house.

"The Lord is great," she said.

"Amen," Henry replied.

171

CHAPTER THIRTEEN

On May 28th, 1937, Margaret Floyd sat in with the Clay High School Senior Class and took her final exams. The Clay County Board of Education had arranged for her to test, after receiving the request for officiating from the Tuskegee University. They were duly impressed that a Negro child from a backwoods turpentine camp had completed all the requirements for a high school senior and was qualified to test, but wanted her finals exams to be proctor-supervised. They were skeptical of her achievements and wanted to see for themselves if this young girl truly possessed the knowledge to graduate from high school.

Delores and Claire were invited to sub-proctor, but only Delores could make it. After the tests were all completed and collected, the students were excused and several of the facility members gathered in the room to witness the test grading. Henry waited for Margaret outside and walked her to the truck, to wait for Delores.

The tests were distributed among four teachers, who began grading, with answer templates in hand. No one knew who had the stack with the young Negro girl's test, so went straight to work. All tests would be graded prior to any results being announced. Besides the four teachers grading the tests, were the principal, the guidance counselor, Delores and the school secretary. When all the tests were graded, they were placed in a stack and set on a separate table. Mr. Tulson, the Guidance Counselor, began flipping through the tests and calling out names with their scores.

"Mike Hillard 82%. Carol Miller 76%. Bob Harper 84%. Gale How..."

"Oh, good grief, people!" the Principal exclaimed. "Let's cut to the chase! This lady has come a long ways. Flip through your stacks and see who has Margaret Floyd's test."

"Mrs. Hodges has it," one of the graders announced.

"Mrs. Hodges?" Mr. Maloney, the Principal, asked. "Can you please let us know something?"

Mrs. Hodges thumbed through the graded tests until she came to the one she sought. Her facial expression did not change. There were one-hundred questions on the test, with each question counting one point. The subjects covered Math, World History, Geography, Science, English, Civics and General Knowledge.

"Margaret Floyd... 99%. She missed *one* question."

"What?" three teachers asked in unison.

"That can't be!" Miss Arnold, the math teacher said.

"And why not," Delores said as she looked straight at her. "Are you saying the proctors didn't do their jobs and Margaret got away with cheating?"

"No...I'm not saying that," she stammered. "I don't know *what* I'm saying, really. I'm just saying that it is nothing short of remarkable!"

"Mrs. Clayton," the Guidance Counselor said. "Let me be the first to congratulate you on a job well done."

"I appreciate the compliment," Delores said. "But I've done nothing remarkable. That child sitting out in the truck with my husband, right now, is a genuine gift from God...a prodigy."

Several other teachers nodded their heads in agreement. They passed the test around, so they all could view it for themselves. Terri Hodges was the math teacher. She stared at the test and marveled.

"My Lord, there aren't even any eraser marks or math problems worked out!" she said. Even *she* couldn't do some of the more complex math problems without a pencil and paper.

"Oh, she's real good at doing math in her head," Delores replied. "She can figure out an algebra problem faster in her head, than I can on paper."

"Now I see why Tuskegee University has taken such an interest in her," Mr. Maloney remarked. "Well, we'll get the results back to them straight away. You can count on it. One thing that confuses me, though..."

"What's that?" Delores asked.

"Tuskegee mentioned an *art* scholarship, is that correct?"

"Yessir."

"Why an *art* scholarship?"

"Why, Mr. Maloney," Delores scolded. "Do you mean to tell me you haven't seen the artwork on the side of some antique shops in Riverside?"

"Oh, my God," the Guidance Counselor said. "She's *that* Margaret?"

"Yes, the one and only," Delores smiled. "Now if ya'll will excuse us, we have to head back to Turpentown. There's still a lot of work to be done, before sundown. Can we expect her diploma in the mail?"

"I'll drive it out there, myself," Mr. Maloney said.

Delores walked merrily out the door and smiled all the way back to the truck. When she got there, Margaret slid over to let her in.

"Well?" Henry asked.

"Well what? Delores teased.

"You know well what!" Henry scowled. "How'd she do on the test?"

"She made a 99% and only missed one question."

"Which question did I miss?" Margaret asked.

"Honey, I'm sorry," Delores apologized. "They didn't tell me."

"It's okay, Miss Delores," Margaret said as she dropped her head. "I think I know which one."

Delores looked over at Henry who glanced her way, then turned back to focus on the road. She noticed a slight grin as he began to whistle.

"So, what happens now?" Henry asked.

"Well...the principal said he would drive Margaret's diploma out to the camp. Once we have that...we wait."

Back at the camp, Margaret thanked Henry and Delores then went back to her unit of the blockhouse. There she told her mother that she had scored well on the test. Agnes wept, while hugging her daughter tightly.

174

"See, child?" she said. "Jesus is watching over us and He will guide us where to go."

"I know, mommy, I know."

The following Tuesday, Mr. Maloney drove down to Turpentown. He had never been down that far, and was curious to see for himself, what the camp and its workers were all about. Both Claire and Delores were working in the commissary, and heard him drive up, as did Henry who was filling out reports next door. Delores went out to greet him.

"Hello, Mr. Maloney," she said.

"Hello, Mrs. Clayton," he replied as he handed her a folder. "I brought out Margaret's diploma."

Delores took folder and looked at the certificate inside. She was disappointed that it didn't read "West Tocoi Private School for African Americans." Instead, it stated "High School Diploma" at the top and Margaret's name below it. Still, it was certified by the county board of education and had their seal.

"Mr. Maloney, I appreciate you taking the time to drive this down to us," she said.

"My pleasure," he said. "I was hoping that maybe you could show me your schoolroom. If you're too busy, I certainly understand."

"Not at all," Delores said. She *was* too busy, but felt his efforts justified the time. "Would you like to see the operations as well, or just our schoolroom?"

"Whatever you have time for," he replied.

"I'll give him a quick tour," Henry said, walking up behind them. Honey, you can meet us at the schoolroom."

"Mr. Maloney, this is Henry, my husband and operations foreman," Delores said.

"Hello, Henry," Mr. Maloney said, extending his hand. "And please…call me Roger."

"Hello, Roger."

"I don't want to be no trouble to ya'll," he said.

"No problem at all," Henry said. "I was just finishing up some paperwork and need a break."

175

After Henry brought the truck around, he and their guest rode out to crop three, which was currently being chipped. Roger gazed out at the sweating bodies as they gouged catfaces or scraped bark off the sides of the longleaf pine trees. He noticed a singular white man among the large number of Negroes. They paid them little attention as Henry drove the truck by.

Once, they had toured the turpentine work, they cut across to the lumber operations, where teams of horses dragged trimmed pine logs forward to the saw mill. After passing through the mill, Henry looped the truck back around the pens holding three pigs, to schoolroom, where Delores waited. Roger was duly impressed with the work that went into transforming a turpentine shanty into a church and schoolroom. He was especially impressed with Margaret's artwork on the walls. There were images of Jesus walking among peasants and of school children sitting in classrooms, some with their hands raised. He marveled at the infinite detail and brilliant use of colors.

"So this is where it all started," he said.

"Well, no," Delores said. "It started on the walls, inside the blockhouse up front. It started with sticks charred in a fire, then used to draw on the wall."

"Amazing!" he said. "Well, I've got to be getting back. I mailed out Margaret's test scores and transcripts to Tuskegee. I sincerely hope she does well, but I don't think any institution would pass up a chance to accept a girl with her talents. Thank you for what you've done!"

"No, thank *you*, Mr. Maloney," she said.

"Please call me Roger, Delores."

"Well, okay Roger," Delores smiled.

Before Roger climbed back into Henry's truck, he turned to Delores. She saw that he had something on his mind, but wasn't sure what that could be.

"I want to tell you something before I leave," he said. "Look, I know Margaret is an extremely gifted child and all, but it took a mighty fine teacher to give her the education she has and recognize her intelligence. So, if you ever run out of kids to

176

teach around here, we sure could use your skills back at the one of the county schools, especially the high school."

"Why, thank you, Roger," Delores said. "I'll keep that in mind."

"I sure hope so, and good day to you Miss Delores."

"Goodbye, Roger."

Henry drove Roger back up to the block house, where they bid farewell, before Roger got in his car and drove off. Delores tidied up a bit then returned to the commissary, where Henry was waiting. She went up and hugged him.

"You done good, woman," Henry said.

"Well, if there's any way I can help a person improve on their future, it's a blessing." she said. "Margaret's accomplishments are all because of Margaret. I just pointed to the door."

"I don't think anyone could expect any more than what you've done here with these children, not to mention many adults."

"I know, I just wish there was more I could do."

"There's time," Henry said. "There's time. Now, let's go give Margaret and her momma her High School diploma!"

"We can't yet," Delores said. "Next Friday is June the 11th. I'd like to have a small graduation ceremony for Margaret."

"I like that idea," Henry said. "We could make a grand affair of it."

"No, I don't think she would like that," Delores said. "I'm thinking a small ceremony, with whomever she wanted to invite, and then maybe some drinks and cookies after."

"Sounds good," Henry said.

That Friday, after evening cant, and after everyone had a chance to clean up a little, Margaret walked the center aisle of their schoolroom. Surrounded on both sides, by parents and children, there wasn't a dry eye in the building. At the podium, Delores smiled down at a very special child.

"Good evening everyone," she said. "And welcome to the

177

first graduation ceremony of the West Tocoi Private School for African Americans. Today, we are honoring the Graduating Class of 1937."

Applause burst out in the small room. Delores smiled and let the noise subside before continuing.

"Today, we are honoring our only student in the class, who has successfully completed all the requirements for graduation and passed all her final exams. Today, we are honoring Margaret Floyd."

Again, a short burst of applause.

"But today is much more than a graduation ceremony. Today is a day that we also recognize all of the parents and students who are also working hatrd to obtain an education, receive their diploma and better themselves to take on all of lives challenges in the future.

Today Margaret now shines. She shines as a beacon of light, which represents hope. She shines as a beacon to all those who will follow in her footsteps and struggle to rise above the concept of *what is*, to become *what can be*.

Margaret Floyd, please step up here."

Margaret stepped up in front of Delores as she handed her, her diploma.

"Ladies and gentleman," Delores continued. "May I present Margaret Floyd of the Class of 1937, and High School Graduate."

Everyone started applauding and many began crying. Several people rushed up to shake Margaret's hand and congratulate her teacher.

Afterwards, everyone gathered at the back, where Stella had set up a table with lemonade and cookies. Many of the workers would remember this night for the rest of their lives. The children gathered around Margaret, begging for a peek at her diploma and excitedly chatted about their aspirations and plans for the future.

Two weeks later, on a Wednesday, a letter came in the mail, addressed to "Margaret Floyd." The return address label indicated that it was from the Tuskegee University. Delores stared at it as her hand shook a little.

"Where's Margaret today?" she asked.

"She's tallyman for crop three today." Claire said. "Why, what is it?"

"It's Margaret's scholarship request!"

After evening cant was rung and the workers had all drifted back to their quarters, Delores, Henry, Claire and Ben waited in the commissary. Claire had asked Agnes to bring her family down after they finished their supper. Soon, Margaret, her mother and three brothers were gathered in the commissary. Delores gave Margaret the envelope.

Margaret looked down at the envelope then held it to her chest.

"What is it, child?" Agnes asked.

"It's from Tuskegee University, momma," Margaret said. "About my scholarship application."

"Well open it child!"

Margaret tore the envelope open and began to read.

"It says I've been accepted," she said quietly.

Every cheered and threw their arms up. Agnes hugged her and then allowed everyone present to hug her as well, starting with her brothers. Tears of pride streamed down Agnes' cheeks, who was not the only one overcome with joy.

"That's good news, sis!" one of her brothers said.

After everyone had given Margaret hugs, Delores asked to see the letter then began reading all the details of the scholarship.

"Margaret," Delores said, looking serious.

"What is it, Miss Delores?" she asked.

"This is a full scholarship, with complete amenities," Delores said.

"What does that mean?" Agnes asked.

"It means that her entire education will be paid for, along with room and board, books, supplies and free dining," Claire smiled as she held her baby. "She won't need a single penny to

179

buy anything."

"Praise Jesus and his precious gifts," Agnes said.

"Amen," the brothers said in unison.

"When will I have to leave?" Margaret asked.

"It says here by this semester, which is August 20th," Delores said. "You'll need to check-in four days ahead of time."

"In less than two months," Ben said.

After leaving the commissary, Agnes and her children went to the schoolroom/church, where they knelt down at the altar to pray. On the back wall of the building, behind the altar was a ten-foot image of Jesus that Margaret had painted.

The next day, Delores sent back the letter of acknowledgement, which she helped Margaret and her mother fill out. Margaret was to travel to Tuskegee by train, then catch one of the institute's shuttles back to the school's dormitory. Henry had called Larry the night before to update him. Larry told Henry to have Delores take Margaret into town and buy her some new clothes. He said he would reimburse them the next time he was down.

Back out at crop three, two men were dripping with sweat as they toiled in the increasing heat of the day. Willy and Dennis had been working together, as Willy showed the new worker the methods of chipping, scraping, hacking and dipping. Dennis was becoming quite good at each of the processes and Willy knew he would soon be turpentinin alone.

"Well, sir," Willy said. "I believe yer gettin' damn near as good as me, doin' this shit."

"Son, ya flatter me," Dennis grinned. "I was taught by the "King of Turpentine.'"

Willy stopped chipping and became momentarily lost in thought.

"Say...I like that." he said, smiling.

Just then, the camp bell rang for lunch. Workers from both camps were heard yipping like coyotes, spreading the word to those who may not have heard the bell.

At the break area, the cook had grilled up over thirty cut-up chickens and a pot of beans. Many of the lumber workers still brought their own lunches, refusing to pay the dollar-a-week fee, which was deducted from their wages. Word had gotten out that the Negroes from the turp camp didn't have to pay anything to eat. Henry had already argued the point with at least three of the workers, saying they made almost three times the wages of the black workers. Henry was tired of arguing the point and vowed to terminate anyone bringing it up again.

"Sumtin' smells mighty tasty," Dennis said as they approached the grub line.

"Why, thank ya," Shorty said. Shorty was the new cook hired to cook lunch for workers of both camps. They still ate where the break area roof had been erected.

"Men, I want everyone to step aside as "King Turpentine" receives his chow," Dennis said, as he and Willy approached. The two men that were ahead of them bowed down graciously to let them by. Most of the men found the antics amusing, while two or three of the white men, did not. Ben sat on his horse nearby and took mental notes of those who did not.

Over the years, Ben had come to understand the body language that workers often exhibit when they were joking, irritated, pensive or resentful. It was his job to be able to read people, although he wasn't aware of the skills he had developed. He had been involved in situations where blacks and whites worked together, but that was years ago, when the prisoner leasing system was still active. He was genuinely surprised that their workers today, seemed to be working well together for the most part. Still, he watched and missed very little.

He found it interesting that Dennis, a man who refused to "sit next to a nigger," was now acting like Willy's best friend. Henry was a genius, he thought again. He made a mental note to speak with him about Dennis, tonight.

"So, how's it going with the turpentine lessons, Dennis?" Bert asked.

"I'll tell ya what, son," Dennis began. "I have nothing, but respect for any nigger who's been doing that their whole lives. That shit ain't easy and I still have the blisters to prove it."

After saying that he realized the term he had used and looked over at Willy, sitting next to him. His face became as red as his hair.

"Sorry 'bout tha name I used," he said quietly to Willy.

"It ain't nothin' but a word," Willy whispered back. "I don't know of any man in our camp who ain't been called that his whole life. It don't cut and I ain't bleedin'"

"Yeah, but still…"

If Willy hadn't already respected this man for his hard work and ability to learn, he did now. This was the first time in his life he could ever remember anyone apologizing for being disrespectful, even if the apology was whispered. Most everyone, however, hadn't even noticed the reference.

"How much sap you boys get out of them trees?" one man asked.

"About a hundred and sixty barrels per week," Ben said, sitting on his horse behind him.

"A hundred and sixty *full* barrels a *week*?" the same man asked. "Holy shit! That's a lot of resin!"

He tried doing the math in his head, to determine how many barrels *per day* that was, but only managed to confuse himself. Many of the turp workers sitting around nodded their heads in agreement. It *was* a lot of resin.

That evening, after cant, Ben approached Henry to speak to him about Dennis.

"How much longer do you want Dennis turpin?" he asked.

"What do you think?" Henry asked.

"Well," Ben replied. "He knows turpin pretty well and I think he's learned a good lesson."

"Then have a talk with him and move him over to the sawmill side next Monday. He could probably use the pay increase. I'm sure he's got rent to pay and and maybe a family."

"Yeah, I heard him talkin' about his kids one time," Ben said.

182

"Okay, then make it happen," Henry said. "Besides, he knows how to run a carriage saw and we could use a backup. Also, we're gonna start another crop and will be hiring maybe six or eight more niggers, probably eight because we're losing Margaret next month. We may even hire some white boys, depending on how many applications we get. We still have a couple empty shanties back there, so they'll have a place to live."

"You gonna hire more men on the sawmill side?" Ben asked.

"Nope, plenty of men there," he said. "We'll be cutting lumber long after the trees have been sapped out. "There's no rush to get them sawed up."

"Okay," Ben said. "I'll see ya in the morning."

"Okay."

Ben led his horse across the road and Henry went in to help Delores close up. Inside, Stella was helping Delores sort through boxes and put things on the shelf as she nursed her baby. Henry walked in, saw Stella feeding her baby, and then turned away politely.

"Aw, Mr. Henry," Stella smiled. "I's just feeding my little bundle."

Delores smiled at her husband.

"Henry, we're getting an awful lot of business with both camps working full time," she said.

"That's a good thing," he said. "Stella, you ain't cooking tonight?"

"I cooked early, Mr. Henry, so's I could help Miss Delores with puttin' things away. Last I seen Willy, he couldn't talk cuz his mouth was so full of cornbread."

"Yer a good woman, Stella," Henry smiled. "I wish I had ten more just like you."

"If they jes' like me, you wouldn't need but five," she giggled.

They all had a good laugh.

"You and Willy, both, are two of my hardest workers,"

Henry said.

"Why thank ya, Mr. Henry. That was a kind thing to say."

"I think I'm getting soft," Henry said.

"It don't matter, we still love you." Delores said.

"Amen," Stella agreed.

The next morning, Larry drove up right after sun-up to collect the end-of-month reports. Henry briefed him on operational status and his plans to hire more turp workers. Larry agreed with Henry's plans to start another crop and promised to bring more turpentine tools for the additional workers, and replace the ones that were worn out. Later, he was introduced to Chuck, the sawmill foreman, and was impressed with the man. After they all had lunch at Henry's house, Larry left and said he would be back the following week. He also walked out and personally congratulated Margaret on her acceptance to Tuskegee.

The next morning, Ben spoke to Dennis about working over at the saw mill, starting Monday. Dennis said he would welcome the change and more money.

"You may not believe me, but I enjoyed working with ya," he later told Willy. "I learned a lot...and not just about turpentinin."

"And I learned some off'n you, hoss," Willy said.

"I'm probably gonna catch shit, over there," Dennis said. "Some of them boys can be spitefully mean."

"You jes' let that shit roll off, like water off a duck's back. If they think it bothers you, they'll keep's on doin' it. Be stronger than them." Willy said.

Just then, the noon bell rang. Since it was Saturday, it meant quitting time, so both men bumped fists and wished each other luck. Only the turpentine workers, worked on Saturday. Dennis headed home. He was a little exciting about telling his wife he would be making almost thirty dollars a week, starting next week. Willy headed back to the block house, where the smell of white pork and fried hoecakes caused him to walk faster in anticipation of a good meal.

That Monday, Dennis was unhitching the harness of the team of horses used to drag logs back to the saw mill from a distant crop being harvested for lumber. As he reached down to unhook the clamp, one horse of the team was stung by a bee on the hindquarter, causing it to bolt upright and spooking the other horse. As the team lurched forward, Dennis was knocked down as his left foot lodged under the logs dragging the dirt. He screamed out in pain and the horseman pulled back urgently on the reins to stop the team, but couldn't calm them. Many men heard Dennis and came over to help, but were confused as to how remove Dennis from under the logs.

Ernest Floyd had heard the commotion from the cooperage area on the far side of the block house and came running over. He immediately went in front of the horses to stop their forward motion and sooth them.

"Whoa, baby. Whoa…darlin', he said gently. As they settled down, he spoke to the men standing around.

"Unhook the harness as I back these mules up," he said firmly. He then made clicking noises and pushed the front harness back, causing the horses to step back two steps. This was enough to cause slack in the dual chains attached to the logs and two men disconnected the clamp. As Ernest heard the chains drop, he urged the horses forward and led them around to the back end of the logs. There he yelled for a man to wrap the chain around the other end of one of the logs pinning Dennis' leg. Once that was accomplished, Ernest urged the horses forward, pulling the log back off of his leg.

By that time, Henry had arrived and asked what was going on.

"The man got his foot broke," Ernest said. "I'll get the flatbed, Mr. Henry. He's gonna need a doctor."

"Go, man!" Henry said. He went over to Dennis to see how bad it was. Chuck came running up with towels and wrapped up the injury. Henry looked over at him.

"It's pretty bad," he said.

"Looks like it," Chuck replied.

185

Ernest drove the flatbed truck over and four men gently picked up Dennis and laid him on the bed. Chuck had a man, climb up on the bed to ride with him to the doctor. Henry told Ernest he would drive the man to the hospital and thanked him for his quick thinking action. Within minutes, the truck drove off and everyone else returned to work.

That evening, Henry returned with the truck. Ben heard him arrive, so he, Claire and the baby came over to see how Dennis was.

"They had to amputate his left foot, just above the ankle," Henry said wearily. "He'll be laid up for two to three weeks."

"That ain't good," Ben said.

"No," Henry said.

"How long will he be in the hospital?"

"Just until next week," Henry said. "Then he'll be moved to his home in Middleburg."

"Middleburg?" Ben asked. "That's where he's from? That's a hell of a drive."

"Yeah, I need you to drive with me out there tomorrow and get his pickup back to his house."

"No problem," Ben said. "What are you going to do about his job?"

"Well, I don't know," Henry replied. "I know he knows how to run the circular carriage saw, which is pretty much a sit down job, but we have Ed there and it wouldn't be fair to him."

"Too bad he don't have experience on the band saw. We're losing that operator to the Army. But then, that's more of a stand up job."

Henry's face lit up.

"But Ed started out on the band saw linebar," he said. "We can move him there and put Dennis on the circular!"

"Hmmm," Ben said. "That might work."

"You bet yer ass that could work!" Henry smiled. "We'll talk to him about it tomorrow. Meanwhile, I'll have a chat with Ed and see how he feels about it running the linebar."

"Great!" Ben said. "Now I got to bed. Today was rough."

"Okay. Make sure you let Willy know he'll be

186

woodsrider until you get back tomorrow."

"Will do."

That evening Henry sat on his porch and thought about everything that had happened that day. He lit a cigarette and blew clouds of smoke, as he watched them drift across his porch a fade into the night. He thought back, over the last couple of years and let his mind drift.

He thought about Ben getting snake bit, Margaret and her drawings, getting a new truck and of the man who lost his leg today. He remembered the expressions of the new workers as they saw the ocean for the first time in their lives. He thought about President Roosevelt's promises to lead the nation out of depression and of the new refrigerators and phone lines they now had at the camps. He thought about reading an article in the newspaper, which reported something about a new electrical box called a "television," and that would bring images and sound into people's homes.

He wondered…where was the world going in such a hurry?

CHAPTER FOURTEEN

On August 16, 1937, Margaret was driven to the train station in Green Cove Springs by Henry, Delores and Agnes. It was a tearful departure, but Margaret couldn't help but feel excited as she contemplated her future and the paths that lay before her. She was placed on the train to Jacksonville, where she would have an hour layover before she caught the train to Montgomery, Alabama. There, she would be met by the Tuskegee shuttle driver, who would transport her and other new arrivals to Tuskegee University, forty-two miles to the east.

After her layover in Jacksonville, Margaret boarded a Southeastern Railroad passenger car and sat in a window seat in the middle. She wanted to watch the trees, houses and small buildings roll by. She opened the book Delores had given and, after turning to the page she had marked with a small hair ribbon, began reading. There were only six other passengers.

About a half-hour after the train pulled out of the station, a man from behind her and across the aisle got up and stepped forward next to Margaret's seat.

"Excuse me," he said. "But I believe you need to be sitting in the back three rows of the car. That area is reserved for coloreds."

Margaret turned up to look at the man. The other passengers looked on with mild interest.

"I'm not "colored," Margaret said, looking up at the man. "I'm black."

"Same thing," the man said, raising his voice slightly.

"Friend, sit down," came a voice from behind him. A massive hand rested on his shoulder.

The man turned and had to look up at another man looming above him. He was huge and had the arms of a goliath.

"This girl needs to move," the man insisted.

"Sit down," the other man said forcefully. "She's fine where's she's at."

188

After glaring at Margaret for a second, the first man returned to his seat. The lady next to him began whispering.

"Hello, young lady," the giant said to Margaret. "My name is Paul. May I sit next to you."

"Yes, Mr. Paul," Margaret said to her new friend. "My name is Margaret."

As the man sat down, he turned to her and smiled. Margaret saw in his eyes a gentle strength.

"Hello, Margaret. Where's a young lady like you headed all by herself?" he asked.

"I'm going to Tuskegee University to get an education and learn more about art, Mr. Paul," Margaret replied.

"Wow," Paul said. "That's gonna be an adventure, huh?"

"Yessah," Margaret said. "Never been away from my family before."

"You're a brave young lady," he said. "Where are you coming from?"

"Turpentown," she said. "My family works in the turpentine mill."

"Really?" he said. "I'm a lumber jack and I cut down trees."

"That must be why you're so big," Margaret smiled.

"Yes, ma'am," he smiled back. "Been doing it all of my life. My daddy and grand-daddy did too."

"My daddy died when a tree fell on him," she said. "But he's in Heaven now and he watches over us."

"That's right," Paul said quietly. "Our daddies in heaven look down and watch over us. Say, what book are ya reading?"

"It's "Little House in the Big Woods," by Laura Ingalls Wilder," Margaret said, showing Paul the cover. "It's about a family who made their life way out in the country."

"Sounds like a good story." He said.

"It is!"

The two made small talk for the next couple hours, before Paul settled back to take a nap and Margaret continued reading her book. At 9:20pm the train pulled into the

Montgomery, Alabama train station. As Margaret struggled to reach her bag, which the conductor had placed in the narrow rack above the seats, Paul reached up and pulled it down for her.

"Thank you, Mr. Paul." Margaret said.

"You're welcome, Miss Margaret," Paul said. "May I escort you to your ride?"

"Why, thank you," Margaret blushed. "Only, I'm not sure where they will pick me up at."

"We'll find them."

The man who told Margaret to move was glaring at them from behind. As he and his wife exited the car from the back, Paul and Margaret headed to the front exit to disembark.

"At least I didn't call her a nig…" he shouted from the rear of the car. His words were cut off as he tripped on the top step and fell out of the car and unto the platform, dislocating his shoulder.

Margaret and Paul were oblivious to his fall as they exited and moved forward on the platform. Up ahead, Margaret saw a man in a black uniform holding up a sign, which read "Tuskegee U." After Paul loaded her bag in the open trunk, he turned to Margaret, held out his hand and shook hers gently.

"Miss Margaret, have a good life and get a good education," he said warmly.

"Thank you, Mr. Paul. Be careful cutting down those trees," she said sternly.

"I will," he smiled and then, turning to the driver. "You take good care of this lady. She has a very bright future."

"I will," smiled the Negro driver. "We'll be at the school in about an hour."

"Okay," said Margaret's friend as he gave her one last smile. He then turned and walked away.

Margaret shared the shuttle ride with three other students reporting to Tuskegee, with two of them returning from summer break. They shared with the two new students, what to expect. They reported the food was good and the dorms were most comfortable. They also said the University had very strict rules and that everyone was expected to obey to them, without

190

exception. No talking in classes unless called upon, no boys in the girls' dorm and punctuality were just a few of the things they discussed. Margaret took it all in and was very excited to start her first class on Friday. Until then, there would be student orientation, book check out and indoctrination classes.

After pulling up in front of the Douglass Hall dormitory for girls, Margaret and the other girl in the car got out and were met by a female student, who escorted them to their rooms. Margaret's room contained one bunk and three single beds, with two girls occupying the singles. Margaret quietly looked around then placed her bag at the foot of the bunk beds. One of the girls sat up in her bed directly across from her and looked at Margaret.

"Are you Margaret?" she asked.

"Yes."

"Hi, Margaret," she said. "My name is Priscilla, but my friends call me *Pretzel*. The girl over there is Roxanne."

"Hi, Pretzel," Margaret said. "It's nice to meet you. Do you know which bed is mine?"

"Either one," Pretzel said. "They're both open."

"Thank you."

"You're welcome, Margaret," Pretzel smiled sleepily. "If you need anything, let me know. That cabinet at the end is for your stuff. There are towels in it too. The bathroom and showers are at the end of the hall on the left. You'll see the double, swinging doors."

"Oh, good!" Margaret said. "Thank you again!"

"You're welcome. Morning bell is at 8:00am. See you in the morning."

"Okay, goodnight," Margaret smiled as she unpacked the few personal items she brought.

Pretzel would become a good friend. They would study and have their meals together. They both shared stories of their lives and the events which lead to their eventual acceptance into the most prestigious African American University in the country.

At the end of her first year, Margaret excelled in all of

191

her classes. She had never imagined a life where everything was so orderly and people treated you for the person you were, instead of preconceived stereotypes. She learned a lot in her first year. She learned that a beam of light was actually comprised of every member of the color spectrum. She learned of an evil man in Germany who imprisoned his own people and sought to control his country with Totalitarian rule. She also learned that from 1508 to 1512, a master artist by the name of Michelangelo labored to produce one of the most wondrous paintings ever created in our world.

On July 28, 1938 she went on summer break. She planned on visiting her family at Turpentown, then return two-and-one-half weeks later for the following semester. She had just turned eighteen years old and had saved up for her round-trip train ticket by doing odd jobs sponsored by alumni groups around campus. She wrote her family almost every week and was anxious to see them again. She had received a letter from Delores and once, one of her brothers, but they couldn't write very well. They sent her news of home, but she still had so many questions.

At the train station, Delores and Henry picked her up. Henry had purchased a car for daily transportation, allowing passengers to travel in relative comfort and did not require the load capacity of the flatbed truck. Delores told Margaret of her family and of some of the changes that had taken place back at the camp.

The block building now had electricity, which afforded residents certain luxuries they never had before. Many of the units now had an oscillating fan, and all but one of the apartments, now a single-bulb light fixture in the middle of the ceiling. Two units even had AM radios, which gave them news of the outside world and provided different genres of music, depending on one's taste and the availability of broadcast stations.

Agnes heard the car approaching the camp and rushed outside to greet her daughter. She carried with her a plate of brownies, which the family had chipped in to buy the ingredients for. Brownies were Margaret's favorite.

"Momma," Margaret mumbled as she wrapped her arms around her.

"Margaret," her mom replied lovingly. "It's so good to see you, child."

"It's good to see you, momma!"

They sat down on one of the benches in front of the block house. Henry and Delores gave them some time alone and asked Margaret to come see them later on. Margaret's brothers were out in the crops, but Ernest had seen them drive up from the cooperage, where he built the barrels for the pine sap. He came over to greet his sister.

"Ernest!" Margaret exclaimed. "You've gotten bigger!"

"Well, I've been working while you've been sittin' in a desk all day, ya little brat," he teased. He was amazed at how much his baby sister had matured. They hugged each other as tears welled up in both their eyes. Soon, he excused himself to get back to work.

That night, Margaret was reminded of what it was like to sleep in the cinder block building. Even though a rotating fan now kept the apartment a little cooler, the July heat was relentless and the occasional mosquito still found its prey. Margaret noticed her drawings on the wall of their apartment had all faded and the charcoal was streaked due to condensation. Her mind drifted back to her studies of Michelangelo and, as she fell off to sleep, a rat crawled across the floor.

The next morning, she enjoyed her old job recording the workers as they shouted out their names for each tree chipped, scraped or dipped. She had pleaded with Henry to assign her the duties of tallyman, which he had reluctantly given. Occasionally, she pulled a tick off her skin as they started to burrow. She wore a hat to shade the sun and keep insects out of her hair.

On Saturday, a group of workers gathered in the jook to celebrate Margaret's visit, if for only a short while. Many of the camp's women cooked and baked an assortment of dishes for everyone to enjoy, as Margaret shared with everyone her experiences at the school and of the outside world. Most workers had little concept of a life where someone isn't telling you where to go and what to do. Many parents listening to Margaret, vowed to encourage their children to get as much learning as their single room schoolhouse could provide. In the morning, they attended church.

Delores would see a rise in the number of children wanting to attend classes. She and Claire would double up their efforts to teach them, and Claire started having one of the wives watch her child so she could dedicate more time to teaching. Many of the camp's children had exhibited signs intelligence and a yearning to learn. After the positive results and notoriety Margaret brought to the area, the Clay County Department of Education sent out more school books and a few supplies. The Superintendent of Schools had also included a hand-written note to Delores renewing their offer to teach in one of the county schools.

All too soon, it was time for Margaret to return to Tuskegee. On the morning of her departure, she sat on a bench in front of the block house and watched the steam drifting up off the packed-dirt road in front. She kept her sketchpad with her everywhere she went and attempted to draw the view. She had made twenty or so sketches during her visit and looked forward to coloring and detailing them upon her return to school. She had drawn camp workers as they labored in the scorching sun, to bleed the resin from the longleaf pines. She had sketches of the camp dogs, Pete and Bonnie, and of the horses struggling to pull a wagon with barrels full of sap. She had drawn many portraits.

"Are you ready to go?" Delores said from behind her.

"Yes ma'am," she replied. "Let me go say goodbye to momma and get my bag."

"Okay, Henry and I will be over at the car."

Margaret went back into her unit and found her mother fixing her a light lunch to take with her.

"Momma, you didn't have to make this," she said.

"It's jes' a snack for along the way." Agnes replied. "I'm

gonna miss you."

"And I'm going to miss you," Margaret said as she hugged her mother. "Momma, I'm going to take you away from this. I swear momma...you won't be here forever."

"Child, God will watch over us. You have a special gift and He has shown you the road to your salvation," Agnes said tearfully. "You jes' do the very best you can, and make this world a better place in any way you can."

"I will, momma. I love you."

"And I love you, child."

Henry and Delores dropped her off at the train station once more. She slept during most of the train ride back.

Back at Tuskegee, she went to bed as soon as she got back to her room. The next day, she found things pretty much as she had left them, except for some disturbing news. The dormitory director told her that her friend Pretzel was one of three people who were killed because of a fire at the public housing unit on the outskirts of Atlanta, Georgia. Her father had managed to carry her down the fire escape, but she had already succumbed to smoke inhalation. Margaret was devastated and spent the next two hours sitting on her bed, staring at the bouquet of flowers someone left on Pretzels bed, next to her favorite stuffed animal. She hadn't noticed them last night.

After eating lunch by herself, Margaret stopped by the art department, and asked for a canvas board and paints. After she told the instructor what she wanted them for, he readily helped her gather everything she would need. After returning to her room, she searched her sketch pads until she found the one she wanted. Margaret spent the next six hours sketching, painting and detailing a portrait of the best friend she would ever know. She let it dry for two hours, and then placed it on Pretzels bed next to the flowers. It was exact.

The following Tuesday, Pretzel's older sister was escorted to their room to collect the few personal effects Pretzel had left behind. She picked up her sister's portrait and sat on the bed staring at it. She began crying uncontrollably. The dormitory director could only place her arm around the woman in an effort to comfort her. She too, could not help but cry while looking at the portrait. There was no signature by the artist, only a simple image painted at the bottom of a pretzel.

"Who painted this?" the sister asked. "It's stunning!"

"I have no idea," the escort said. "I think I know, but can't be sure. Take it with you, it was meant to be a gift. I'm sure of that."

"If you ever find out, please tell them thank you from a very grateful family."

"I will do that."

Pretzel's sister took the portrait with her and it was displayed at Pretzel's funeral services the next day. It brought most of her family to tears, and became their most valued possession.

Margaret focused her attention on her studies and struggled desperately not to become obsessed with the passing of her friend. If she wasn't attending classes or studying, she was recording all of her thoughts and experiences in the journal she had been keeping ever since she learned how to write. She would sometimes skim through the entire journal to see how her writing had improved over the years. She would smile at some of her earlier misspellings.

On January 10, 1939 she started her third semester at Tuskegee University. She had signed up for six classes, the maximum allowed during a semester. They included Physics 2, Advanced Oil Painting, English Composition, Spanish 101, World History 2 and US Government. She was most excited about English Composition because she wanted to improve her writing skills.

Back at Turpentown, Chuck was watching Dennis run the circular carriage saw as he cut four sides, trimming the bark and squaring the log. The squared log was then moved down the rollers, where the linebar saw cut it into boards. They were six, eight and ten inches wide. Some of the eight inch boards were ripped in half, yielding a four inch board.

After the linebar, the boards were run through the planer, which gave them a smooth, finished surface. These boards, referred to as "old-growth pine" were popular in lumber yards because of their ruggedness, resistance to warping and long-lasting characteristics. Chuck was extremely pleased at how well Dennis Hamm was operating the carriage saw, considering he only had one foot. Dennis considered himself the luckiest man on Earth and was steadfastly determined not to let his handicap keep him from doing the very best job he could. He would strap a narrow board to his left leg, which allowed him to depress the clutch when he drove his truck. It took some getting used to, but he was determined.

CHAPTER FIFTEEN

In Boone, North Carolina, Scott Carter unlocked the front door to his hardware store then flipped the sign around, indicating that he was "OPEN." He rubbed his belly, having just finished a meal of eggs, hash browns, biscuits and bacon at the diner up the street. He lived above his store in a small apartment, and had been there ever since his wife Ellen, had passed away some six years before. He looked at his watch as he went over to the counter and opened the cash bag he brought with him from home. He took the cash out and started placing the bills of different denominations in their proper slots. There was no need to count it, as he was the one who had counted it at closing time, yesterday evening.

Just as he was finishing up the coins, his cashier, Theresa came in the front door.

"You're late again, Terri," he said without looking up.

"Why, Mr. Carter, I ain't been late since Christmas time of last year," she objected.

"That was December the sixteenth, young lady, and only seven months ago," Scott smiled. "And what's your excuse *this* time?"

Terri realized he was teasing her, so decided to play along.

"The subway was packed!" she said.

"This town ain't never had no subway," he said, as he saw the grin on her face. "Oh, I get it."

"Well," she said. "If it did have a subway, I'm sure it would have been packed today!"

"I'm sure it would," he said. "Okay, I got the money all counted, so watch the counter while I go in the back and bring out some more bird feed. Evelyn Wright about cleaned me out yesterday."

"I know, I rang her up," Terri said. "You might want to

get some more clothespins while you're back there. I noticed yesterday we're about out of those too. Oh, and a couple bags of fertilizer. I can't lift those heavy bags."

"Fertilizer," Scott mumbled. "Cow shit! That's all it is…and you can get all that you need just outside of town."

"Well, you best be proud they're coming in here to buy it from you!"

Scott headed to the store room in the back of the store and picked up five bags of bird seed. He then went over to the pallets of fertilizer, stacked the seed on the top bag, then reached down to pick it up. Just as he lifted, he felt a sharp bolt of pain rack through his chest.

"Ellen!" he shouted, as he passed out. He fell to the side and knocked over several empty jars before hitting the concrete floor.

"Mr. Carter?" Terri said as she rushed to the back. "Are you okay? And why'd you call me Ellen?"

Terri saw Mr. Carter lying on the floor, next to the broken glass, with one hand clutching his chest.

"Mr. Carter!" she screamed.

Ben was out on the far side of crop three, when Claire received the call about his dad. She knew how much his dad meant to him and was not looking forward to telling him of his passing. Ben had not been home in four years and they were planning on going up there for Christmas this year. She readied the toddler and walked over to the commissary, where Delores was working. Delores saw the expression on Claire's face and stop what she was doing.

"What's the matter?" she asked.

"Ben's father passed away. I just got the call," Claire said.

"Oh, no," Delores said. "Henry's over at the house. Do you want me to tell him?"

"Probably," she said. "He's going to need to know. I don't know what Ben will want to do."

"Okay, I'll call Henry."

Delores told Henry the news and asked him to come over. Claire cuddled her son until he arrived. Henry said that he would ring the bell for Ben then give them some privacy so Claire could break the news to him in the commissary. He walked across the road and rang the bell three times, followed by two more. Ben heard his call and came riding back to the cinder block building. He saw Claire standing at the back door. He dismounted his horse and went over to her.

"What's the problem?" he asked Claire.

"Honey," Claire cried. "I'm afraid I have some bad news."

"What is it?" Ben asked.

"Honey, your pa passed away," Claire said. "Terri called a little bit ago."

Ben became quiet and stared at the ground. He knew this day would eventually come, but you never expect it when it does.

"How?" he asked.

"Terri said he had a heart attacked as he was lifting something."

"Stubborn old man," Ben said. "I knew we should've moved back up there, so I could keep a better eye on him."

"What do you want to do," Claire asked.

"We need to talk about it some." Ben said. "Where's Delores and Henry?"

"They're next door. Do you want to talk to them?"

"Yeah, why don't you call them to come over. We're gonna need to go home."

"Okay." Claire said.

Claire called Delores on the phone and asked them to come over. Ben walked out back to think about things as Henry and Delores came over. Delores went into the commissary, while Henry walked back to where Ben was standing.

"I'm sorry about your loss, Ben," he said quietly.

"Thanks, Henry," Ben said. "I'm gonna need the rest of the day off. Claire and I have to figure out what we're gonna do."

"That's no problem at all, Ben. You take as much time as you need."

"Thanks. We're gonna go, now," Ben said.

"Okay, partner," Henry said as he reached out and shook Ben's hand. "Just leave the horse. I'll get Willy to finish up riding today and he'll put her up."

"Thanks again." Ben said. He grabbed his rifle and then headed back into the commissary to get Claire.

Henry mounted School Duster and rode back out into the pines. He handed the horse over to Willy and told him that he had the reins for the rest of the day. He also told him about Ben's dad and that he would be woodsrider when Ben went up north to make funeral arrangements. Willy told Henry to give Ben his sympathies if he did not see him before he left.

There would be little sleep for many of Turpentown's residents that night. Ben spent close to an hour on the phone with Terri. She told Ben she had pretty much left everything the way it was when his father had died, and that it was at opening time and they had no customers. She also told him which mortuary had his father and gave him the phone number. She cried frequently and he knew that she loved his father almost as much as he did.

Ben and Claire talked for hours and made a decision regarding their future, which they felt would work out the best for them. The next morning, Ben approached Henry.

"Henry, we need to talk," Ben said.

"I figured we would," Henry replied.

"Me and Claire talked long and hard last night," Ben began uncertainly. "I don't know any other way to tell you, but we're going to have to pull up stakes and move up north. Daddy left me the store in his will, so I'll need to deal with that then figure out what we're going to do from there."

"I understand," Henry said. "Ben, you're a good man...the best. I'm proud to have worked with you and honored to call you my friend. Life is all about change and our ability to deal with those changes. You do what's best for you and your

201

family. Nobody will ever fault you for that."

"Thanks, Henry," Ben said quietly. "And I am honored to have you as a friend as well. We will keep in touch and I'll write ya'll to let you know how things are going. Now, we don't have a lot of personal effects here, so if you don't mind, Claire, myself and the baby will need a ride to the train station tomorrow. There's a one o'clock leaving Green Cove Springs, headed north."

"We'd be happy to take you to the train station tomorrow," Henry said. "Just let us know when you want to leave."

"We're thinking about eleven-thirty or so."

"Not a problem. In the meantime, why don't you pull Willy aside sometime today and let him know that he'll be replacing you as woodsrider."

"You're going to give the position to Willy?" Ben asked.

"Yes," Henry replied. "Why? What are your thoughts?"

"I think he's the best man for the job," Ben said. "Willy knows the duties as well as I do and he knows the people better than I do."

"Well, I wouldn't go that far, but give him time, he'll be just fine."

"Okay!" Ben said. "I should let him know as soon as possible."

"Agreed," Henry said. "Where you got him today?"

"Crop three…I think he's dipping today," Ben replied. "I think I'll head out there now. The sooner he knows, the sooner he gets used to the idea."

"Good idea," Henry said. "Now, I got a ton of paperwork, so I'll see you at evening cant."

Ben mounted School Duster then headed out to crop three, where Willy was dipping. He asked the tallyman where Willy was then headed over in his direction. He saw him on the back side of a streak and rode up next to him.

"Willy," Ben said, as he dismounted. "Hold up a bit. We need to have a talk."

202

"Hello, Mr. Ben," Willy said. "I's sorry to hear about your pa."

"Thank you, Willy. It part of the reason I wanted to talk to you," Ben said. "Claire and I will be going up to Boone to take care of things."

"Yessah," Willy said. "Mr. Henry said I would need to be taking over as woodsrider until you gets back."

"We won't be coming back," he said. "You will be the new woodsrider for good."

Willy looked at Ben. He wasn't expecting to take over the duties of woodsrider permanently, but was more disappointed that Mr. Ben would not be returning.

"Are you sure?" he asked Ben. "I never heard of a Negro woodsrider befo'. Are you sure Mr. Henry is okay with this?"

"It was Henry who told me to come and tell you," Ben said. "You're the best man for the job, Willy. Don't let anyone ever tell you different."

"Yessah, Mr. Ben," Willy said. "I'll do my best to cover this."

"Okay," Ben said, as he handed the reins over to Willy. "Now, I'll let the tallyman know as I head back to the front. Just make sure everyone does their job."

"Yessah," Willy said as he took the reins. He watched Ben walk away and head back to the front of the camp. Ben felt his eyes tear up as he walked back. He needed the walk and some time to himself.

"Mr. Ben!" Willy yelled. "You forgot your rifle."

Ben turned around for a minute then yelled back.

"It's yours, now," he said. "It comes with the job and I don't need it anymore."

He then turned and continued walking back to the camp with Bonnie at his side. Ben had another rifle, a shotgun and two pistols. He really didn't need another item to carry clear up to North Carolina. Willy looked down at the custom engraved side of the Henry rifle, then turned School Duster and headed across the crop. This was the nicest thing anyone had every given him, besides his baby daughter.

203

Ben, Claire and Jacob made the long train ride up to Boone, North Carolina. At the train station, Ben used the payphone to call Terri to let her know they had arrived. He said they would catch a taxi and for her to meet them at the hardware store. After collecting their luggage and Bonnie, they packed into a taxi for the trip to the hardware store. The taxi driver was not thrilled about the dog in his cab, but said nothing. Fares were few and far between.

They met Terri at the front door. She had arrived ahead of them and had unlocked the store. After Ben placed the pit bull in the fenced-in area behind the store, they went inside. There, they hugged a greeting and stood there silent for a moment.

"I'm so sorry about your pa," Terri said. "I loved that man, like he was my own."

"We know you did, Theresa," Ben said.

"Well, I'm sorry it's under these circumstances, but it's good to see you again," Terri said. "And you guys call me Terri, okay?"

"Okay, Terri."

"So this is Jacob?" Terri asked as she peered down at the little blue eyes peering up at her.

"Yes, it is," Claire said proudly. "He turned three years old last month."

"He's a very handsome young man," Terri said. "Ben, will you be staying in your dad's apartment upstairs or at the house."

"What house?" Ben asked.

"Your dad's house."

"The one on Miller Street?"

"Yes. What other house did he have?" Terri asked.

"But I thought he sold the house on Miller."

"No," Terri said. "He put it on the market, but it didn't sell. Between you and me, he was asking too much for it and refused any offer below what he was asking."

"And he lived in the upstairs apartment?"

"Yes. He went out to the house on occasions and made

204

sure the place was kept up, but it has been empty since your mother passed."

"Where are the keys to the house?" Ben asked.

"After they took your father away on the day he died, I took the cash out of the drawer and put it in his filing cabinet in the apartment upstairs," Terri said. "Everything is there. The keys to the house, his files, the keys to his car and everything else. I don't know what the combination to his safe is, but here are the keys to the store and his apartment."

Ben and Claire attended his father's funeral on Tuesday, as Terri babysat Jacob. She told Ben it was just too much for her to attend another funeral of someone she loved, and that she would pay her respects later.

On Thursday, Ben began sorting through his father's personal effects and files. He had a locksmith come in and drill the safe open. He discovered his father was quite the businessman and had built a portfolio that most investors would have envied. At the county clerk's office, Ben provided his father's will, insurance policies and banking information, and then filed the necessary paperwork to have himself designated as the sole beneficiary of his father's estate.

He contacted a prominent realtor and placed both his father's store and the Miller Street house on the market. He instructed the realtor to offer the structures at below a fair market price, but do not waiver from those numbers. He also asked the realtor to look for property for him and his family to settle, somewhere up among the nearby Blue Ridge Mountains. He gave her the specifics on what he was looking for. Claire and Jacob mostly stayed in the apartment upstairs or walked to the park, as Ben sorted through the process of liquidating his father's estate. There was no kitchen, so they ate at local diners around town.

The house was sold almost immediately, as several buyers had already expressed an interest. The realtor also located two properties not far away, which met the prerequisites of what

Ben was looking for. He had not mentioned this to Claire as he wanted to surprise her.

One morning, the following week, Ben loaded up Claire and their son, and headed north to view the properties. Claire was anxious to see what Ben was so excited about. After a forty-five minute drive Ben stopped by a diner along the route, and was met by a man who led them further up a road weaving through the forest at the base of Fontaine Mountain. They entered a gate and followed a road leading to a massive, two-story log cabin. Next to it was a huge stable with a second floor apartment. Surrounding the cabin and stables were green pastures, and behind them was a picturesque stream winding down from the mountain ridge, which served as a background for the entire property. It was the most beautiful property Ben or Claire had ever seen.

"Why are we here?" Claire asked Ben.

"I thought you might like to raise Jacob someplace where he had plenty of room to run around," Ben said coyly.

"Are you kidding me?" Claire exclaimed.

She immediately jumped out of the car and the two of them were given a grand tour of the property. It was more than they ever dared to dream about. The house was expansive, yet comfortable. The kitchen every woman's dream and the fireplace was surrounded by overstuffed leather furniture, with end tables carved from Walnut. The stables too, were equally impressive.

"Well, how do you like it?" the man asked.

"We like it very much," Ben said looking over at his grinning wife. "And we'll prepare an offer as soon as I have news about the selling of the hardware store back in Boone."

"Oh, I meant to tell you," the man said. "Carol, your realtor called just as I was leaving to come over here. It seems you have a buyer who's agreed to your asking price. You're set there."

Another week of working out the minor details and a deal was struck. Ben and Claire Carter signed the papers to purchase their mountainside horse ranch and celebrated that evening with a bottle of wine. Ben was able to liquidate his father's estate and pay cash for their mountain ranch, with enough money left over to buy twelve breeder horses and two Arabian's for sport. Ben had dreamt about working on a horse ranch ever since he was a child. It was be hard work, but an exciting new life. There were nearby churches, stores and a school for Jacob. The mountain air was exhilarating and scenic views were plentiful.

Ben had loaded up the car with all of their belongings and his father's personal effects. He would return for Bonnie later on. He, Claire and Terri sat in the diner as Terri's cousin babysat Jacob. They drank coffee and nibbled on cinnamon biscuits.

"Well Terri," Ben said. "What will you do now?"

"Well, I'm still living with my cousin," Terri said. "I have a job interview tomorrow at the JC Penney store they're fixin' to open on Main Street."

"That's wonderful," Claire said. "I hope you do well on the interview."

"I think I'll do okay," she said. "I know the HR Manager and he said I had a good chance of getting hired, because of my experience in retail."

"Good," Ben said. "You be sure and come visit us when you have the chance. We have plenty of space."

"I look forward to seeing your new place," Terri said. "Claire was telling me about it."

They made small talk until finally Ben reached into his pocket and pulled out a check.

"Terri, Claire and I would like for you to have this," he said as he handed the check to her.

Terri looked at the check and her jaw dropped.

"But, Mr. Carter…this is for one thousand dollars!" she said, trying to hand it back to Ben. "I can't take this. Ya'll are just starting off on your new ranch."

"Terri, you took such great care of pa over the years, and we would like very much if you would accept this as a gift of our love and appreciation," Ben said. "I only wish it could be more.

Now take it!"

"Well, thank you!" she stammered as tears rolled down her cheeks. "This will help me get my diploma. I never finished high school."

"Then it will be money well spent," Claire said. "And we do look forward to you coming to visit."

They dropped Terri off at her cousin's house and picked up Jacob. After saying good-bye one last time, Ben, Claire and Jacob headed back up the mountain road to their new home. The front wooden gate now had three wooden logs on either side, which stair-stepped up to support another log spanning the entrance. Below that log hung a wooden, hand-carved sign that Ben had arrange to be made without Claire's knowledge. The sign read "Claire's Ranch." Claire looked over at her grinning husband and playfully slapped him on the shoulder.

"You've been up to no-good, I see," she said sternly.

"How do you like it?" he asked.

"It's beautiful and you know it."

"Well, actually this is the first time I'm seeing it too," he grinned. "But it does look beautiful, just like my wife."

"Well," Claire whispered. "Maybe…just maybe later, after Jacob is sleeping, I'll show you my appreciation."

Ben smiled. "THAT, woman, is exactly what I was hoping you'd say!"

Ben worked ten, sometimes fourteen hours a day, setting up his ranch exactly the way he wanted. Claire made herself busy with the interior of their new ranch home. She had stocked their pantry with enough food to prepare some tasty home-cooked meals for her ranch-foreman husband. At times, their thoughts would drift back to Turpentown and the friends, and work they had left behind. They had never known the happiness they now shared together and looked forward to the adventures each and every day presented. Claire took to sewing and made her family some nice outfits as her skills improved. They found the people in nearby communities were decent, friendly people and attended social events, and the town church services every

Sunday.

One day, Ben felt compelled to ride a horse up into the hills at the base of Fontaine Mountain. He took with him the five foot length of bamboo cane he had carried with them from Florida. He didn't know why he had saved it or brought it with him to the mountains. Claire never asked him about it, knowing it somehow meant something to him.

He rode upwards, until he found a small clearing overlooking his ranch down below. He dismounted and sat on a rock with the cane in his hand. He looked down at the bamboo and thought of all the times he had used it and ones like it, over the years as woodsrider. He remembered during his early years, the times he had used it to encourage workers to get back to work or work faster. He had beaten the workers so bad, it had left bleeding welts on their backs or the side of their faces.

He had seen the bloody footprints of those who did not have shoes, but were still forced to work in the sometimes rugged terrain of Florida's forests. He had seen the wretched interiors of the shanties where the workers lived and windows without screens, which encouraged armies of mosquitos in the stifling summer heat of night.

He wept as he looked down and whispered, "Lord, forgive me."

He then took the bamboo cane, broke it in two across his knee and tossed it aside. Quite suddenly, a mountain breeze washed up through the valley below, up the hill and blasted him in the face, blowing his hair back. He felt both refreshed and exhilarated, at least for a few moments.

More importantly, he felt forgiven.

CHAPTER SIXTEEN

In 1941 the West Tocoi steamboat dock was still used by the steamship Rose Marie, which offered limited room for passengers and was the primary means of transportation for barrels of turpentine, pine resin and lumber along the western side of the St. John's River. Its route ran from Palatka to Jacksonville, with several stops in between. Turpentine camps which still utilized field distilleries, shipped barrels of refined turpentine and naval stores up north, while many camps sent raw pine resin up north to Jacksonville, where their massive units distilled it into turpentine and pitch.

In March, the holding field of the loading docks was packed to capacity and needed to be shipped north. After the Rose Marie docked, over three hundred barrels of resin were stacked three-high on the first two decks of the steamer, with passengers crowding the third. The steamer had been constructed fourteen years prior, when steamboats were a main mode of transportation for both passengers and cargo. In their haste to produce as many steamers as possible, sometimes shortcuts were taken and quality control overlooked. The double-walls of the boilers weren't always welded as well as they could have been.

The captain usually had lunch and sometimes a nap during the docking at West Tocoi, depending on how much cargo was taken onboard. Afterwards, the Officer of the Deck would wake him when the ship was ready to steam. On this day, he noticed the horizon through his porthole looked unusually high. Up on the bridge he gazed aft and was startled at the number of barrels packed into the first and second decks.

"Good God," he said to his helmsman. "How much cargo have we taken on?"

"Three hundred and twelve barrels," he said. "And about twenty bundles of lumber. The waterline is about eight inches below our high-water mark."

"Eight inches?" the Captain exclaimed. "I don't like this. I don't like this one bit!"

"What do you want to do?" the helmsman asked.

The Captain stepped to the back of the pilot house and peered aft. The hog chains were as tight as a violin string and the decks groaned under the weight of the load.

"Passengers?" he asked.

"Ten hearty souls," the helmsman replied.

The Captain leaned out the side windows and looked up at the twin smokestacks forward of the pilot house. Thick, black smoke billowed up. Below he saw decks hands awaiting orders to cast her off. The Captain shook his head and called over to the helmsman.

"We'll be taking her out," he said.

The order was given by the Officer of the Deck to cast her off, as the linesmen and deck hands worked together to loosen the lines. This was usually done at the exact same time, but the tension on the aft lines prevented the dockhand from unwrapping the cleat. The sheer weight of the massive ship drifting out, ripped the aft cleat clean away from the dock. The deck hands gathered quickly to pull in the line, along with the cleat still attached. This happened from time to time with big loads of cargo.

After the lines were secured, the Captain grabbed the handle of the engine order telegraph or "EOT," which allowed him to communicate with the engine room. He pushed it all the way forward, and then pulled it back and stopped on "Ahead/Slow."

"All ahead slow," the Captain relayed through the ship's communication lines. The "1MC" was the ship-wide communication system.

The paddlewheel at the back of the ship groaned as the paddles slapped the water in succession. At first it didn't seem as if they were moving at all. Slowly, the ship began inching forward and further out into the St. John's River. The Captain observed all operations with moderate concern. Below deck the men in engineering shoveled coal feverishly into the furnace beneath the boilers. The steel sides vibrated with the energy they contained as the Engineering officer monitored the gauges. Soon, the EOT rang to "Ahead/Half" and he turned the flywheel valves accordingly.

The Engineer complied with the order and opened the boiler valve even further. The boilers groaned in protest then it happened…an explosion erupted below, so massive and powerful that the engineering personnel were literally blown to pieces. The smokestacks toppled as the explosion surged upward through the decks and ripped the ship in half.

Of the fourteen crewmembers and ten passengers, only four survived. The Captain, helmsman, Officer of the Deck and most of the crew were killed instantly. Many bodies were never recovered as the water of the St. John's burned for hours. Barrels of turpentine and pine sap added to the resultant fire, with many more sinking to the river bottom.

The explosion could be heard for miles, as far south as Palatka, and as far north as Green Cove Springs. Henry looked in the direction of the loud boom and shook his head. He wasn't sure as to what caused the loud explosion, but had his suspicions and could only think that regardless of the source, it wasn't good.

It took Larry Larson three hours to hear about the explosion and another hour to drive down to Turpentown. There he met with Henry, who was expecting his visit.

"I suppose you heard the news," Larry asked Henry.

"Not officially, but we damn sure heard an explosion," Henry replied. "Was it what I think it was? I know they were scheduled pick up some barrels sometime this week."

"We lost three hundred and twelve barrels…two hundred and sixty were from here." Larry said. "Not to mention twenty people who were killed."

"Good God Almighty," Henry said. "Do they know what caused it?"

"The boiler exploded, that's about all they know."

"Those poor souls," Henry said remorsefully.

"It's horrible," Larry said. "I cannot imagine what that must have been like."

Larry and Henry stood there, silent for a moment. It was incomprehensible.

"What will this do to us?" Henry asked.

"I ain't gonna lie to you, it hurts," Larry said grimly. "That cargo was not insured. The demand for turp is fading and prices are down. It takes us almost twice the production to make what we made five years ago. The only thing that's keeping us afloat financially is the lumber. Are crops one and two complete?"

"Yes," Henry replied. "They're finishing up on the last of the tree-cutting on crop two. Crops three and four have about three, maybe four seasons left."

"Well, don't be hiring any more workers, until we get through all of this. Also, you know we can't legally hold any of the workers here because of debt, right?"

"Yeah, I heard about that," Henry said. "But we haven't had any workers even think about leaving. I know we've come out of the depression, but jobs for Negroes just ain't in that high of demand, except for maybe picking oranges. I see some of the orange groves are making a comeback."

"Well, I'm not too worried about the orange industry," Larry said. "They pay by the crate and you'd have to pick a hell of a lot of oranges to make what they make here, even though it ain't very much. How's Willy doing as woodsrider?"

"He's doing great," Henry said. "I can't say he's as good as Ben was, but he keeps them boys working and watches the chipping real well. We have a good group of workers."

"I know," Larry said. "We've been very fortunate."

"Yes, we have."

"Have you been reading the paper?" Larry asked, changing the subject.

"Some," Henry said. "Why?"

"All hell is breaking loose in Europe. That asshole, Hitler is trying to take over Europe. He's invading other countries and creating a bad situation over there. If we get sucked into all that trouble, who knows what it will do to production."

"Well, I'll keep an eye on it," Henry said. "I read about some of the stuff he's doing, but I only get the paper about twice a week."

"Well, I read the paper every morning, so I'll give you a call if anything bad happens."

"Okay," Henry said as he walked Larry out to his car. "Meanwhile, it's business as usual."

"Good enough," Larry said. He started up his car and drove away.

Henry watched Larry drive back up the road towards Green Cove Springs. He stood there a while thinking about what they had talked about.

"Fucking Germans," he mumbled as he walked back inside.

On December 7th of that year, the Japanese attacked Pearl Harbor, killing over twenty-four hundred people, including sixty-eight civilians. Eleven-hundred seventy-seven sailors were killed on the Arizona alone. On December 8, 1941 President Roosevelt declared war on Japan and the United States entered into World War II. The news spread quickly around the camp and, after evening cant, everyone was glued to the two AM radios. Many would not sleep that night.

The next day Wilson asked Willy if he could speak with Henry. Willy led him back to the commissary, where Henry was handing out the tallyman sheets.

"Mr. Henry, could I speak to you?" Wilson asked.

"Why certainly, Wilson," Henry replied. "What's on your mind?"

He couldn't remember the last time he had spoken directly to Wilson, so was a little curious and hoped there wasn't anything wrong.

"Mr. Henry," Wilson said. "Most everyone heard on the radio last night that we have gone to war with Japan."

"Now Wilson," Henry said. "We don't know how or even *if* any of that will be affecting our work here."

214

"I know, Mr. Henry, but I was wondering how you would feel about me joining the Army. I want to fight for our country."

"Why, Wilson...that's a very commendable notion," Henry said.

"There's two others that said they want to join too," Wilson said.

Henry thought about this for a while. Losing three workers would be a setback, but he could replace them with no problem.

"Wilson, you and the other two can join the service, but I want to warn you, it may be no easy task." he said.

"I know, Mr. Henry, but we want to try," Wilson said. "Will we be able to leave if we's debted to the company store?"

"We can no longer force you to stay here if you owe money. The laws have been changed."

Wilson hadn't known the laws had changed and they were legally free to move on, regardless of debt. None of the other workers knew this either.

"Mr. Henry, I'll pay my debt when I gets paid. I don't know what the pay is, but I'll get it back to you, I promise."

"I believe you, Wilson," Henry said. "And when you join to serve our country, your debt is forgiven."

"Thank you, sir."

Wilson and the other two workers joined the Army two weeks later. The Navy, at the time, was still not accepting black enlistees. They were sent to segregated combat support groups, and transitioned to combat a year after. The African American infantry divisions were known for their aggressiveness in combat and took no prisoners. Many battles were won due to the fierce fighting characteristics of the black infantry divisions. Many lives were saved because of their gallantry.

Turpentine demand actually increased during the beginning of the war. Solvents and sealants were developed from the pitch, which contributed to the war effort. Turpentine was used in the production of medicines, disinfectants, paint thinners and solvents. Turpentown was working crops three and four of about six hundred and forty acres or about twenty thousand longleaf pines. Word had spread about the laws be revoked, which required workers to stay on the property if they were indebted to the company store, but few even considered the option of leaving. Where would they go? What would they do?

Willy continued as woodsrider and had little problem encouraging workers. Most were hard working and knew their jobs well. On the sawmill side the old growth pine boards flowed smoothly, even as workers began enlisting in the service. They were replaced by others seeking work, who for one reason or another, were not eligible for enlistment into the military.

Exports for lumber increased as the demands rose to accommodate the construction of military barracks and base housing abroad. The workers were pushed to maximum output. Larry had sent two flatbed semi-trucks to transport both the turpentine barrels and the lumber to Jacksonville. It was a costly way to get their product to market, but demand was high and their efforts paid off.

In early December of 1942, the turpentine and mill workers were having lunch in the break area between the two yards. They mostly talked about the war and the recent events they had heard on the radio as they understood them. They cursed the Japanese, although most of them had never met a person from Japan. Occasionally, an aircraft in training for the war at nearby Lee Field would fly overhead.

As an F6F Hellcat flew over their covered break area, the workers heard the plane's engine sputter loudly. They ran out from under the roof to see the aircraft soaring by as thick, black smoke trailed behind. The engine stopped, causing many of them to gasp.

"Oh, Lord," one worker shouted. "He's going down."

All of the workers watched as the disabled plane quickly lost altitude. Soon, the pilot's canopy slid backwards and the pilot pulled himself out of the cockpit and jumped. The workers watched in disbelief as the pilot plummeted.

"Lord Jesus, help that man," Curtis yelled.

Finally, a parachute deployed and they could see the pilot sailing slowly to the ground. They each breathed a sigh of relief.

"Do we need to go help him?" one worker asked.

"No," Henry said. "That plane went down way north of us and you can bet there are rescue crews on their way to fetch that pilot as we speak."

After calming down, the workers returned to finish their lunch before heading back to work.

"Men," Henry said. "We are all concerned about what's going on in the Pacific. We all want to help, but hear me out. The best we can do to help with the war effort right now is sapping these trees and cutting the lumber. They need this stuff more than ever."

Many workers felt a new sense of patriotism, knowing their work was helping their country. They worked harder than ever.

The next day men sat out from under the covering to watch the skies better. They saw more aircraft, but no more problems. Soon, someone mentioned the Christmas gathering in the jook, coming up next week. Willy turned to the white man sitting next to him and nonchalantly invited the mill workers to the celebration.

"You boys are invited to the Christmas gathering in the jook next Friday," he said.

Many heads turned at this unexpected invitation. Willy himself, was unsure why he had mentioned it, but the spirit of the season and the workplace comradery they had come to embrace, supported the notion.

"I'll see if the wife has plans," the white man replied.

Most paid little attention to the invitation, but some had mixed feelings at the thought. A few, even considered it. Willy spoke with Henry about it later, who told him not to worry about it. What would be, would be.

As it turned out, eight of sawmill workers showed up at the jook on Friday night. Seven of them even brought a plate of food or cake. One worker's wife brought scented candles, which

217

were lit and placed on tables around the room. Out front, where they had parked their cars, one man argued with his wife.

"Come on, Ethel," he said. "These are men that I work with. It ain't no big deal."

"Billy Ray, when you said we were going to a Christmas party, you didn't say nothing about celebrating the birth of Jesus with a bunch of niggers!" Ethel said.

"Then you can just sit your ass in the truck," Billy Ray scolded. "I don't believe Jesus would approve with your stubborn ways, either!"

Billy Ray turned on his heel and went back inside, where he enjoyed the evening immensely. The food was grand and the music, soothing. Memphis strummed Christmas melodies on the guitar the turpentine workers had given him several Christmas' ago. He was accompanied by Camden Wilson on the fiddle.

The eggnog was spiked and people began swaying to the rhythm of the Christmas spirit. Quite suddenly, Chuck stood up and walked over to where Stella was sitting.

"Ma'am," he said. "May I have this dance?"

Stella looked up and was more than a little surprised at his invitation. The whole room turned her way to see how she would react. Willy and Chuck's wife looked on with equal curiosity.

"Why thank you, Mr. Murray," she replied. "I'd be happy to dance with you."

She stood and the two began to dance to the Christmas song, "Oh Come All ye Faithful." Soon, other men in the group, both black and white, began to rise and asked the ladies to dance. For many of them, it was the first time they had even touched the flesh of a different race, but the Spirit of Christmas was far too powerful for the destructive sentiments of racism. Everyone enjoyed themselves and capped off the evening by singing Christmas carols in near perfect harmony.

CHAPTER SEVENTEEN

January of 1943 was one of the coldest months anyone could remember in recent years. Some workers kept busy scraping hardened resin from catfaced pines. Most had good shoes with socks by then, but only half of the workers had coats. Those with worn shoes did not work the winter months, because of the possibility of cutting their feet and not knowing it. Workers could not afford antibiotics and infections could be deadly.

Willy had a tattered old coat that he had brought with him from the camp in North Carolina. It was fourteen years old, but it still kept him warm. He rode up behind Curtis who was scraping resin on the backside of crop four. He saw that he was shivering, so dismounted and went over to him. Curtis only had a thin, worn out sweater with many holes.

"Son, you okay?" he asked.

"Freezing my ass off," Curtis replied. "I can't remember it ever being this cold."

Willy took off his leather glove and placed the back of his hand on Curtis' neck. Curtis was burning up with fever.

"Curtis, yer sick," Willy said. "You need to git yo ass back to the shack."

"I can't," Curtis said. "I gots too much debt."

Curtis turned to face Willy, but staggered a little. Willy grabbed him so he wouldn't fall. He looked Curtis in the face and was alarmed at what he saw.

"Look here, friend," Willy said. "I'm the woodsrider here and you'll do as I say. I know you and me are about the same size, but I swears to Jesus if you don't get back to your place and get to bed, I'm gonna kick yo ass all the way back to the block house."

"I reckon I'll have to do what you say," Curtis said as he stumbled forward.

Willy took off his coat and draped it around Curtis. He then helped him up on the horse and led them back to the quarters. As they neared, he saw Stella out back, boiling clothes. It was impossible to get sap out of clothes, but boiling them dissolved most of it.

"Stella!" Willy shouted. "Run get Curtis' bed ready and get an extra blanket."

She had his bed ready as Willy helped Curtis inside. She helped put him down and could feel the heat off his body.

"He's got the fever," she said. "I'll run down and see if Miss Delores has any medicine. There's soup on the stove, Willy. Get him a bowl and feed it to him."

"Okay, but hurry it up," Willy said. "I have to git back out."

Willy propped Curtis up and spoon fed him some possum soup. Stella came back with a glass of water and two pills that Delores had given him. She took the bowl from Willy to finish feeding Curtis.

"I *have* to git back," Willy said.

"You go," Stella said. "I'll watch him."

As Willy rode School Duster back out to the crops, Stella placed a cold, wet cloth on Curtis' forehead and took his temperature. It was 102 degrees. She didn't tell him about the thermometer and made sure she had cleaned it off real good before sticking it in his mouth. She sat with him the next two days until his fever broke and was able to eat on his own.

In October of 1943, fourteen year old Thomas Wright sat on an empty half-barrel outside of the block house. A heavy fog hung over the camp and surrounding woods, providing a surreal setting. It was as quiet as cotton and Thomas strained to hear any noise at all. There was none.

Catface had delivered a powerful sermon in their schoolroom/church earlier. Most everyone in the camp knew that change was coming. Crops three and four were still being worked, but no new crops had been started, which concerned many. Catface had preached there would be new paths to follow

220

and that the world was going to be a different place in the years ahead.

Feeling an itch, Thomas looked down at his arm and saw a tick. He casually plucked it off, flattened it between his finger nails and flicked it away. In the distance, he heard a truck approaching. He stood and backed up behind a tree until he saw who it was. It was Mr. Larry's truck, so he relaxed and headed back to the shanties to look for someone to play pine cone tag. It would be such fun in this fog.

Henry had heard Larry's truck approaching as well, so went out to meet him. Across the street, he saw smoke billowing out of the woodsrider's chimney and knew Stella was probably cooking up something tasty for lunch. She and Willy had moved over there after Willy had been assigned as woodsrider. Larry stopped the truck on the road in front of him.

"Good morning," Henry greeted.

"Morning, Henry," Larry said.

"Have you had lunch, yet? Delores made up a big pot of pinto beans and rice. We have plenty."

"I just had breakfast not too long ago, so I'll have to pass," Larry said. "I will take a glass of her sweet tea if any's been brewed."

"We *always* have sweet tea," Henry smiled.

Sitting on Henry's back porch they talked about the weather and the war. After an hour, Larry's face became serious.

"Okay," Henry said. "What really brings you out this way on a Sunday?"

"I'm afraid it isn't good news, Henry," Larry reported.

"Shutting her down?" Henry asked. He had been expecting this conversation.

"Yes," Larry said. "The cost of transportation is beginning to exceed profits. The fuel rationing system is killing us. The war is changing everything."

"How long we got?" Henry asked.

"Three, maybe four months."

"Will we finish out the crops?"

"Yes," Larry said. "Get them sapped out as soon as

221

possible. Start chipping 20 streaks per tree, but only on trees you've already started. There will be more dipping, but we want to extract as much resin as possible before cutting them down."

"Gotcha," Henry said. "What else do I need to be aware of?"

"Towards the end, you'll need to start transferring equipment and supplies south. The sawmill will be the last to be broken down and the equipment sent to the camps in central Florida," Larry said. "How's the paperwork looking?"

"I've kept all the files and documents current," Henry said. "Birth certificates, personnel records and equipment ownership papers...all in order."

"Good!" Larry said. "When the time comes, we may rent out your house, but you can stay as long as you like. I may have a position coming up that you might be interested in. We can talk about it later."

"Okay," Henry said.

After Larry left, Henry went back inside and broke the news to Delores. She was as upset about it as Henry, but somewhat relieved that he said Larry may have a job for him after they shut down.

The following week, as lunch was ending, Willy asked Curtis what his tally was for dipping that day. After Curtis told him, Willy looked shocked.

"Dayum, son!" Willy exclaimed. "That's a lot of dippin."

"Dayum right," Curtis said proudly as he extended his arm with his hand in a fist. Willy bumped his extended fist with his own. The other men watched with idle amusement.

"Wait a minute," one of the white workers said. "Why do ya'll do that?"

"Do what?" Curtis asked.

"Thump each other's fists like that," the man said. "Not trying to be rude or nuthin', but is that a black thing?"

"It's a turp worker's handshake." Willy replied.

"Why do ya'll shake hands like that? How come ya don't just shake hands normally?"

Willy held out his massive hands and showed the man his palms.

"See these?" Willy asked.

"Yeah," the man replied.

"What you see on them?"

"A bunch of sap," the man laughed.

"Yessah," Willy explained. "After working all day chipping and scrapping and dipping, we gots a *lot* of sap on our hands. If we shook hands *normally*, like you call it, our hands would stick together."

"Well hell," the man smiled. "I never thought of that. How long ya'll been doing that?"

"For as long as we've been sapping the pines," Curtis said. "My pap did it and his pap before him. Long before that, even."

Many men looked at each as if the answer to an ancient riddle had suddenly revealed itself. Soon, everyman there began bumping fists as they left to go back to their assignments. It became the standard handshake among friends and workers, both black and white, for generations to come.

CHAPTER EIGHTEEN

The Turpentown mill closed in early 1944, after every tree in all four crops had been harvested. The sawmill workers would be the last to go and no other crops were started. The war was still raging around the globe and the economy suffered as America concentrated on wartime production. Turpentine was still used in lamps, medicines and paint products, but demand waned after the use of the pitch became less popular.

Slowly, the turpentine workers packed up their belongings and followed whatever paths destiny had presented to them. Most of the workers migrated south to where many turpentine mills remained in operation until the 1950's. Willy had purchased an old car and was tying down the last of their belongings on a trailer, hitched to the car. Henry stopped by to bid him farewell.

"What kind of plans do you have for your family?" he asked.

"I bought a restaurant, on the outskirts of Green Cove," Willy smiled. "We'll be serving up home cookin' just like Stella has been cookin' here for the last nine years."

"You bought a restaurant?" Henry asked. "How in the hell did you manage *that*?"

"Well, Mr. Henry, I'll tell ya," Willy began. "Remember some years ago when I found that Civil War belt buckle out in the pines? I asked if I could have it and Mr. Larry said that I could keep anything I found in the crops as long as it didn't belong to the turpentine company."

"Yeah," Henry said. "He *did* say that."

"Well," Willy smiled. "I found something else too. While raking back the pine needles from trees way out on the backside of crop two, I found a heavy, leather pouch. It had mostly rotted away, but was still full of coins, Mr. Henry. It was full of *gold* coins."

In 1864, as the Civil War was coming to an end, a group of five men stole the payroll for the entire Southern Confederate Army, and disappeared into the Florida terrain. They were never heard from again. The only mention of this in Civil War history books, was that the payroll had been stolen. The payroll was in gold coin, because many soldiers began refusing the Confederate paper currency toward the end of the war. Gold coin had become the standard method of payment for the fighting members of the Confederacy.

"Well, I'll be damned." Henry said. "Worth a lot of money?"

"Enough for a down payment on a restaurant," Willy smiled.

"Well, good for you," Henry said as he extended his hand to shake Willy's. "What will you name your restaurant?"

"Stella's Home Cooking," Willy said, shaking hands. "And yer welcome to visit any time you and Miss Delores want some good southern cookin."

"We'll take you up on that."

"Mr. Henry, I wanted to thank you," Willy said. "You and Miss Delores have always treated us good and we 'preciate that. You're a good man and Miss Delores is a kind and decent woman."

Henry thought for a minute and then replied.

"Willy, I haven't always been a *good* man," he said. "But over the years, people change. I learned that we can compare ourselves to trees. We may be different kinds of trees, but in God's eyes, we're all still trees, and I thank him and people like you for showing me how life truly is."

They shook hands one last time as Willy joined Stella in the car and drove off.

After working for several months in the flooring department of a home improvement store, Delores accepted a teaching position with the Clay County School System, and would eventually work her way up and become Assistant

Principal of Clay High School. Henry accepted a job as assistant foreman at the National Truck Driver Training School Larry Larson had developed right up the road, where crop four had been.

After three years, they would accept a standing invitation from Ben and Claire to move up to North Carolina. They lived in the apartment above the barn and enjoyed living in the mountains. The pit bulls, Pete and Bonnie, were reunited once more and spent most of their time chasing rabbits or laying around the ranch. Henry and Ben went on several hunting trips together and brought home elk, deer, rabbit and squirrel. During the summer, they fished the stream behind the property.

Two of the units of the block house remained occupied for some time, and the men living there with their wives, were hired as laborers at the truck school. Curtis even went on to obtain his CDL license and made a living driving trucks.

On January 13, 1997, Wilson Sanders and five other African Americans were posthumously awarded the Medal of Honor by the President of the United States. Even though he was seriously wounded, Wilson had scaled Frocker's Hill and killed eight Japanese soldiers occupying a machine gun nest at the top. His heroic bravery saved countless lives and he later died of his wounds. He also received the Purple Heart, but because they were African Americans, the awards came fifty-two years after the war's end.

Margaret Floyd went on to serve as the Assistant Director of African American Art in the Philadelphia Museum of The Arts. She eventually moved her entire family up to Philadelphia, where she rented a four bedroom house. Her brothers found work, commuted daily on the city's bus lines and were required to sit in the "Colored" section of the bus. Margaret would sometimes contract with different cities to paint murals on buildings in historical districts. She made an honorable living in a segment of society which had adjusted to having people of color employ their skills and talents, providing they were exceptional.

In 1955, she visited Ben, Henry, Delores and Claire up in the North Carolina. She stayed for two weeks as she sketched, then later painted some of the scenery she observed up in the Blue Ridge Mountains. She sketched close to one hundred scenes, which she would later complete with her memories of the mountain colors.

In 1962, Margaret Floyd published her first book. It was an autobiography entitled, "Turpentine Child ~ The Story of Margaret." It was listed on the New York Weekly's Top Ten books in print for six months straight.

That same year she was contracted to paint a wall mural on the outside wall of the Boston Maritime Museum, facing a restored tall masted sailing ship. The mural depicted turpentine workers chipping and scraping longleaf pine trees. It was entitled "Turpentown."

THE END

Made in the USA
Middletown, DE
05 December 2022

17131676R00129